Faith of a Cowboy

Triple J Ranch Book 4

Jenna Hendricks

Books by Jenna Hendricks (Clean & Wholesome Romance)

<u>Triple J Ranch</u> –

Book 0 - Finding Love in Montana (Join my newsletter to get this book for free)

Book 1 - Second Chance Ranch

Book 2 – Cowboy Ranch

Book 3 – Runaway Cowgirl Bride

Book 4 – Faith of a Cowboy

Book 5 – Cowboy Blessings

Book 6 – The Cowboy's Game

<u>Big Sky Christmas</u> –

Book 1 – Her Montana Christmas Cowboy

Book 2 – Her Christmas Rodeo Cowboy

Book 3 – Her Mistletoe Cowboy

Book 4 – Her Sleigh Ride Christmas Cowboy

Crooked Arrow Ranch –

Book 0 - Wounded Hearts Ranch (join my newsletter to get this free)

Book 1 – A Broken Heart Mended

Book 2 – Hope's Healing Love

Book 3 - Love's Healing Balm

Book 4 – A Crooked Arrow Christmas

Book 5 – Tripping Over Christmas

Saguaro Bookshop Mysteries –

Book 1 – Saguaro, Snowflakes, and Murder

Standalone Novels –

Christmas Crazy in July

Rebel Hearts Anthology

See these titles and more: https://JennaHendricks.com

Contents

Newsletter Sign-up

By signing up for my newsletter, you will get a free copy of the prequel to the Triple J Ranch series, Finding Love in Montana. As well as another free book from J.L. Hendricks.

If you want to make sure you hear about the latest and greatest, sign up for my newsletter at: https://jenn ahendricks.com/newsletter/ . I will only send out a few e-mails a month. I'll do cover reveals, snippets of new books, and giveaways or promos in the newsletter, some of which will only be available to newsletter subscribers. You'll also get a heads-up when I'm running sales on my books!

JENNA HENDRICKS
Finding Love
In
Montana
A Triple J Ranch Prequel

Chapter 1

Leah Hayes was pretending to straighten the shirts on the double rack near the front corner of the store so she could watch the checkers tournament out of the corner of her eye. If she did it right, no one would know how much she enjoyed watching the old men in town play checkers and share their stories of former glory. Once in a while she'd even get some good gossip from those old coots.

Charlie Macon, Cindy Macon's brother-in-law, looked to be winning. He usually did. But in this case it was very important for the group of older cowboys to ensure Charlie won instead of George Cannon. Mr. Cannon was the worst griller in three counties, and everyone knew it.

The cowboys always made some sort of wager on their games, never money. But they would decide that the winner would have to either buy the meat for their next barbecue or he would have to cook it up. Last year, the checkers group did a week-long championship series and the winner had the privilege of getting to ride in the mayor's convertible during the Fourth of July parade. The *prize* was always something fun.

The current prize for this month's competition was that the winner provided the beef for their monthly dinner. The men would have a barbecue for all the players and their dates. Some men were still married and others were widowers, like Mr. Macon. But they always found a date. And lately Mr. Macon had been dating the retired school teacher, Ms. Barton. The entire town was talking about the two of them, and everyone wanted to know when they'd finally tie the knot.

When the little bell above the front door jangled, Leah looked up. Her friend Harper Bensen, the nurse over at the town's clinic, walked through the door with a huge smile on her face. In her hands were two sweet teas. She too had been looking forward to watching the checkers game.

Leah waved her friend over. "Hey, Harper. Thanks for the tea." She took the offered drink and almost melted when she tasted the chilly sweetness as it went down her throat and cooled her overheated body.

The store's air conditioner was on the fritz again, and it was a very hot day for so early in the year. Winter was over and spring was just getting started, but it was looking to be an extremely hot summer if the temps didn't let up soon. It was good for the flowers, though. Shoots of what would be yellow daffodils were peeking through the formerly frozen ground. It wouldn't be too much longer before they began to see the wild yellowbells.

"You're welcome. What did I miss?" Harper looked over at the group of four men sitting in the window on old barrels with the checkerboard painted on the top of another barrel.

Leah took another long sip of her tea. "I think it's time for a new AC unit."

"No, I meant with the game." The nurse pointed her drink toward the men in the front window.

A few others stood outside, fanning themselves with their cowboy hats and watching the game through the front window. Leah wondered why they didn't just come inside. Even with the AC on the fritz, it was still cooler inside than it was outside.

"So far it's Mr. Macon's game. He's got half his pieces kinged. Mr. Cannon only has one kinged. And he's lost a lot more than his opponent." She took another long drink and sighed. If her brother Logan didn't get the AC fixed soon, she was going to call in a repair man.

Since her brother had returned to town almost two years ago, they had worked hard and saved a little bit of money. They'd even gotten out of the red with the store. When her dad started getting sick, he didn't manage the store as well as he should have. Then on top of everything, the online markets had really taken away a lot of their regular sales. But Logan had come in with his big city marketing experience and turned things around. Even while wooing his old high school girlfriend and helping their pa get back on his feet again after the heart attack.

Now they had a fantastic line of clothing as well as a top-notch website that competed with the online stores. Most of the women in the area came to their general store before heading to Bozeman to shop. Leah had started to bring in women's and men's clothes that were more in line with today's fashion. They still sold work clothes, but now it was so much more.

In fact, she had unloaded a batch of brand-new cowgirl shirts that just happened to appear in the current month's issue of *Cowgirl Today*. She didn't even know that line of clothes was going to be featured in the magazine almost all women in the area subscribed to. It truly was a blessing from God. Once word got out those shirts were here in stock, she'd sell out.

Those were the shirts she was straightening on the rack. With the checkers tournament going on in the front window, the ladies who stopped by were sure to notice the rack of new clothes and start coming in soon. By tomorrow, everyone in a fifty-mile radius would know to come into the Beacon Creek General Store. Then one more day, and the news would spread to at least a hundred-mile radius. Leah hoped she'd be sold out by week's end.

If only she could get the AC fixed before everyone started coming in.

"Oh, look. Mr. Macon is setting himself up nicely. If Mr. Cannon isn't careful, he's going to lose within two more turns." Harper smiled before sipping on her tea.

"You're right, you know. You've got to get the AC in here fixed or no one will come shopping."

Leah worried on her bottom lip and wondered who she could call on short notice to fix the AC. Her brother was all wrapped up in newlywed bliss with his new wife, Elizabeth Manning—now Elizabeth Hayes.

Chapter 2

"It's been over two years since he returned home. Has John said anythin' to any of you as to why he left college?" Mark Manning looked across the table at his brothers Matthew and Luke.

They were all at Rosie's Diner having lunch and discussing their younger brother John. He had always been a happy boy. When he first left home, it was to attend college and rodeo for his school. He had always been the best in his family at rodeoing. His best sport was bull riding. After two years he'd quit college and joined the circuit. Everyone expected that within a few years he'd be winning left and right on either the Professional Bull Riders (PBR) circuit or the Professional Rodeo Cowboys Association (PRCA).

"When he was injured he was supposed to only come home to recover. He's been fine for over a year, but he's said he's not going back. John refuses to talk to me about it." Matthew was the oldest of the Manning brothers, and all of his siblings had always gone to him first with any issues they had...until now. He set his sweet tea back on the table and looked to his brothers.

Luke scratched his chin. "Maybe he's spoken with Roman? The two of them are pretty close."

Mark shook his head. "Nah, I spoke with Roman before he went back to college in January and he said John wasn't speakin' to him, neither. He hoped we'd be able to figure it out."

"Well, until he's ready to talk we can't make him. All we can do now is support him and be there for him when he is ready to talk." Matthew took the last bite of his burger and followed it up with two fries drenched in ketchup.

Mark shook his head. "I don't know. It's got to be somethin' more than just his injury. He's not even looked at a woman since he healed up. At first I thought he didn't want to go out with any of the cowgirls in town because he was injured and didn't want any of them to fuss over him. But now?" He dragged three fries through his barbecue sauce and ate them without finishing his thought.

He knew there was much more going on with his younger brother than anyone knew, but until John opened up he could only guess. The fact that his normally outgoing brother, who never went a weekend without a date, hadn't been on a single date in almost two years bothered him. At least John was attending church regularly. And reading his Bible on a daily basis.

Mark had walked in on him more than once early in the morning at the kitchen table with his Bible open. While he didn't want to pry into his brother's life, he did want to know what had caused him to completely change his personality.

John had been in all the Manning brothers' prayers, and would continue to be so until the young man opened up and told his brothers what had really caused him to drop out of college and bull riding.

"Oh, look," Cindy Macon exclaimed, and pointed at the table full of Manning brothers. "Luke's back from his honeymoon." She tittered and giggled while her pink pouf, which must have just been done up, bobbed around. Every hair on her head stayed in place thanks to a generous dollop of Aqua Net.

Mark chuckled. "Man, I'm glad I've not succumbed to a woman's charms. Those Diner Divas are always up in your business, Luke. And poor Callie. She can't walk down the sidewalk in town without being practically jumped by the gossipmongers wanting to know this or that." He shook his head and took a gulp of his sweet tea.

"Just wait, they'll move on when the next couple is announced." Matthew Manning, also recently wed, gave his younger brother a commiserating look.

"Yeah, they only left you alone because they turned their gossip onto me and Callie." Luke scoffed and turned away from the group of four elderly women making their way to the Manning table.

"Luke, you look great," Lou Ann Dobbs gushed.

Martha Stanhope looked Luke over and with a knowing grin and blurted out, "That's because his wife took such great care of him." She waggled her brows.

Mark just about threw up in his mouth. Then coughed. "Ladies, what did the pastor say about gossip?"

Merry Walters sighed. "I know, I know. But we aren't wagging our tongues to everyone on the street, we're here talking to the source."

Luke put his head in his hands. "Will they never learn?"

Matthew chuckled. "Doubtful."

"This is enough to keep me single—forever." Mark grinned.

Chapter 3

With spring in full bloom, the entire town of Beacon Creek, Montana was preparing for the annual Spring Fling. Not only did they have a yearly dance, but they also had a rodeo and craft fair. It was the highlight of spring. A lot of people hibernated with the bears and did crafts all winter long. But the moment the yellow shoots of the flowers popped up, everyone was outside and preparing for this first large event of the year.

The town would be inundated with residents from all over Montana, as well as other western states like Wyoming and the Dakotas. Rodeo was the lifeblood of so many ranchers and farmers, including the Mannings.

"John, why aren't you going to compete this year?" Caleb Manning, John's dad, asked at breakfast.

He shrugged. "Just don't feel like it."

"But ever since you were four years old and I took you to the Spring Fling rodeo you've wanted to ride bulls.

As a local, I'm sure it's not too late to get in this rodeo." Caleb pushed his sons, but only because he loved them and wanted them to make something of their lives.

"Dear, leave John alone. If he's done with rodeo, let him be." Judith Manning, John's mom, never liked him riding bulls to begin with.

Mark walked into the kitchen and grabbed a coffee mug off the counter and sat at the table. Once his mug was full, he looked around at his parents and John. "You know, if John doesn't want to ride we shouldn't push him. You know how stubborn he is. He'll get back on the bull when he's good and ready."

John stood up. "What he said." He pointed to his brother and scowled at his parents before leaving to begin chores.

Once John was clear of the house, Mark looked to his dad. "Dad, you really got to let him be. When he's ready to tell us what happened, he will."

"Son, you know I'm not good at sitting back and watching my kids when they hurt." Caleb looked out the kitchen window toward the barn, where John was heading. "And that there boy"—he pointed out the window—"is hurtin' something awful."

"I know. It most likely has to do with a woman. So what do you say we leave him be?" Judith took a sip of her coffee, but watched her husband over the brim of her cup.

Caleb shook his head. "It's more than that. Since he fell off that bull and broke his leg, he's not been the same. I know my son, and he's in need of help."

"Maybe he needs the kind of help we can't give him." Mark looked out toward the window, even though he couldn't see his brother from where he sat at the table. "I think prayer is all we can do for John right now."

Caleb sighed. "You're right." He turned around. "When did you get so wise?"

Mark's chest puffed out. "I've always been wise, you've just never noticed."

His dad threw the kitchen towel as his middle child and laughed. "I've noticed more than you realize." Caleb arched a brow.

"What's that supposed to mean?" Mark took the towel and handed it to his mom.

"Just that you're not as invisible as you think." Mark's dad smiled at his wife and winked.

Judith picked up the message. "So, when are you going back to Bozeman with Elizabeth and her friends?"

Mark looked between his parents, brow furrowed. "Ah, I think Lizzie has a trip planned for next week. Why?"

"Oh, no reason." Judith smiled and took another sip of her coffee.

Later that night, Elizabeth and her husband Logan came for dinner with the Manning family. "So, I think we should head back up to Bozeman on Tuesday afternoon." She looked around the table at her entire family.

Judith had invited all her kids and their spouses who lived in town. The only Manning child missing was Chloe, and that was because she lived a few hours away in Frenchtown, Montana.

Callie, the town's sheriff deputy who was married to Luke, smiled. "I've got Tuesday off next week. I'd love to join you."

Luke shook his head. "I thought we were going to spend the day packing so we can move into the house we rented in town?"

"Don't you think helping Elizabeth with the homeless is more important?" Callie tilted her head and batted her eyelashes.

"You know, I'm catching on to your sultry ways. One of these days, batting your pretty long eyelashes at me won't affect me so much." Luke took his wife's hand and brought it to his lips.

"But for now, it still works." Callie leaned in and kissed her husband's cheek.

"Gross, get a room," Mark gagged.

Everyone at the table laughed, except for John. Mark noticed the sadness in his brother's eyes and the way his shoulders drooped. He wished John would talk to him about what was bothering him. Maybe he just needed a project.

"Hey, John. What do you say we team up and help Elizabeth on Tuesday?" Mark had other reasons for wanting to go, but if he could get his brother involved it would help John. He just knew it.

The youngest Manning brother present shrugged. "Sure, I guess." He looked to his dad. "As long as you're fine with me leaving for the day?"

Caleb smiled and clapped his hands. "I think that's a perfect way to spend the day. Just don't leave until the animals have been fed. I can manage the rest that day."

It was settled, all the Manning children and their spouses would take the day and head up to Bozeman to work with the homeless.

Mark had spent a good amount of time during the winter working on the new bunkhouses so they would have the space to bring back more of the homeless women who were ready to change their lives for the better. They even had one bunkhouse ready for men, if any wanted to get away from Big Bart.

The next day, Mark had to head into town for supplies. They were supposed to share the supply run job, but lately Mark had volunteered himself more and more.

"Hey, cowboy. Fancy seeing you here." Leah Hayes, sister to Mark's new brother-in-law Logan Hayes, greeted Mark with a huge smile.

"Hey...there." Mark's reply even sounded awkward to his own ears. Leah had been a friend his entire life. He'd even taken her out on a couple of dates, as friends, in the past. But now that they were kinda sorta related, Mark wasn't really sure how he should greet her. Was she his sister now? Or was she still just the pesky little kid who followed him around when they were in school? Whatever the situation, he did enjoy talking to her. Especially when she gave him the blow-by-blow of the latest checkers match.

"So tell me, who won this time?" Mark's cheese-eating grin spread from ear to ear.

Leah tried to hide her smile. "Who do you think it was?" She tilted her head and waited for him to answer.

"Not Mr. Cannon, or I'd have heard about it already." Mark didn't bet on the winners and losers, but he did like to think he could pick the winners, and he'd chosen Charlie Macon. Charlie won most of the time, so it really was a no-brainer.

"Ok, Mr. Smarty Pants. If it wasn't Mr. Cannon, who do you think it was?" She put a hand on her hip and smiled.

Mark's breath hitched, and he shook his head to clear his thoughts. "Ahhh, I... Um..." He couldn't speak. When he looked at Leah, all he saw was a beautiful young woman. Where had she come from? What had happened to the girl with pigtails he used to tease and torment?

Today she wore tight jeans, a red tank top, and a form-fitting black-and-red checked shirt that was tucked in. Her auburn hair was silky and hung in long curls around her shoulders. And her scent. Mark's senses were on overdrive. Leah smelled like spring flowers, vanilla, and something a bit woodsy that he wouldn't have expected on a woman. Was it wood chips? That would only make sense if she had been working in the garden.

Oh, he couldn't think straight.

"Mark? Did you hear me?" Leah's brow furrowed as she gave him a worried look.

"Huh?" He scratched his chin. "Sorry, my mind was elsewhere. What did you ask?"

"Are you alright?"

"Yes." He shook his head and chuckled. "Guess I was woolgathering. Sorry about that."

"Uh-huh." She blinked and crossed her arms over her chest. "Who do you think won?"

"Charlie Macon, right?" If Mark had been thinking straight he would have teased her, but as it was he was having a hard time not leaning in closer to Leah and taking a better whiff of her alluring aroma.

If he did, she'd probably slap him. And he'd deserve it.

Leah chuckled. "You really weren't paying attention, were you?"

He winced. "I guess not. What did I miss?"

Leah laughed and shook her head. "Not much, I guess. Just that it wasn't Charlie who won."

With wide eyes, Mark refocused on the conversation. "Please tell me it wasn't Mr. Cannon?"

"Nope, it wasn't."

Mark searched his addled brain, trying to figure out who it could have been. Mr. Addison never won. The only other person it could be was Lou Ann Dobbs' husband, Ditson. "No way, Mr. Dobbs won?"

"Nope." Leah smirked.

With a slack jaw, Mark stared in amazement at Leah. "You mean to tell me that our old postman Tom Addison finally won a tournament?"

Leah nodded. "Yup. And I'm surprised you hadn't heard about it. It's been the talk of the town for several days now."

"Wow, I guess I've really been out of the gossip lately." Mark rubbed his chin. "Good for ol' Mr. Addison. He deserves a win."

"Yes, he does." Leah walked to the feed supply section of the store with Mark on her trail. "Now, what can I get you today?"

"We have a list of items." Mark pulled a piece of paper from his pocket and handed it over to Leah. "Also, I wanted to check and see if you've heard about the trip to Bozeman on Tuesday."

She nodded. "I can pull this together for you. Give me twenty minutes? I can text you if you want to head over for coffee?"

"I can help." Mark put his hands in his front pockets.

Leah looked up at him. "Really?" She scrunched her nose. "You've never wanted to help me pull items before."

His shoulders slumped. "Well, now that we're related I figured I should act more like a big brother."

The smile left her face, and she turned around. "I already have one big brother. I don't need another five."

"Well, John and Roman would technically be your younger brothers." Mark gave her a cheeky grin, which she missed.

"Still, I don't need any more brothers. Go ahead and get your coffee; I'll text you when the order is done." She walked away without a backward glance.

"What'd I do?" Mark ran a hand through his hair and stood watching Leah walk away from him.

Sheriff Roscoe stepped up to Mark and chuckled. "Looks like the little lady wants something other than another big brother."

Mark turned a confused gaze on the sheriff.

Chapter 4

"**M**en, pft." Leah shook her head and went to the back of the store to pull the order for the big lughead. "Why do they always think that I'm some little girl needing a big brother?"

"Hey, what's going on?" Elizabeth walked in from the back door.

"Oh!" Leah jumped and put a hand over her heart. "You scared me. How'd you get back here without me seeing you?"

She held up a keychain. "Logan gave me the keys. He asked me to grab something off his desk."

Leah nodded. "Oh."

"What's wrong? Who are you grumbling about?" Elizabeth joined Leah and followed her to the back storeroom.

"Your brother."

"Which one?" Elizabeth raised a brow.

Leah pointed over her shoulder. "The big lug who thinks I need another set of brothers."

A glint shone in Elizabeth's eyes. "Ah, I see. Mark's out front?"

"Wait." Leah stopped and looked to her sister-in-law. "How'd you know it was him?"

"Because he's the only one who elicits that kind of reaction from you these days."

Leah got a sour look on her face. "What's that supposed to mean?"

Waving a hand in front of her face, Elizabeth ignored the question. "So, Tuesday. Are you in? We're heading up to see the girls in Bozeman."

"I wish, but if Logan's going then I have to stay here and watch the store." Leah frowned.

"Bummer. I'll tell you all about it. How about lunch on Wednesday?" With her schedule lately, Elizabeth had been able to stick around town more often and do lunch with her friends and sister-in-law.

"Perfect." With that settled, Leah got to work filling the Manning order.

When Tuesday rolled around, Leah found herself meeting up with her brother and his wife thanks to her dad coming in and watching the store for the day. Over the past few months he had taken on more and more shifts. Her dad was doing much better with Logan home and married to his childhood sweetheart. His heart attack was in the past, and even though he had to be careful, work was one thing the doctor had said he could do as long as he didn't lift anything more than forty pounds.

"Remember, Dad. Let Stevie do all of the lifting." Leah pointed a knowing finger at her dad. Typical of most men, he usually did try to lift things he shouldn't. "Stevie, be sure to keep an eye out for my dad and don't let him lift anything," Leah ordered.

The part-time helper saluted Leah. "Aye, aye, Captain."

She rolled her eyes but said nothing before leaving to join the caravan to Bozeman.

"Leah. I thought you couldn't make it?" Mark smiled and hugged her.

She shivered when Mark's arms wrapped her in a warm hug. He smelled of spices that pricked her nose, pine, and leather. Leah loved the scent of leather. One thing she had noticed was that most cowboys smelled like leather. But none smelled as good as Mark Manning.

"Hey, are you cold?" Mark took his denim jacket off and wrapped it around Leah's shoulders.

"I'm fine. Really." She tried to take the jacket off, but when his scent enveloped her she halted and left the jacket on her shoulders.

Mark smiled. "Please, I insist."

"Thank you. I should have brought a jacket today." Even though she really wasn't cold, Leah decided it would be nice to wear Mark's jacket. She tilted her head to take in another whiff of him and closed her eyes. It was like smelling perfection.

Elizabeth walked to the front of the group. In addition to the Manning family and Leah, Harper and Sophia were also there. "Alright"—she looked around the group—"you all know the rules. No one goes off on their own, and there's always at least one guy in each group just to ensure that Big Bart and his guys don't get any ideas."

"What about Georgia? Are you prepared to bring her home today?" Sophia asked. Georgia was one of the homeless women they had all been speaking with lately. The woman was new to the area but not happy about being there. Bart and his guys had practically gang-pressed her into working for them.

Elizabeth nodded. "I'm always ready to bring anyone home who wants to come with us. But we won't force anyone into leaving. They have to want to leave this life in order for it to work for them."

Everyone nodded. They knew all too well the problems with forcing someone to clean up their act. It never worked. The last time they tried to make someone leave the streets, she ended up back there and hadn't spoken to anyone from Beacon Creek since.

"I hope Alana talks to us today." Callie had been the one to persuade Alana to leave the streets, only to have her run away a few days later when Mrs. Manning tried to get the young girl to help with chores.

Luke took his wife's hand. "Don't worry. At least you tried. That's all we can do. If Alana isn't ready to clean up her act and contribute to society, then we can't force her."

"I know, I just feel bad that I talked her into coming home with us before she was ready. I should have known better." Callie sighed and put her head on Luke's shoulder.

"We can only learn from the past and move forward." Elizabeth smiled at her sister-in-law.

Everyone piled into the SUVs and trucks heading to Bozeman, and Mark was pleasantly surprised to find himself seated next to Leah in Logan's SUV. It wasn't a long drive, only about thirty minutes, but it did mean that he would most likely be paired up with her for the day. They all usually worked with whoever they rode with.

The time went quickly, and Leah was surprised to see they were already closing in on the Burger Basket where they normally parked. "Looks like Bart is expecting us."

Mark looked out the side window and growled.

Bart was standing on the end of a street with several of his thugs, watching their caravan park in the lot.

"Great, I had hoped by coming in on Tuesday we would catch them off guard." Elizabeth pursed her lips.

"Do you think he got a heads up that we were coming?" Mark asked.

While Logan focused on the road, the rest of the group in his vehicle looked out the window at Bart.

"No, I think it's just bad luck." Elizabeth watched as Bart's eyes went from surprised to angry when they passed him. "Looks like he might be just as surprised to see us as we are to see him here."

Leah scanned the street for any familiar faces. "Is that Lisa?"

Mark looked around Leah and nodded. "Yes, and it also looks like the local sheriff is talking to one of Bart's goons. Do you think he's finally doing something about these guys?"

Elizabeth shook her head. "No, I doubt it. Sheriff Roscoe has spoken with him a few times, and all he says is that he doesn't have the budget or the manpower to get rid of them."

"But they're always committing crimes. Why can't he arrest any of them?" Leah scowled at the men on the street watching them.

Mark had been involved in several conversations with Sheriff Roscoe regarding this very topic and wasn't happy with the outcome. "The local sheriff has no proof of them committing crimes. Living on the street isn't illegal. Neither is panhandling. Not really. So until some real proof comes in against Bart and his goons, the sheriff really can't do anything."

"But"—Leah pointed to one of the women who had an obvious black eye—"he beats the women who don't do what he tells them to do. That's illegal, isn't it?"

"It is, but none of them will point the finger at Bart or his goons. Until someone witnesses it and reports Bart, the sheriff can't do anything." Elizabeth opened her door and got out once Logan had parked.

Everyone gathered around Elizabeth and her team.

Bart sauntered over to the team with a cocky expression on his unshaven face. Leah noted that he could have been handsome if he wasn't so evil. That must have been how he was able to get so many people to follow him. He was kinda like the pied piper, but instead of playing a flute he smiled and charmed people into doing what he wanted.

Then he stabbed them in the back. And threw them down and jumped on them.

Bart looked Leah up and down. "It's good to see you again, Leah. It's been a while."

Mark stepped closer to Leah and narrowed his eyes at Bart.

"Another Manning brother acting as chaperone? Really, you guys are too much." Bart snorted. "I'd never hurt a woman."

At that lie, Leah laughed. "Really? Then why are there so many women under your *care* who look as though they need to be under a doctor's care instead?" She crossed her arms over her chest and glared at the brute.

He held his arms up and acted innocent. "Living on the street is dangerous. I do what I can for my people, but sometimes things are just out of my control." Bart turned to his men. "Isn't that right, Rocko?"

Rocko flexed his muscles. "That's right, boss. It's very dangerous out here. Especially for women." He narrowed his eyes at Leah and his lip curled up.

Leah did all she could to keep from showing any fear. But right then and there she decided she'd not allow herself to be alone with Rocko, ever. The giant brute looked like he wanted to scare her. And he'd probably beat her up if he was ever given a chance.

Mark put an arm around her shoulder. "Knock it off. There's no need to act like an animal. Unless of course you're nothing more than Bart's dog?" He arched a brow.

When a growl emanated from Rocko, Bart pulled him back. "Calm down. These nice people are just here to help the poor and destitute. Let them give out their money and treats. Our people can use their help." He nodded back toward an alley where more of their crew stood watching.

Leah hadn't been on too many of these outings, as she always had to stay back and watch the store. But she had been on enough to know that Bart and his gang would watch them. If they gave out anything of value, his goons would take it from the homeless—by force, if necessary.

They had moved away from giving out gift cards. Since those who needed them most never ended up with them, it wasn't worth it. Besides, too many of the women and even a few of the older men ended up with bruises all over when they refused to give up the valuable cards.

Instead, they now handed out bags of food. Usually a sandwich of some sort along with fruit and a small bag of chips. They always put a gospel track in the bags so there was something to use for witnessing to the people who lived on the streets. And when it grew cold, they handed out warm socks and thermal underwear.

Now that spring was on their doorstep, they'd hand out t-shirts and tube socks. If Bart took those items, well, there really wasn't much he could do with them. Unless he just wanted to be mean. It wouldn't do to let the people die; Bart and his goons needed them to beg and steal for them. So as far as Leah knew, Bart let the folks keep the clothing items.

Once Bart and his guys walked over to the side street, Elizabeth set her teams to work. They worked in teams of four that day. Leah, Mark, Elizabeth, and Logan took off down a street that they preferred to work. The homeless were creatures of habit; they tended to stick to the same places, so this team wanted to see if any of the people they were trying to befriend were around.

Georgia was on Leah's mind. The last time she joined the group in their effort she had met Georgia, a homeless woman from California. Plus, Elizabeth had been talking about the woman a lot recently. The last time Lizzie and her brothers came out, Bart had beaten the middle-aged woman badly.

One of Bart's goons hovered close by that day, according to Logan, and they didn't get much information out of Georgia. Of course, everyone knew what had happened, but she refused to confirm it. Today, Leah was hoping the woman was in better shape.

A blonde ponytail swished in the distance, and Leah's eyes widened. If that was Georgia, she was looking much better than she'd expected.

"Oh, no. It's worse than I thought." Elizabeth scowled and grabbed Logan's hand.

Leah looked to Mark for an explanation, but he shook his head.

Chapter 5

The team walked toward where Georgia was looking through a window. As they passed by a side street, Mark heard two men whispering.

"She's perfect for the job." The voice wasn't familiar to Mark.

The second guy disagreed. "No, she's not. If she's not willing to do it then she'll do a bad job. We need someone who's willing to work."

"What?" Leah started, but was cut off by Mark's finger to her lips.

Mark nodded toward the street. The two of them watched Logan and Elizabeth continue on to Georgia, but Leah and Mark stayed out of sight and listened in on the conversation.

"I'm tellin' ya, she'll do just fine. We only need her to distract the guard." The first guy was adamant.

"We'll get caught if we use Georgia. She's too lazy." The second guy broke out into a coughing fit.

"You really should have that looked at."

The cougher said, "Nah, it's just smoker's cough. I'm fine. But what are we going to do about the job tonight?"

"Make Georgia do it. And if anything goes wrong, she'll take the fall." The first guy cackled.

Mark looked to Leah.

She returned his worried gaze and nodded.

They headed toward Mark's sister and Leah's brother, whispering about what they had just heard. "They're going to force Georgia into something illegal."

"I know. We have to get her out of here, and now," Leah agreed.

"Hey there." Elizabeth's perky voice belied her worried expression.

Mark knew his sister well enough to know that she was worried, and he had to agree with her. Georgia was in some serious trouble.

The woman was clean and her hair had been recently washed. She was even dressed in clothes most street people wouldn't be caught dead in. Mostly because it wasn't warm enough to wear jeans and a light blouse while being outside all day long. The woman only had on a light denim jacket. She'd catch a cold or worse if she didn't get proper clothes on soon.

The temperature had been going back and forth between hot and cold the past week. Leah wished it would make up its mind and either be cold or warm.

"Georgia, it's good to see you again." Leah walked forward and handed the homeless woman a bag.

Georgia turned fearful eyes on Leah and Mark. She mouthed, *Help*.

Elizabeth pulled out her cellphone, but Mark couldn't hear her conversation. He turned his attention back on the poor woman in front of him and thought how he could get her away from here.

"There's some food inside the bag. You might want to eat it now." Leah watched as Georgia pulled out a ham and swiss and took a bite.

"Mmm, it's good. Thanks." She looked around and froze.

Leah looked over her shoulder and noticed a man standing at the entrance to the side street they had passed. He must have been one of the guys they'd overheard. She looked to Mark and willed him to do something. Anything to help the poor woman.

Mark looked at his sister and nodded back toward the guy behind them.

His sister stared at him and gave a slight nod toward Georgia. Then mouthed, *Stall*.

Realization dawned on him. Elizabeth had already started a rescue plan.

"So, Georgia. What did you used to do when you lived in California?" Stalling wasn't exactly something Mark did best. But he would do whatever came to his mind if it meant getting this woman out of trouble.

She shrugged. "I did a lot of different things. Mostly just office help."

Leah joined in. "What was your last job?"

Georgia looked at her and a small smile crossed her lips. "I was a file clerk for a law office. It wasn't anything glamorous, but I did enjoy working in an office."

"Why aren't you still working there?" Mark asked. He knew he was being too nosy. In his experience, the homeless rarely spoke about their past and what put them on the streets.

Georgia sighed. "My boss was caught embezzling funds from clients. When he lost his job, everyone on his team did as well. Even though I had nothing to do with it, I was guilty by association." She sighed.

"I'm sorry. But why couldn't you get another job in the same field?" This time it was Leah who was being nosy.

"The story of my life. Guilty by association meant that I was unhirable. No matter where I tried, I was treated as though I had participated, or at the very least had turned a blind eye. It didn't matter that I couldn't have known, since those records weren't even something I had access to."

Leah scrunched her nose. "I'm sorry. That sucks." She looked the woman up and down. "Are you preparing to head out for a job interview?"

"I gotta go." All of a sudden, Georgia looked around and began to fidget. She tried to walk away from Leah and Mark, but with the four of them surrounding her it was difficult.

Elizabeth held her hands up in a placating manner. "Whoa there. We're sorry if we pried. We didn't mean to."

A pair of frightened eyes stared back at them, and Georgia licked her lips. "Look, I've gotta go. I don't need any more trouble." She looked down the street before turning pleading eyes on Mark and Leah. "Please, let me pass."

Tires screeched, and Logan's SUV came to a quick stop in front of them.

"Hurry up and get in," Matthew called to the group.

Elizabeth took Georgia by the arm. "We're getting you out of here, to somewhere safe."

Georgia pulled back. "It's not safe anywhere."

Logan looked back and noticed the man on the corner coming toward them with a scowl on his face. "If you don't come with us, I think you're gonna be in a lot of trouble."

Georgia looked over her shoulder and cried out, "No." But she scrambled into the back seat of the SUV along with everyone else.

Matthew was behind the wheel. The second the doors closed, he hit the gas and took off like a bull straight outta the chute.

"Did everyone else get in their cars safely?" Elizabeth asked.

"Yes, they should all beat us home." Matthew kept his eyes on the road but also watched his rearview mirror as they left town.

"Will Bart come after me?" Georgia's fearful voice barely made it to Matthew's ears.

"I don't think so. We've taken others home with us, and he's never come to Beacon Creek before." Elizabeth turned around from the front seat to smile at Georgia. "You'll be safe with us."

Once they were back at the Triple J Ranch, where Elizabeth and the rest of the Manning family had set up bunkhouses for the women they planned on rescuing, Mark took Leah back to town.

"I can't believe that all happened so fast." Leah shook her head. "We didn't even get to give out more than like two bags of sandwiches and socks."

Mark chuckled. "I know. It's never been like that before. It went so fast, it feels like all we did was rescue Georgia."

Leah looked to Mark and pursed her lips. "Do you really think she's gonna be safe here?"

"I do. Even if Bart shows up, Sheriff Roscoe won't allow him to hurt anyone. Not to mention all of us can protect the women on the ranch. Georgia will be just fine." Mark turned down the main street and headed toward the general store. "Besides, it's not like Bart knows where we live exactly."

Leah thought about it for a minute. When they stopped, she turned to him before getting out. "You're right. All should be just fine. But I have a feeling we won't be welcomed back in that neighborhood for a while." She chuckled.

"Yeah, I think we should hold off a few weeks before going back." Mark smiled and waved to Leah as she closed the door and headed inside.

When Leah entered the store, all thoughts of Georgia and Big Bart left her mind. Her dad was inundated with shoppers. She should have known; it was spring, and the ranchers would be ready to begin planting. Which meant a lot of business.

"Oh, honey. Thank goodness you're back already." Her dad sighed and motioned to the chaos surrounding him. The store was packed with people wanting to place orders as well as pick up those they had placed online.

Leah put on a smile and jumped right in and helped. When the day finally ended, her stomach rumbled and she placed a hand on it.

"I heard that," a familiar voice said when he entered the store.

She turned around and felt her cheeks warm. "Mark. What are you doing here?"

"I had to come to town for an errand and saw the lineup of trucks outside. Knowing you and your brother the way I do, I figured you hadn't eaten anything all day." Mark held up a takeout bag of food.

The scent caused Leah's tummy to rumble again. "Oh, you're a lifesaver."

He chuckled. "Don't worry, I brought enough for everyone." Mark moved to the back room and laid out four sets of burgers and fries from Rosie's Diner down the street.

Mr. Hayes, Leah, and Stevie all smiled when they saw their dinner waiting for them.

Mark looked around. "Where's Logan? I got him a burger and fries, too."

Stevie chortled. "He went home when his wife called about an hour ago."

Mark raised a brow, but didn't comment even though he sorely wanted to crack a joke about Logan already being whooped by a woman. Or maybe he would have said that Logan was stuck to his wife's apron strings. He wasn't exactly sure what would have come out of his mouth, but since Logan was married to his sister, he figured he should keep his trap shut. She'd hear whatever he said and then he'd have to pay.

Leah watched the expression cross Mark's face and did her best to hold in a laugh. "You want to say something, don't ya, cowboy?" She smiled at him before taking a bite of her burger.

"You know me well."

"Of course—you're practically my brother." Leah wished she could have taken that statement back. He wasn't her brother. She didn't need another brother, nor did she want one.

"Brother?" Mark raised a brow and sat down next to Leah. "I seem to remember someone stating that I most certainly wasn't her brother. And that she had zero use for another brother-in-law or otherwise." He winked at her.

A funny feeling entered Leah's stomach. One she didn't want to acknowledge. Instead, she took another bite of her burger and looked away from the handsome cowboy.

Chapter 6

Mark stopped short when he entered his kitchen the next day. Georgia stood in front of the stove with his mom, fixing breakfast. "Good morning, ladies." He walked over to the coffee pot and pulled out the carafe. It was empty. He scowled.

"Oh, I'm so sorry about that." Georgia put the pan she was cooking with to the side and headed over to the coffee maker. "I had set it all up to make another pot but forgot to turn it on."

He waved a dismissive hand. "I got it. No worries." Mark turned on the coffee maker and waited for the brown liquid of the gods to begin dripping. Once there was enough in the carafe, he pulled it out and poured himself a strong cup of joe. "That's the stuff. Thanks, it's cold outside today." Mark had just come in from feeding the cattle outside where it wasn't even thirty degrees yet.

His mom looked over her shoulder. "Mark, you might as well take a seat. It's going to be a few minutes before breakfast is ready."

He sat at the table and looked at the spread they were fixing up. "Looks like we're gonna have a nice breakfast today." Mark smiled and took a sip of his coffee and sighed. This was exactly what his cold bones needed to get moving again. "Can I help with anything?"

Georgia smiled and put the toast into the toaster. "No, I think we got it all."

"Ma, you must like having someone to help again in the kitchen."

Judith Manning smiled and nodded. "It's very nice to have a second pair of hands that know what they're doing." She looked to Georgia. "I hope you're going to stick around for a while."

Pink tinged Georgia's cheeks and she tilted her head down. "Thank you. I really appreciate you giving me a place to stay. And it's nice to cook again. I haven't done that in...gee, I don't know how long." She pulled the butter from the fridge and set it on the table along with three different jam jars.

Before Mark could pipe in, his brothers and dad joined them. All of the Mannings who currently worked the ranch got themselves a cup of coffee and sat down at the table.

Georgia, without even being asked, went over to the empty coffee pot and began making a fresh pot. "You really go through a lot of coffee, don't you?"

Mark laughed. "You know it. A rancher has to be up very early and works hard. The caffeine helps to keep us going in the morning and afternoon. And the hot drink helps warm us up throughout the day."

"Plus"—Luke took a drink—"coffee is the nectar of the gods." He grinned when he placed his mug on the table next to his plate.

"Hear, hear." Caleb saluted with his mug before taking a drink.

John had been quiet, but looked to Georgia after taking a bite of his country scramble. "This is really good. I hope you'll be staying with us for a while. Ma can really use help in the kitchen."

"Hey, now," Caleb practically growled.

John's eyes widened. "Oh, I didn't mean it to sound like that. What I meant was that we eat a lot. There's a lot of us. It's all too much work for one person." He looked to his mom. "Ma, you know I love your cooking. But Georgia is a much better helper than any of us boys have ever been."

Judith laughed. "I know exactly what you meant, son."

Mark chuckled. "You know, John, it might have been better if you'd just kept quiet."

Sitting next to Mark, it was easy for John to backhand his brother.

"Boys, what I have said about fighting at the table?" Caleb arched a brow.

Mark looked down at his plate. "Sorry, Dad."

John sighed. "I'll save the rest for when we get out to the barn."

"That's my boys." Caleb grinned.

"Is it always this rambunctious?" Georgia turned wide eyes to her hostess.

Judith smiled. "Yes, it is."

That afternoon, Sheriff Roscoe stopped by looking for Caleb.

"Sheriff, come on in and I'll call my husband." Judith directed their old friend to the sitting room. "Would you like some coffee while you wait?"

"Did I see the sheriff drive up?" Mark and his dad walked into the sitting room and greeted the sheriff.

"Judith, if you've got some fresh coffee I'd love a mug." Roscoe sat down in one of the easy chairs and faced the two men in the room with a scowl.

Once they both sat, Caleb looked to his old friend. "What's goin' on, Roscoe? You don't look too happy."

The sheriff rubbed a hand down his face. "That's cuz I'm not, Caleb. Why didn't you tell me you'd rescued one of Bart's girls?"

Mark looked to his dad and back to the sheriff. "Is something wrong? You know that we do this once in a while."

With a sigh, Roscoe sat back in his chair. "But this time Bart's out for blood."

"What?" Georgia said as she entered the room with a tray carrying three mugs and a carafe of coffee.

All three men turned to the middle-aged woman and saw the color drain from her face.

"I knew leaving was a bad idea. I should have just done what they wanted me to do." Georgia put the tray down on the coffee table and practically fell back onto the sofa.

Sheriff Roscoe stood. "Are you the one Bart's looking for?" He looked at the woman who could easily pass for any of the town's ladies. "You don't look homeless."

Georgia wore he hair up in a ponytail, had on clean blue jeans, a pink sweater, and pink fuzzy socks. She had also fixed her makeup. The woman may have been in her mid-forties, but she looked more like she was in her thirties.

"That's because she's not." Judith entered the room holding her own coffee mug and walked over to where Georgia sat. "She lives here with us now."

"That's not what I meant, and you know it." Roscoe shook his head. "Why is Bart chasing after you when he hasn't set foot in our town before yesterday, that I know of?"

The shy woman bit her lower lip and looked to Mark.

"Sheriff, I think Georgia might know something she's not supposed to. When we rescued her, Bart and his gang were trying to force her to help with some sort of heist or theft." Mark rubbed the back of his neck. He knew that rescuing Georgia the way they did was dangerous, but she had asked for help. None of them could have turned their back on her that day.

When the sheriff took his seat again, he scratched the stubble on his chin. "Care to tell me what Bart is up to?"

She shook her head.

"If you tell me what you know, I'll keep you safe. Don't worry about Bart."

Georgia turned frightened eyes to Mark and bit her lower lip. "What should I do?"

Of everyone in the house, Mark was the one she knew best. Not that she really knew anyone in the Manning household, but she had spoken to Mark on multiple occasions since she joined Bart's crew last year. So when she turned to him, Mark knew it would be up to him to help her feel safe. And he was going to do whatever it took to ensure she never went back on the streets again.

He moved to sit next to her on the couch and put a hand on her shoulder. "Georgia, you're safe here. And if you tell the sheriff what you know, he just might be able to arrest them. If they're taken off the street, they won't be able to hurt anyone again."

"But if I stay quiet, they'll leave me alone." She began to pick at her fingernails.

The sheriff shook his head. "Darlin', I'm sorry. But if they think you have information on them, they won't leave you alone."

"Then I'll go back to them and stay quiet." Georgia looked to Mark and winced.

Mark shook his head. "That will be worse. You can never go back to Bart or the streets. We can keep you safe here. Tell the sheriff what you know so he can arrest Bart and his crew."

"But what I know won't put Bart in jail, just two of his crew." Georgia stood up and began to pace in front of the sofa.

Mark stood up and took her hand. "Georgia, listen to us. We *can* help you."

Georgia pulled back from Mark and winced. "I'm afraid."

"I know. Anyone in your shoes would be. But do you trust us?" The sheriff's soft voice seemed to get to her. He put a light hand on her shoulder and looked her in the eyes.

"I know I should, but trust isn't easy to come by on the streets."

"Give me a chance to show you I can be trusted. Stay here with the Mannings and tell me what you know. I'll do everything I can to get Bart and his entire crew off the streets and into jail where they belong." The sheriff had wanted that band of thieves off the street for the past two years. Even if it meant he could only pick them off one at a time, he'd still do it.

Georgia looked at everyone in the room. She squared her shoulders and did her best to stand taller, even though all the men in the room were taller than her. "I'll do it."

"I knew you could." Sheriff Roscoe smiled warmly at the woman. "Now, let's sit down and you tell me what you know. Even if it's not about Bart directly, tell me everything you can remember."

They sat there and went through two carafes of coffee before her story was finished.

"Do you think it's enough to put Johnny and Bob away?" Georgia gnawed on her bottom lip and picked at her fingernails.

"If we catch them in the act it will be. I'll coordinate with the Bozeman sheriff to make sure we have a trap set for them." Roscoe stood up.

"But, isn't the Bozeman sheriff working with Bart?" Mark asked.

Georgia scrunched her nose. "I doubt it. He's always sniffing around and hassling Bart and his gang. He just hasn't found anything substantial to charge Bart with yet."

"Why didn't you report him for beating you up?" Matthew asked.

Georgia winced and looked down at her hands in her lap. "Because I was afraid. They said they could get to me no matter where I was. Even in the hospital they have friends."

The sheriff sat back down and put a hand over Georgia's. "They can't get to you here. I don't know who all they know in Bozeman, but I do know that the sheriff there is fed up with Bart and his gang. If they try to pull this heist, it will be the biggest one they've attempted. And there's no way the law in Bozeman will stand by and let it happen."

She nodded, then looked up into the sheriff's eyes. "Thank you. I really do appreciate your help."

The sheriff cleared his throat. "Of course. That's what I'm here for." He stood up looking dazed.

Mark hid a smile. "Sheriff, I'll walk you out."

When they were leaving the room, Sheriff Roscoe looked back over his shoulder and smiled at Georgia, who was watching him leave. Her cheeks pinked and she turned her head.

Mark caught the exchange out of the corner of his eye and chuckled. When they were outside, he patted his friend on the back. "Roscoe, looks like someone has caught your eye."

With hat on his head, he turned back to look at the house. "I... She's just a witness who needs our protection. That's all." He cleared his throat and got in his police SUV.

Laughing, Mark waved and called out, "You keep telling yourself that."

Chapter 7

That night Leah was closing up the general store by herself. A niggling feeling in the back of her mind told her something was off, but she wasn't sure what it was. She kept a can of bear spray in her purse. Not that they were close enough to the areas bears frequented, but it also served well as a human deterrent. In all her years she'd never had to use it.

Once she was certain all the doors were closed, she turned on the store alarm, exited the front door, and then locked it. She took the can of bear spray out and primed it to make sure it still worked. The entire time she looked around and tried to see if there was in fact anyone watching her.

The hairs on her arms stood on end when she walked into the lot where she'd parked her truck. In that moment, she wished she would have called her brother to come and get her. Like most of the single women, she had taken self-defense classes at Sophia's gym. But that didn't mean she wasn't a tad bit afraid of what, or who, might be watching her.

Earlier that evening she'd heard from Mark, who'd told her that Georgia told the sheriff what was going on. If Bart and his crew knew, then she could be in danger from him. Or it could be anyone out there casing her store to break in. Not that they had much crime in her little town, but it was possible.

She made it to her truck and was about to open the door when something told her to turn around. "What?"

A tall man, dirty and stinky, stood right in front of her. He brought his hand up.

Not wanting to wait and see what he was going to do, and since he was in her personal space already, she put up her own hand and sprayed. She prayed the wind was in the opposite direction and she wouldn't get any of that spray in her face.

He screamed and backed away from her.

Leah scrambled inside her truck and locked the doors before she started the engine. As she pulled out of the lot, she noticed a familiar face smirking back at her—Rocko. Bart's men were in town and stalking her. Using her truck's Bluetooth device, she called the sheriff.

Part of her wanted to complain when he told her to go home, but another knew it was the right thing to do. But instead of going straight home, she took many turns and even left town before turning around a few miles outside of town. Leah didn't want anyone following her home in case they didn't already know where she lived.

As she drove home, she kept her eyes peeled for anyone she didn't know. And she called Mark to let him know that Georgia might be in danger.

"Are you alright?" Mark asked, his voice laced with worry.

"Yeah, I'm fine. I'm just glad I thought to take my bear mace out of my purse before I walked outside. Who knows what that creep would have done if I hadn't sprayed him before he could get his hands on me." Leah shivered. She was going to talk to Sophia about more self-defense classes. One couldn't be too prepared for something like that.

"So am I." The phone went silent for a moment before Mark came back on. "I think you shouldn't be alone in the store. At least, not until Bart and his gang are arrested."

"That's taking it a bit too far, don't you think?" She didn't need a babysitter. Some more pointers on how to defend herself would be all she needed. Well, that and a new container of bear spray. Or maybe she should get a stronger concentration of pepper spray? It was legal in Montana.

Mark sighed. "Leah, please. Be safe. If Bart's gang tried to attack you tonight, do you think they'll just move on because you sprayed one of his goons with bear spray?"

She knew he was right, but it still stung that she might need an escort, or protector. Or whatever Mark was going to call it.

"Look, I'm not saying you can't take care of yourself. Because I know you can." He chuckled, thinking of the time Leah had kneed the town bully when he yanked on her hair in high school. She'd showed him. He always gave her a wide birth after that. "What I'm saying is that you shouldn't be alone. It's much easier to defend against a few men when there are at least two of you."

"Uh-huh. And that second person you mentioned. Would that have to be a man?" Leah wasn't a feminist, but she was a strong, independent woman who didn't think women in this day and age had to have a man to protect them. Sure, men were generally stronger. Well, except for Sophia. Not too many men were stronger than the woman who owned the local gym.

Leah would love to see any of them try anything stupid with Sophia.

"Not necessarily. But you know that Bart and his gang have always been deterred when you had men around. It might not make sense, but they seem to think that you women can't take them down."

Leah chuckled. "Well, I proved them wrong tonight."

Mark laughed. "Yes you did, sweetheart."

A funny feeling swarmed through Leah's chest when he called her sweetheart. Mark had never used a term of endearment with her. He'd called her plenty of names over the years, but never anything like sweetheart.

He stumbled over his words. "Ah, I... Ah, I mean kid-do."

Leah could hear the sigh coming over the phone, and if she hadn't been confused by his words and how they made her feel, she might have teased him over it. But as it stood, she just wasn't sure what to say.

After a few seconds of dead air, Leah spoke up. "I think I'll talk to Sophia tomorrow and see what she has to say. And besides, the next few days I will have a closer with me. We have some restocking to do after hours, so Stevie or Logan will be with me when I do close." She didn't always close; sometimes she was the opener. But the rest of this week she was on the schedule to close along with one of the guys, since they had several shipments coming in for spring product.

"That's good. I'm glad you won't be alone. I'll talk to Logan tomorrow, too, and see if there isn't anything else we can do."

When they said their goodbyes, Leah was already in her driveway. Before she got out, she looked around to make sure no one was at her home waiting for her. The lights were on inside, as well as the outside security lights. Nothing seemed amiss, so she got out and quickly walked inside, locking the door behind her.

She knew she'd have to tell her parents. They would need to keep an eye out at home, and when they were at the store as well. Why couldn't Bart just leave them alone?

The next day, Leah left early. She planned on visiting her friend, Sophia. Not too many people knew what the local gym owner did for the Army, but she knew her friend had been a part of the Army's secret intelligence division.

The only reason her friends knew this was because Sophia had spilled the beans about her training before she even left for boot camp. When she came home, she said she couldn't talk about anything. Leah was actually surprised that the Diner Divas hadn't sussed out exactly what Sophia did in the Army. There wasn't too much they couldn't figure out.

Sophia always got a faraway look in her eyes when she spoke about her time in the Army. Well, what little she did say. But when Sophia came home, she had bulked up and opened her gym. The cowgirl taught self-defense classes for free on the first Monday night each month to anyone who wanted to learn. You didn't even have to be a gym member to take these classes. Sophia was on a mission to ensure that each woman knew how to defend herself.

There were even men who took these classes. A few high school boys did it to meet girls, but when they realized they were going to be the ones getting beat up, most stopped going. Sophia did have a few men who volunteered to be the punching bags. They were pretty big and beefy cowboys who didn't mind women hitting them or throwing them over their shoulders.

Leah had even seen a few of the men date some of the women who attended these classes. But she had never been interested in the cowboys who helped, or those who came to learn. Something about dating a guy she'd met at a self-defense class seemed...weird.

"Leah!" Sophia called out from across the gym floor as she made her way to her friend.

"Hey, Sophia." Leah smiled and hugged her friend. "How's it goin'?"

"I'm fine. But I want to hear about you. The grapevine is all abuzz about you getting attacked last night. What's going on?" Sophia linked her arm with Leah's.

"I wasn't actually attacked." Leah looked around and lowered her voice. "I kinda did the attacking."

Both cowgirls laughed.

"Come on. Let's head into my office where we can have some privacy." The gym owner led them to the back room. Once the door was closed, she turned on the electric kettle to make tea.

"Sit down and tell me what really happened." Sophia crossed her arms over her chest and arched a brow.

Leah complied. Once she had told her story, the kettle whistled and Sophia began to make tea without even asking Leah what she wanted. They'd spent enough time chatting over the years for Sophia to know how Leah liked her tea.

"So, what do you think? Should I get a bodyguard? Or do you think another can of bear spray will be fine?" Leah had even considered getting a guard dog. It might be a good idea for the house, but not for the store.

"Mark's got a point." She held up her hands when Leah began to complain. "Hear me out." Sophia gave Leah a mug of hot tea and then took one for herself and sat in her chair across from Leah. "I think being alone isn't smart right now. But"—she held up a finger—"I also don't think you need a man watching your back."

A slow smile spread across Leah's face. "Are you volunteering to help me when I'm alone at the store?"

Sophia shrugged. "I could definitely help. But what I was thinking was that we could put together a schedule. Get all of our friends to volunteer some time to hang out with you, and anyone else who might be alone, until these guys are arrested."

"I didn't even think about others needing protection." Leah took a sip of her tea. "Do you think they'll go after anyone else here in town?"

"Hmmm, I'm not sure." Sophia narrowed her eyes. "Was there anyone else that day in Bozeman that Bart and his guys seemed to not like?"

"Yeah, Elizabeth. But they've never liked her." Leah chuckled.

Since Elizabeth was the one who had originally started this endeavor to help the homeless women in Bozeman, she'd come up against Bart and his goons too many times to count. She'd almost broken his thumb once.

Sophia nodded. "I doubt they'd try anything with her. She's married to Logan, and she's also come up against Bart a few times and won." She shook her head. "I think if they target anyone it would be you, since you're single and Logan's sister. Plus, you close the general store by yourself a lot. If they've been watching, they would know you're the easiest target right now."

"What about Harper? She's single, and she's not you." Leah pointed to Sophia.

The women chuckled.

"But she works in the clinic with other people. I don't think she ever walks out at night by herself." Sophia tapped a finger to her chin. "And she's got a shotgun at home. So anyone who tried to break in wouldn't get far."

"We've got several guns at home." Leah grinned. "And also in the store."

"That's why they'll wait for you outside. But I don't think guns will help you if there are several guys coming at you from different directions. A second person, even if it's a woman, will help deter them."

"Yeah, these guys are cowards. They seem to like to gang up on a woman who appears defenseless. I fought back last night, so they'll probably think twice before coming after me again." While Leah knew the greasy guy had been arrested already, Rocko was still out there. He was the one who worried her more than any of the rest.

She doubted Bart would come at her directly. He was too weaselly and wouldn't want to get his hands dirty if he could help it. If what Leah knew about Bart was true, he was just the face of the operation. Bart directed everyone else, who did the dirty work for him.

"True, but that doesn't mean they won't send three guys next time. All you need is one more person to stand with you. You just let me know what nights you work alone and I'll get a schedule set up. Don't worry, we protect our own."

Leah went into work after her time with Sophia. It was a busy day, and an even busier evening.

Mark brought them food from his mom after dinner.

"Thanks, Mark. I really appreciate having a good homecooked meal instead of fast food." Leah took his offered bag and brought it to the back.

He followed her and checked the locks on the back door before joining her in the little office/breakroom. "So, have you seen any of Bart's crew here today?"

Leah shook her head. "No, they haven't been around. Or at least, I haven't noticed anyone out of the ordinary."

"Good, good. If they don't come around again for a few days, it probably means they've given up on harassing you." Mark took a seat near Leah at the table.

"How's Georgia holding up with all of this?" Leah had worried about the girl all day. If Bart was mad at Leah, he had to be livid with Georgia. Especially if his guys got busted.

"She's doing really well." Mark ran a hand down his face. "Except for tonight."

"Why tonight?"

Mark sighed. "Tonight's the night of the heist. Or at least, the night she thought it was supposed to happen. The sheriff isn't sure if they're going to go through with it or not since we have Georgia."

"You mean, they might suspect she spilled the beans?" Leah sipped a bit of the taco soup and sighed. She loved the combination of spices, cheese, beans, beef, and corn. It was almost like a beef stew and taco combined.

He nodded. "They would have to be either very stupid or desperate to hit up that warehouse now."

"Or cocky?" Leah guessed. She knew Bart thought he was all that and a bag of chips. So maybe he thought they wouldn't get caught?

Mark looked at his watch. "We'll know in a few hours."

Chapter 8

Turned out Bart was smarter than the average thief. The stakeout was a bust; no one showed up.

"Well, that sucks," Leah said when Mark called her the next morning to tell her the situation.

"Yeah, it does." Mark had hoped it would have been all over the previous night. He should have known that Bart was smart enough to stay clear of the target now that Georgia was no longer under his control. "Sheriff Roscoe said they'll keep an eye out on that warehouse just in case they show up later."

"Okay, thanks for the update." Leah hung up and headed into work. At least she would have Stevie with her that night. He was scheduled to come in later in the afternoon and help her close and then restock.

She went in earlier than usual so she could head over to Rosie's Diner and see if there was any gossip. While Leah hated the way gossip spread faster than wildfire, she did appreciate being in the know on something as important as her own safety. If Bart and his gang were hanging around the area, the divas would know.

The bell above the door dinged when Leah walked in, and a pink pouf shimmied when a familiar face turned to look at her. "Leah Hayes, it's good to see you, girl."

"Hiya Mrs. Macon, Mrs. Dobbs, Mrs. Stanhope, and Mrs. Walters." Leah smiled at the retired women who held court at the diner counter. If anyone wanted any information on what was going on around town, all they had to do was come into the diner and sit near these four women. They gossiped like it was going out of style.

And they weren't quiet about it, either.

Last year the pastor did have a talk with them, and their gossip had slowed for a while. They even got involved in charitable work around town. But since Christmas they hadn't had much to do. Except gossip.

Leah thought they might want to help with the Spring Fling dance, and maybe even the carnival. Elizabeth had said that these ladies meant well and needed something to do.

The pastor had said that idle hands were the work of the devil.

Leah had to agree with both of them.

"Leah, sweetie. How are you doing?" Lou Ann Dobbs turned worried eyes on Leah and put a hand to her heart. "I heard some men tried to kidnap you the other night. Please tell me you're alright?"

Leah snorted. "Kidnap? Really? Come on, ladies. You know better than that. It was just a homeless guy hanging around the store."

"But didn't you mace him?" Merry Walters raised a brow.

"It was bear spray, not mace." If they knew that detail, then they knew she wasn't in any real danger.

"I heard there was another rascal watching the whole thing. But he's not been seen since." Martha Stanhope sniffed and reached in her purse for a tissue.

"Really? What do you know about that one?" Leah hadn't heard about Rocko from anyone else, nor had she told very many people. Just the sheriff, her family, Mark, and Sophia. And she knew none of them would gossip about Rocko.

"Oh, yes." Cindy Macon's pink pouf wobbled as she nodded, but not a single hair dared to move out of place. It was as though her hair was a jello mold and wobbled as she moved. "Tom Addison said that the bank's camera points directly at your store's parking lot. The sheriff went over and took a look at the footage. They saw a beefy man watching the whole thing." She tilted her head and her molded hair moved, but never fell over. "It looked as though you saw him. Did you recognize that man?"

Leah knew exactly who they were talking about. She also knew that the sheriff wouldn't have shared that detail with anyone outside of his team. Shoot, even Callie Manning hadn't said a word to her about it. "How did Mr. Addison hear about this?"

"Oh, that's easy." Mrs. Walters smirked. "He was in the bank when the sheriff was there with the bank manager reviewing the footage from your attack. When the sheriff left with a copy of the video, Tom and Eddie watched the footage."

"Eddie should have been told by the sheriff not to share that information with anyone. Especially not the old postman. He's no better than..." Leah almost said Mr. Addison was just as much of a gossip as the Diner Divas, but she held her tongue. "Well, I'd appreciate it if you wouldn't spread any more gossip about me." She arched a brow.

The four women gasped and put their hands to their chests, almost like it was choreographed.

Mrs. Stanhope spoke for the group. "We'd never gossip about you, Leah."

"Uh-huh." Leah pursed her lips. "Say, I heard the Spring Fling planning committee needs some help this year with planning. Have you ladies offered up your services yet?"

Mrs. Macon waved a hand in front of her face. "Oh, they don't want our help. They've got plenty of volunteers."

The rest of the ladies nodded.

Leah hadn't heard anything like that. In fact, she had heard Fannie saying she needed more help this past Sunday at church. "Did you offer to help?"

The ladies tittered and turned around.

"Ah, you haven't offered your help yet, have you?" Leah had caught them. When the pastor and Elizabeth had a talk with them in the past about their gabbing too much, it was said that they needed something to do. But these women did love their free time at the diner. If they did go help with the planning, they wouldn't be in the center of the town's gossip.

"You know, there's quite a bit going on over at the barn." Leah looked around at the almost empty diner. Granted, they were between breakfast and lunch, but if the ladies wanted to pick up on gossip, this wasn't the place to be right now.

It may have been sneaky on her part, but Leah was going to entice the divas to head over to the barn and livery, where the planning committee was working. A hundred years ago, the livery was the center of town. Once cars became commonplace the use of a livery was less and less important, but the town did keep the livery. Now, it was more of a local meeting place and less of a place to keep your horses when you were in town. And behind it was an old red barn where they held monthly dances.

Leah sidled up next to Cindy Macon, the unofficial leader of the divas. "You know, if you want to know what's going on in town right now, the livery really is the place to be." She winked and walked out of the diner.

Once she was clear of the place, Leah couldn't help it, she broke out laughing. Those women were irksome, but also hilarious. If she knew them half as well as she thought, they'd be over at the barn volunteering within the hour.

"What's so funny?" a very masculine voice asked.

Leah stopped in her tracks and put a hand to her heart. "Mark. What are you doing in town?"

"Oh, that hurts." Mark put a hand over his own heart. "Is that any way to greet your friend?"

Leah arched a brow. "Excuse me. Mark, it's so good to see you." She gave him a droll look. "Now, what are you doing in town?"

His deep, throaty chuckle sent chills all down her back and into her toes. He walked up close to her and set a stray hair behind her ear. "I came to see you."

Leah had always had a crush on Mark, but he had never touched her like that before. He used to pull on her hair, or he'd slap her shoulder, but he never touched her the way she'd seen Logan do with Elizabeth. Her stomach did somersaults, and her breathing grew ragged.

When he didn't say anything else, just kept staring into her eyes, Leah hoped he wasn't about to play one of his practical jokes on her.

"Hey, guys. What's going on?" Logan's voice broke the mood, and Mark took two steps back.

Leah wasn't sure if she should kiss her brother for saving her or punch him for interrupting.

"Oh, good. You're here, too." Mark turned to look at his brother-in-law and shook his hand.

Logan looked at his little sister. "Are you alright?" His brows furrowed, and he took a step closer to Leah.

"Hm? Oh, yes, I'm fine. Just wondering what's going on." Leah rubbed her sweaty palms against her jeans and headed toward the general store. "Logan, I thought you had today off. Aren't you taking Elizabeth out on a date tonight?"

"I am, but I'm working the store with you until about three. Then Stevie's coming to finish the night with you." Logan got in step with his sister as they crossed the street.

Mark was right behind them. "And I'm here to check out the security cameras."

Once they were across the street, Leah stopped. "The security cameras? Can't Logan do that?"

Logan chuckled. "Yes, I can. But Mark insisted on checking them himself. Plus, he wanted to add a couple to the area just to make sure every inch is covered." He patted his brother-in-law and friend on the back. "You know, I can take care of my little sister. But it's nice to know that you're looking out for her, too."

"We're family. And family always takes care of each other." Mark cleared his throat and looked at Leah sideways.

"You aren't going to spout off something about you being my big brother again, are you?" Leah put her hands on her hips. "I swear, if you do that again I'm gonna knock you into next year." She narrowed her eyes and leaned forward with a menacing look on her face. There was no way Mark Manning was ever going to be her big brother.

Mark put up his hands and gave Leah his biggest, pearliest grin. "But Leah, you wouldn't want to hurt your big brother-in-law, now would you?"

She slapped his bicep and pulled back her hand. "Ow. Since when did your arms get so hard?" The moment she said it, she regretted it.

The cheese-eating grin that spread across Mark's face was enough to send her packing.

Leah turned around and ran into the store. "Stupid dingleberry," she griped under her breath. "Big lughead." She shook out her hand and made a mental note not to hit his arm again. At least not without some padding on her hand.

Mark followed her inside. "Leah, any time you need my big guns"—he flexed his arms and kissed his biceps—"you just let me know."

"Oh, brother." Leah rolled her eyes and went to the back room to get her apron and put her purse away.

"That's right, *big* brother." Mark chuckled and looked around at all the eyes in the store watching him. "What?"

Mr. Addison scratched his chin. "Son, I don't think women like it when a man who's trying to court her refers to himself as her brother."

"Ah, no one ever said I was trying to court her." Mark's cheeks warmed, and he looked to Logan.

Hi brother-in-law shook his head and chuckled. "Come on, you big... What'd she call you? Dingleberry?" Logan waved for Mark to follow him to the back, where they kept a computer to view the backup of the security footage that was stored online.

"Hey, Logan. You know I'd never make a move on Leah, right?" While Mark and Logan were friends and had only gotten closer since he'd moved home almost two years earlier, he wasn't sure what Logan'd think about him dating his sister. Shoot, Mark wasn't sure how he himself would feel about it. But something had changed recently, and he wasn't sure what he wanted from Leah.

"Mark"—Logan put a heavy hand on the cowboy's shoulder—"as long as you treat my sister with respect and don't lead her on, I'm fine with the two of you dating." He turned around to turn on the monitor. "Just don't go hurting her. Make sure she's what you want if you do ask her out."

"Whoa, I never said I wanted to ask her out." Mark held up his hands, and he felt sweat begin to form on his forehead.

Logan turned around. "Uh-huh." He chuckled. "Everyone sees it. The divas have already chosen your wedding date."

Mark slumped in a chair. "NO! They didn't, did they? Does Leah know?" He picked up some papers and began to fan himself with them. "Is it hot in here? I heard your AC was on the fritz. I can fix it if you can't get a repairman out here."

Logan smirked. "Sure, if you want to fix it, go right ahead. And no, I don't think Leah's heard the chatter yet."

Mark smacked his forehead. "Oh, please tell me Elizabeth hasn't heard it yet?"

"Nope. Mrs. Macon said something to me yesterday and I shut her up." Logan narrowed his eyes at Mark. "At least, I think I did. But if the divas saw what I did outside

Rosie's Diner earlier, then I don't think they're gonna keep quiet."

Mark pinched the bridge of his nose and closed his eyes. "Man, I don't know what I feel. But I do know that I'm not ready for marriage. Not even close. Especially if those divas start wagging their tongues."

"Yeah, we've got to get them busy on a project." Logan had taken them with him to Bozeman a few times when they passed out bags of lunches and clothes. But the ladies hadn't gone with him and Elizabeth since the fall. And he didn't think it would be safe any time soon to bring them. He wasn't even sure it would be safe for him and a group of men to go, forget about bringing ladies.

"I heard the Spring Fling planning committee needs help." Mark had planned on suggesting to Fannie that she get the divas to help. "But, do you remember a few years back when Fannie tangled with the divas?"

Logan's face fell. "Yeah, I remember. I wasn't here, but my mom told me about it."

Mark scrunched his nose. "The divas just don't know when to back off. Although"—he held a hand up—"since the pastor spoke with them last year about their gossip, they've been much better."

"Until winter came and they had nothing better to do," Logan added.

Leah stuck her head into the room. "Hey you two wannabe Diner Divas, I could use some help out here if you're done gossiping?"

"I'll be right out, Leah." Logan turned to his sister and shooed her away.

Once she left, Logan showed Mark where everything was located and he joined his sister in the front of the shop.

During a lull in the afternoon, Leah asked her brother, "So, do you think they'll catch Bart and his gang soon?" She bit her lower lip.

Logan sighed. "I really don't know. I'd like to think that evil always loses, but the closer we get to the end times, the more evil is going to win."

Leah was afraid of that. "I know." She pursed her lips. "You know, sometimes I wish we weren't going through the Book of Revelation in Sunday school."

"Yeah, ignorance can be bliss sometimes," Logan agreed.

With a nod, Leah went back to straightening the rack of Wranglers she was working on.

Stevie walked in. "Did you see that strange guy hanging around outside?" He used his thumb to point over his shoulder.

Leah and Logan looked at each other.

"No, I didn't." Leah gulped.

"I'll go check the camera feeds." Her brother headed to the back, but stopped. "Stevie, stay up front with Leah until I get back."

"Yes, boss." Stevie turned worried eyes on Leah. He was only nineteen and not built for defending himself, let alone another person. "Do you think it's one of them?"

"Let's not jump to conclusions." She pulled her cell-phone out of her pocket and held it, ready to dial the sheriff if anything went wrong.

Not five minutes later, Logan joined them, smiling. "It wasn't anyone."

"What do you mean? Of course there was someone there," Stevie argued.

"Yes, there was a man outside, but I recognized him. He's from a ranch about two hours from here. He's come to town before." Logan rubbed his chin. "I think he might be dating Fannie's younger sister. I saw them walk hand in hand toward the diner."

Relief flooded Leah's system. She hadn't realized how worried she was until right then.

"Alright, everything looks fine. I'm heading out to take my wife to dinner. See y'all tomorrow." With a hand in the air and a smile on his face, Logan left the general store.

Chapter 9

L eah sat in her pew on Sunday morning, listening to the pastor's sermon. When she entered the building that morning, something inside her said to pay close attention. Usually when that happened, God had a special message for her. Looked like he was speaking to her again.

As she listened to the pastor, his words resonated through her entire being. He was preaching about the apostle Paul and his shipwreck on the little island of Melita. Not only did Paul barely make it to land after his ship was torn apart on the sea, but a viper latched onto his hand while they were trying to warm up over a fire. Most people would have thought Paul was being punished for something he'd done wrong.

In actuality, he was under attack by the enemy. However, like the footprints poem, God was carrying him through the trials. God isn't here to keep all evil away from us, the pastor explained, but he can help us get through it if we go to him and trust in him.

Leah thought about what she was going through. Most of her life had been pretty good. Her father having a heart attack almost two years ago had been the worst thing she'd ever experienced. But lately, with the taunting from Bart and his crew, she was worried the worst was yet to come.

Getting her head back into the sermon, she discovered that while Paul was on that island the locals treated him very well, even though he was a prisoner on his way to Rome for their version of a trial in front of Caesar. Paul used his gifts to help those on the island, and they in turn used theirs to care for him. According to Acts 28, Paul was on the island for three months before they were able to set sail for Rome again.

She doubted she'd ever go through anything as horrific as what Paul had to endure, but his experience hit her. He never lost his faith in God, and he kept preaching the Word and bringing more and more people to Christ. In fact, his words still brought people to Christ today. Part of Paul's draw was how he never turned his back on God, despite how he was treated.

Not that Leah was considering turning her back on God, but she had started to wonder what was going on. She turned her head and noticed that Mark had been watching her. Her cheeks warmed, and she hoped no one knew she was blushing.

Once the sermon was over and everyone stood to leave, Leah caught sight of Mark approaching her.

"So, what did you think about that sermon?" Leah hoped he had paid more attention to what the pastor was saying than to her.

"I think it was very appropriate for the time. We're all going through a lot right now, and I for one was wondering where God was during all of this." Mark rubbed the back of his neck.

She nodded. "I must admit, I had wondered the same." Leah winced. "In fact, my quiet time with God has suffered lately. I've felt further from him than normal."

"I know what you mean." Mark let go of a deep sigh and looked into Leah's eyes. "I think I need to spend more time in the Word and prayer."

Leah nodded her agreement and sent a silent apology to God for pulling away from him. She should have remembered that during times of difficulty she needed to move *closer to* God, not further away.

"I'm very glad the pastor spoke on this topic today." Mark looked around at his family and some of his friends. "I think we aren't the only ones who needed to hear this, either."

Leah turned around and watched others in the congregation having similar conversations to the one she and Mark were having. "I think I'm going to go home and read through Acts 27 and 28 more thoroughly. I have a feeling God might have more to say to me right now in those chapters."

"Yeah." Mark nodded. "I think you might be on to something."

Without thinking, Mark leaned in for a hug.

Leah felt flutters in her stomach and wished she didn't keep having these types of reactions to Mark. He was just being her friend, that was all. But her heart was telling her otherwise.

When he pulled back, a look of confusion crossed his face, and Leah wondered why he was confused. Did he ask her something? She wasn't really paying much attention to anything other than her traitorous heart and those butterflies that wouldn't leave her be.

"Ah, I think I need to get going. My family is waiting for me." He motioned to his brothers, who were watching them from near the exit.

Matthew had a huge smile on his face, and John was chuckling. It was good to see him laugh. Leah had noticed lately that he wasn't the happy cowboy he used to be.

"See ya." Leah waved to Mark and his brothers as they exited the church. She turned toward her parents and left with them for Sunday supper.

As Mark and his family headed home for their regular Sunday supper BBQ, he thought about Leah and this morning's sermon. Bart was watching her, he knew that. But for what reason, he didn't know. What he did know was that Bart was an evil guy who never did anything nice. And he had an issue with women.

Mark knew that God was in control and would protect Leah from anything He didn't want to happen. Even though Mark was worried about the pretty cowgirl, he knew he had to leave it all in God's hands. But that didn't mean God wasn't going to use him to help protect Leah.

Once he had worked through his thoughts, he realized that the pull he felt toward her must have been God's call for him to protect her. She was not only a childhood friend, but also family. True, they weren't related by blood, but that didn't mean they weren't as close as blood relations.

With a plan in mind, Mark knew what he would do come Monday.

Monday night, he drove into town. He knew that night Leah was closing the store with Stevie. While the boy would work as a sort of deterrent to anyone who might want to hurt Leah, he also knew that Stevie wouldn't be able to do much if that Rocko character was the one who came after them. Blast, he wasn't even sure if *he* could stand up to Rocko and walk away. That guy had some serious muscles, and looked to be the kind of animal that was accustomed to winning fights.

Once he drove into town, he noticed a few unfamiliar cars parked down the street from the general store. While that didn't mean anything, he was going to be ultra-sensitive to anyone new in town. He'd have to be if he was going to ensure Leah's safety.

Once he parked, he looked around before getting out of his truck. He didn't see anything out of the ordinary. But that didn't mean there wasn't danger lurking nearby. He stepped out of his truck and continued to look around as he walked up the steps into the general store.

Stevie waved to the cowboy when he heard the jingle above the door. "Hey, Mark. What brings you in so late?"

"I just thought I'd come in and check on you two to make sure everything was alright." Mark noticed two men in the front corner looking at men's clothes. He took a closer look but didn't recognize them. Again, that didn't mean they were up to no good.

"Mark, hey there," Leah called out when she came in from the back carrying a few pairs of Wranglers. She made her way to the men at the front of the store. "Okay, so I have your size in two different styles. Which one would you like?" She held out the jeans for the shoppers to see.

The taller one smiled at her and picked up the darker pair of jeans and looked at the size. "This is the one I want. Thanks."

"Don't worry, they're just in town visiting family," Stevie whispered as Mark continued to watch the strangers.

"How'd you know?" Mark turned questioning eyes to the young clerk.

"I asked them." Stevie shrugged and walked away to straighten the stack of jeans they had been looking through.

With a chuckle and shake of his head, Mark went to the section of the store where they sold various types of recurve bows and supplies. He and his brothers hadn't been hunting in a while, and they had been talking about going bow hunting lately. He'd have to make sure he polished up his skills.

Once the new guys had made their purchase and left, Mark headed toward Leah at the front counter. "Looks like you've been busy today." He had noticed that the store wasn't as clean as usual. The racks of clothes needed straightening, but so did a lot of the shelves.

She sighed. "Yes, it's been a madhouse here today. Not only are the farmers coming from our area, but the general store over in Three Forks had their roof collapse and they had to close while they fix it. So all of their customers are coming here instead."

"Wow, that sucks for them, but good for you. Right?"

Leah shook her head. "Not good for us, either. Stock is really low, and we don't have the manpower to keep up with demand."

"Why don't you hire more help temporarily?"

"It should only be like this for a week, so by the time we find someone and get them trained, it will be too late." Leah rubbed her lower back. "No, we're just gonna have to deal with it. Tomorrow my dad will start coming back in regularly, which will help. We should be fine for a week."

"And I'm going to work full time until the Three Forks general store is back open." Stevie walked up to the counter. "Boss, I think I need to head out back to get some of the stock that's locked up. Can I get the keys?"

"Sure, hang on." Leah went to the back office and came back out with a small key ring. "You know which ones you need?"

Stevie nodded and headed out back, leaving Mark alone with Leah.

With a hand on his neck, Mark looked around at the store. "So, you need help cleaning up tonight?"

"Thank you, Mark. That's mighty nice of you, but Stevie and I got this."

"I'm not leaving until you do, so let me help." He leveled his gaze on the pretty cowgirl and waited as he watched indecision on her face turn to reluctant acceptance.

"Fine. I can't have you staying up past your bedtime or you'll be too grouchy tomorrow and I'll never hear the end of it from Matthew and Luke," Leah grumbled.

"That's the spirit!" Mark held up a hand for her to high-five. "Oh, come on. Don't leave me hanging."

Leah chuckled and shook her head. "You better get to work. I'm not paying you to stand around chatting like a diva."

"Darlin', you ain't paying me anyways." He grinned and headed over to a rack of women's clothes and began straightening the hangers.

As Mark worked, he kept stealing looks at Leah. After about the tenth look, he noticed her cheeks beginning to turn pink. And he realized she knew what he was doing. Blast it all. He had been caught checking her out. But the fact that she was blushing had to be a good sign, didn't it?

Leah cleared her throat. "I'm going to go check on Stevie, make sure he's doing alright." Without looking at him, she went out the back door.

When he moved to the next rack, he heard her screaming. Mark ran out back as fast as he could.

"What's wrong? What happened?" He looked around expecting to see Bart or one of his guys.

Instead, what he saw made his blood boil.

"Stevie, can you hear me?" Leah was down on her knees next to the unconscious boy.

He hadn't even made it to the storage locker out back that housed some of their smaller items. Mark looked around for danger as he pulled out his cellphone and dialed 911.

Once the paramedics had taken away Stevie, who had come to right after Mark hung up, they went inside the store with the sheriff.

"Sheriff, I didn't hear anything or even see anyone." Mark rubbed a hand over his face. "What would have happened if I wasn't here? Would they have come inside and hurt Leah, too?"

The sheriff shook his head. "Now let's not go borrowing trouble. We don't even know for sure this is Bart and his guys. It could be someone else entirely."

"The video feeds," Leah blurted out. She had been quiet ever since Stevie woke up and said he didn't see his assailants.

Leah had been thinking about all the possibilities for the past fifteen minutes. The sheriff was right, it could have been anyone at all. But something in her gut told her it was Bart and his gang of goons. She just knew he had escalated the situation, and nothing in this world was going to stop her from ensuring that Bart didn't hurt anyone else ever again.

She ran to the back room where they had the camera feeds stored. Not only did they have the feed coming into a computer here at the store, but it was also stored in the cloud with a backup. After scanning the feeds for the past thirty minutes, she came upon the timestamp where Stevie went out back. It had actually been closer to an hour since he'd left the store.

Two men stood in the shadows, avoiding one of the cameras. But the camera that they had just installed across the lot got it all. And in pretty good definition, too. "Look, I would know that build anywhere."

"Rocko," Mark stated, nostrils flaring.

"Well, this confirms that Bart's gang was involved." The sheriff leaned in closer. "But I don't recognize the other guy."

Mark and Leah both shook their heads.

"Neither do I. But Elizabeth might. She knows most of the guys from Bart's crew, and his goons." With fists on his hips, Mark narrowed his eyes at the men on the camera as they watched poor Stevie go down. They had proof that both men had attacked Stevie without provocation. Shoot, they didn't even give him a chance to defend himself; they attacked him the second he walked out the door.

"They didn't even look to see who was coming out, they just slammed him the second the door closed." Leah put a hand over her mouth and turned from the screen.

Mark put his arms around her and held her tight. "He's going to be fine. You heard the paramedic—they're taking him to the hospital in Bozeman so they can get a head CT, but they said that since he woke up so quickly and was so alert, he should be fine. Probably a concussion, but that can be treated."

"I know. But when will they be caught? Will they even be put in jail? So far, no one has been able to get charges against them to stick." Frustration laced Leah's words, and Mark had to admit he had wondered the same thing.

"Well, this time it happened in my jurisdiction, and I'll not rest until they're both in my jail." The sheriff put away his notepad and pen after he finished taking their statements. "I'll need a copy of this video, too."

Chapter 10

The Spring Fling planning committee was in over-drive. Leah had the day off, so she decided to go in and see if she could help. Laying around worrying about everything wasn't going to do her a bit of good. Plus, the excitement of the upcoming dance and carnival should be enough to keep her mind more pleasantly occupied.

Stevie had been checked out and the doctor said he was going to be just fine. The young man would be in pain for a few days, but he didn't even have a concussion. Leah was grateful for that, but she was still worried for him.

The sheriff was going to send his deputies by the store on a regular basis, and he would also drive by whenever he was anywhere near town. Plus, he had brought in a few of the ranchers who had been deputized in the past.

The previous night they had a meeting, and everyone agreed to keep an eye out and to help with patrols around town, and most especially the Hayes ranch and the general store.

The barn where the dance was to be held was chaos, but Leah wasn't sure if it wasn't organized chaos. There was less than a week until the dance, and then the next day was the rodeo and carnival. The entire town would be focused on those two events for three days.

"Oh, are you here to help?" Fannie asked.

"If you could use my hands, I'd like to help." Leah looked around and noted the various people who had come to help, including all four of the Diner Divas.

"Yes, I can use you." Fannie looked to the side and noted someone who looked as though he needed help. "Come on, I've got just the thing for you."

Mark couldn't believe he had been roped into helping Fannie when he saw her at the diner that morning. He was grumbling about flowers and crepe paper when he felt eyes on him.

"Mark, you look like you could use an extra hand." Fannie motioned for Leah to join him before she headed off to the sound of glass breaking. "Now what?"

"Ouch. That sounded like it was going to hurt." Leah winced and looked toward a pink pouf covered in shards of glass.

Mark covered his face with his giant hand. "Oh, Mrs. Macon is going to have a hard time clearing that stuff out of her hair."

"At least she was protected by a mile-high pink pouf that was protected by an entire can of Aqua Net." Leah giggled, then covered her mouth. "Oh, that wasn't very nice, was it?"

"But it was the truth." Mark watched as Mrs. Macon complained about the kid on the ladder above her. He knew she was just fine. "That hair of hers finally came in handy for something."

"Too true." Leah turned back to Mark. "Now, how can I help?"

Mark waved his hands around at the layers of crepe paper he had somehow wrapped himself in. "What am I supposed to do with all of this?"

Not wanting to hurt his feelings, Leah held in a laugh. "Here, let me help."

They spent the next few hours hanging crepe paper banners, streamers, and even some silk flowers around the barn. He got up the ladder while Leah handed him everything he needed and pointed out exactly where the items needed to go.

The chairman of the Cattleman's Association walked in and headed straight to Mark and Leah. "Mark, got a minute?"

"Mr. Brandman, good to see you." They shook hands.

Mr. Brandman looked around and lowered his voice when he spotted Mrs. Walters looking his way. "I saw Logan, and he told me he was going to be staying close to home for the next few months. Are you feeling the same?"

"Ah, I see. You asked him to go on a buying trip with you, didn't you?" Leah's brother enjoyed traveling and was a member of the Cattleman's Association, even though they only had enough cattle for their family's needs. But since they owned the general store, they sold beef and pretty much anything the cattlemen around town would need.

He nodded. "I did. I was hoping to visit Hank Walton and wanted someone who could introduce me to him."

"I think Matthew would be a better contact. He's the closest to Hank." Mark got back up on the ladder to straighten a banner he had hung but was lopsided.

"I did ask Matthew, but he's not interested in leaving his wife right now." Mr. Brandman chuckled and shook his head. "Newlyweds."

"Well, you could ask Harper to give Hank a call for you," Leah suggested.

Mr. Brandman looked up at Mark on the ladder. "How about you, Mark? You know the man, don't you?"

Mark looked to Leah and frowned. Until the Bart situation was handled, he wasn't going anywhere. "I'm sorry, Mr. Brandman, but right now just isn't a good time for my family to leave the ranch."

"Yeah, yeah. Spring. I get it." He waved a hand. "Alright, well maybe I'll ask Harper for a phone introduction. Thanks anyway." He walked away grumbling.

Leah scratched her head. "Is the ranch really that busy right now?"

Mark stepped down the ladder. "Yes and no. None of us want to go anywhere right now for various reasons."

"What about you?" She tilted her head, trying to get a read on the cowboy and why he didn't want to leave town.

He put his hands on her arms and looked Leah directly in the eyes. "I'm not leaving you until Bart and his goons are taken care of. Plain and simple."

Tears pricked the backs of Leah's eyes. The emotions running through her were intense, but she didn't understand them. Mark was a long-time friend. His wanting to protect her was only natural. Plus, her brother had married his sister. So in a way, they were family. But it felt like it was something more. Something she didn't quite understand.

For the past few weeks their friendship had been shifting. Sure, they still joked around like usual. But since Bart had threatened her, Mark had been around much more. He had been protective of her. And now, not wanting to go to Wyoming to see a friend of their family's just because he felt the need to protect her? Did she dare to hope?

Leah had always had a crush on Mark Manning, but she'd known a long time ago that he'd never look at her *that* way. Or could he? The way he was looking into her eyes right then, the connection growing between them, was it all in her imagination? Or was this starting to look like something more?

"Great job, you two." Fannie Stallings smiled and looked around at their decorations, not realizing she had interrupted something between the two. "I knew pairing you up would be the smart move."

"Thanks. I think we're done. Did you need our help with anything else?" Leah pulled back from Mark's touch and cleared her throat. The haze of emotions that had enveloped her was beginning to dissipate, and she could see that it was all in her imagination. Mark cared for her, sure. But it was like he had always teased: she was his little sister.

"Nope, I think we got this covered. Why don't you two head on home. But come back tomorrow, or whenever you have time. We can always use help from good workers." Fannie narrowed her eyes when she looked over at the Diner Divas. "At least you two work and don't spend your time gossiping or distracting others."

Everyone was taking turns ensuring that no one closed the general store alone. It was Logan's turn to close with Leah, but Elizabeth wasn't feeling well. Logan was torn between staying with his sick wife and protecting his sister. Stevie hadn't been released for work yet, and there wasn't anyone else to help Leah.

"Logan, don't worry about me. I'll be fine. Besides, we haven't seen anything of Bart and his goons for close to a week now. I bet with the Spring Fling here, they won't be around to hassle any of us. Too many people here, and with the state patrol coming to town to help out I really doubt those criminals want to be anywhere near here right now." Leah practically pushed her brother out the door.

"I don't know. I would feel a whole lot better if someone were here with you tonight. At least when you close up." Logan looked around him and noticed quite a few shoppers in the store.

"Fine, I'll call one of my friends to come and babysit me. Would that make you happy?" She put her fists on her hips and rolled her eyes.

"How about I stick around?" a very welcomed voice piped up from the crowd in the store.

"Mark, thank you. You're a lifesaver." Logan grinned and left without a backward glance.

"Don't I get a say in this?" Leah arched a brow.

Mark spread his hands wide. "Who wouldn't want me to hang around for a few hours?"

She couldn't help herself, Mark always did make her laugh. "Fine. Just stay out of trouble, will ya?"

"Who, me?" Mark's expression of innocence sent a chill down Leah's back. Not an unpleasant one, either.

"Miss, do you happen to have this shirt in a small?" a visitor to town interrupted, and Leah couldn't have been happier to focus on something, or someone, other than Mark Manning. That cowboy had her confused. One minute she thought he was a pesky older brother, and the next she was battling her old feelings for him again.

Leah had to admit, it was nice having Mark around. He helped customers when they had questions, and also lent Leah a sense of peace and safety.

Chapter 11

M ark wasn't sure if Leah had been right about the Spring Fling keeping Bart's goons away, or if they knew they were in a lot of trouble for attacking poor Stevie so that's what kept them away. Either way, Mark was going to take it and be happy.

That night was the Spring Fling dance, and since the attack on Stevie no one had seen hide nor hair of those goons. Even the Bozeman sheriff said Rocko hadn't been seen in town for the past week. Which had Mark wondering what was going on.

However, he was looking forward to the dance. It was probably the first time since high school that Mark even wanted to attend a dance. The idea of dancing with Leah intrigued him, and he hoped she felt the same way.

He dressed with care that night and wore his black boots, black jeans, and a fire-engine-red shirt with a black bolo tie. His clasp was silver and shaped into a triangle with an eagle stamped on it flying above a waving US flag. He had always liked this particular bolo tie, and actually enjoyed wearing it when he got the chance.

Leah's nerves were shot. And it had nothing to with Bart or his goons, but everything to do with the idea of dancing with Mark that night. She kept going back and forth like a kid making a wish on a dandelion—will he, or won't he? Her heart couldn't decide if it *wanted* Mark to ask her to dance.

She had gone to great pains to look her best that night. Dresses weren't really Leah's thing, but since it was a dance she had found a red dress with a fitted bodice and a flouncy skirt that went down to her calves. When she stepped in front of the mirror, she knew the dress looked great with her black boots. "Well, if he's not impressed with this then he won't be with anything else."

Leah rode with her parents in their truck to the barn. The moment she entered the building, her eyes automatically searched for one cowboy in particular. As she looked around, she noticed a lot of people she knew as well as quite a few new faces. This was one of the things she loved most about their large events—all the new folks in town.

Beacon Creek was small. They had a lot of ranches and farms that they supported, but their sphere of friends was limited. Not that Leah needed a lot of friends, it was just nice to have new people to talk to once in a while. That way she could hear new stories and learn about more than her little part of the world. One of these days she was going to take a long trip around the Earth and meet new people from everywhere. Until then, she was energized by meeting new people who came to town for their rodeos and carnivals.

"You take my breath away." A husky voice behind her sent chills up her spine.

Leah slowly turned and sucked in a breath. "Why cowboy, don't you clean up nicely." She looked him up and down from head to toe.

A sly smile crossed Mark's face. "I know."

With that one little wisecrack, the mood had been broken and she slapped his arm. "You're so vain sometimes, aren't you?" Although, she was pretty sure she was grateful to Mark for breaking the tension building between them.

The band began to play a new song, and he held his hand out to her. "Care to dance?"

She picked up the notes of a waltz and grinned. "I'd love to."

Mark held her hand the entire way out onto the dance floor. Once they were in position, he led her across the floor for the next three songs—the one waltz, and then two-stepping until Leah said she was thirsty. He led her to the refreshment table.

"Thank you. I had no idea you could dance so well." Leah took a sip of the sweet tea he offered her.

"With two sisters, none of us boys had any choice but to learn how to dance." Mark remembered back to his childhood and told Leah about the nights when they were snowed in and Lizzie and Chloe would make them all dance. Whenever the storm was too bad, they wouldn't get any TV reception and there wasn't a lot to do.

"Why didn't you play Monopoly or some other board games?" Leah asked.

"Oh, we did. But we also had to dance with our sisters a lot." He chuckled. "It wasn't too bad. At first we complained, but once we started getting better and the girls at school enjoyed dancing with us, well." He shrugged. "What can I say?"

"You enjoyed all of the attention you got being a good dancer." Leah laughed.

"Guilty as charged."

"Well, Mr. Fred Astaire, if you're ready to show me some more moves, I've had enough tea." Leah set down her empty cup and put her hand out for Mark.

They danced in their own little world the rest of the night, totally ignorant of everyone watching them and whispering. When the night did end and they danced the last waltz, Mark offered to take her home.

"Oh, I came with my parents." Leah looked around for her mom and dad, but couldn't find them. In fact, there were very few people left in the barn.

"I think they left a while ago. I'll be happy to drive you home." Mark stared into her green eyes and felt a pull that wouldn't let him loose.

Mark helped Leah put her coat on and then drove her home. Once he parked in front of her house, he felt like a teenager on a first date. He wasn't sure if he should kiss her or walk her to the door without a kiss.

Leah sat in the front seat, as close to him as the seat-belt would allow. She'd had a marvelous night and didn't want it to end. But there wasn't anything appropriate to do this late at night in Beacon Creek. While it was only a little after midnight, their town didn't have any sort of night life. Nothing like what a big city could offer.

"Well, I have to open tomorrow," she hinted. When he didn't speak, she took off her seatbelt and reached for the door handle. "I guess I better get going."

"Do you want to go to the rodeo with me tomorrow night?" Mark blurted.

A slow smile spread across her face and she felt warmth begin in her belly and spread throughout her body. "Yes, I'd like that."

"Great, how about I pick you up at five?" He got out and went around to open her door. "We can have dinner at the rodeo. I hear Rosie is going to grill steak sand-wiches."

"That sounds great. I look forward to it." Leah walked next to Mark and felt his hand graze hers as they walked up the steps to her porch.

Once they were both in front of her door, he picked up her hand and kissed it. "Until tomorrow."

"I look forward to it." She opened the door and walked in. But she turned around and smiled at him before closing the door.

Mark waited until he heard the latch of the lock be-fore he left the porch. With a smile a mile wide and a spring in his step, he sauntered back to his truck. Never had Mark looked forward to the next day as much as he did right then and there.

He drove home and thought back to the events of the night. They'd never left each other's side. She didn't even seem to want to dance with anyone else but him. And they had a date for the rodeo. The night couldn't have gone any better.

When he arrived home, everyone was already in bed. With a smile on his face he couldn't quite seem to shake, he got ready for bed and looked forward to dreaming about Leah.

Stevie came in for a few hours. The doctor had said he could work, but it had to be light duty. Leah was grateful he was able to spend four hours working at the cash register. She didn't mind doing the heavy lifting since Stevie had been injured. It also meant she and her dad weren't alone.

Since his heart attack, he hadn't worked as much or as hard as he once did. Not that he slacked off, but he was getting older and didn't have the same amount of energy or strength he once did. But he could still sell the pants off of her and her brother. While her dad helped customers, Leah rotated between helping customers, loading product into trucks, and restocking shelves as needed.

Nothing was a better workout then a full day at the store. However, she was glad when her brother walked through the door and said she could leave a little earlier than planned. Somehow, word had gotten out about her date with Mark that night.

"Go home, take a shower." Logan waved a hand in front of his face as he smiled. "You stink."

"Hey!" She slapped her brother's arm. "Stevie can't stay much longer. And Dad's getting tired."

"Don't worry about me. I got this." Logan smirked.

"What's that look for?" She put her hands on her hips.

"Just that I don't want to hear that you made Mark wait."

"Uh-huh. And what are you going to do once Dad and Stevie leave for the day?" Leah crossed her arms over her chest and raised a brow.

"Like I said, I've got this covered." Logan stood up straighter and looked over Leah's head when he heard the bell above the door ring. "Lizzie. Just in time."

Leah chuckled. "I should have known." She turned around to smile at her sister-in-law. Then frowned. Lizzie was her sister, and Mark's sister. This was really getting complicated. She hoped it wasn't also going to be weird for the entire town.

"Leah, I hope you have fun tonight." Elizabeth walked to where Leah stood next to Logan and then hugged her husband.

"What about you two? Will you be attending the rodeo?" Leah hated to make her brother and his wife miss out on the fun.

Lizzie wrapped her arms around her husband. "Actually, we have a nice quiet night planned for us."

"Yes, we do." Logan placed a light kiss on the tip of his wife's nose.

It was almost enough to make Leah feel like she didn't belong, but she had gotten used to seeing the affection between her brother and Lizzie. Especially over the last few weeks. It seemed like they were even more lovey-dovey than usual. It was probably because spring was in the air. In fact, Leah had noticed several new couples around town lately.

"Alright, enough of that. I'll see you both later. Enjoy your quiet night. I'm sure you don't get too many of those."

"Nope, we don't. And the next two nights I'll be at the rodeo on call, in case any of the animals need a vet. So tonight I'm really looking forward to staying in." Lizzie put her head on her husband's shoulder and sighed.

Leah took off without a backwards glance. She knew her brother had everything under control. And he was probably right, she did stink. But in her defense, she'd worked hard that day, being the only one who could lift anything heavy. If business kept up the way it was even after the general store in Three Forks opened back up, they'd have to hire someone else to help.

Even if Stevie got the all-clear to go back full time and lift things again, they were still too busy for just four of them. She'd have to bring it up with her brother after the rodeo left town. For now, she was excited to get ready for her date.

A date with Mark. Who would have ever thought it would happen for her? She'd certainly never thought it would. While she knew the entire town was gossiping about her and Mark's *date* last night, she knew that wasn't an actual date. He hadn't asked her to meet him at the dance, they'd just gravitated toward each other at the beginning of the night and never left each other's orbit the entire time.

Tonight, however, was a real date. That meant she had to put extra effort into getting ready. Since it was a rodeo and carnival, she wasn't about to wear a dress. But she still wanted to look her best. She had just the outfit.

An hour later she was ready with one minute to spare, if Mark was on time. So she used those extra few seconds to look in her full-length mirror to ensure that everything fit right. This was the first time she had worn the outfit. When she purchased it a few weeks back, Leah had no clue that her first time wearing it would be on a date with Mark.

So much had happened over the past few weeks.

When the doorbell rang, her entire body tingled. He was here. She was actually going a date with the one man she'd been more than attracted to since she'd first discovered boys were cute. Not that he'd ever noticed her as anything more than a pesky little girl. Well, that was until last night. The way he looked at her while they were dancing, it was just as she had always dreamed he would look at her. He never once checked out another woman, and she had been paying attention. Mark only had eyes for her last night. Would it be the same tonight?

Last night she'd worn a dress. Her mother had told her that men preferred it when women wore dresses on dates. But for tonight's date, she wanted to make sure she'd be comfortable and warm. So jeans were more appropriate for a night out at the rodeo and carnival. While it was spring, the nights were still fairly cold. The sun had already set, so no warmth would be coming from the sun.

Her mom yelled from downstairs, "Leah!"

The butterflies went into overdrive, and she checked her makeup and hair one last time before grabbing her leather jacket and heading downstairs. Leah didn't want to worry about carrying a purse, so she had packed her necessities in the pockets of her jacket. Her jeans were too tight to hold anything, not even a tube of lip gloss. So instead, she weighed down her jacket with a cellphone, lip gloss, ID, and some cash just in case she and Mark were separated for any reason.

Her mother had always taught her to carry at least twenty dollars and her cellphone. One never knew if they'd be stranded and need to call for a ride. Her mother had told her stories of how when she was a kid they used to carry quarters in case they needed to use a pay phone. Leah couldn't remember a time when she'd ever used a pay phone. While she knew what they were, thanks to TV Land, she'd not seen one in forever. At least not a working one.

When Leah got to the top of the stairs, she could hear voices downstairs. She stopped to take a cleansing breath and then slowly walked downstairs.

Mark heard her on the staircase before he saw her. When he heard the squeak of the stairs, he turned around with a smile on his face. But the moment he saw her long legs coming down the stairs, his mouth dropped open.

She was a vision. Leah had on dark-washed denim jeans that seemed to be painted on. Along with knee-high red boots and a matching red-and-white button-down shirt. Underneath was a white tank top. And to cover her up, she had on a black leather jacket. Her makeup and hair were done up in a way he'd never seen before. She looked as though she was heading to a photoshoot for a cowgirl calendar. He'd buy any calendar she was in. In fact, he'd buy them all up so no one else could drool over her the way he was in that very moment.

"Hiya, cowboy." Leah smiled when she got to the bottom of the stairs.

In his mind he was saying, *hubba, hubba, hubba*, but what came out of his mouth was nonsensical. "I... Ah... You..." He motioned toward her. "Wow."

When Mrs. Hayes laughed, it shook Mark out of the daze he was in. "You two have fun tonight."

"Thanks, Mom," Leah said as she took Mark by the hand and led him outside. If he hadn't stared at her the way he did, she probably would have been the one drooling. He was wearing his dark denim jacket, dark-blue Wranglers, brown boots, and a blue-and-brown button-up shirt. He looked yummy. Any girl would be proud to be with him.

Chapter 12

When they arrived, two cowboys tailgating next to their parking spot whistled and tipped their hats in Leah's direction.

Mark glared at them and took Leah's hand as they walked toward the ticket booth. He had bought his tickets online earlier in the day, so they were able to bypass the ticket booth lines. Turned out he had made the right call. All four booths had lines a mile long. "Looks like we won't have to wait to get in." He showed Leah the barcode on his phone indicating their tickets.

"Smart man. I don't think it would have been fun to wait in those seriously long lines. Plus, I'm betting we're gonna have better seats than most of them." She nodded toward some of their high school friends, who waved and smiled at Leah and Mark.

She wasn't wrong. Mark had decided to pay for the VIP seats. He could have joined his family in their box, but he didn't want to share the date with his family. Instead, he directed Leah toward the center of the ring where they had seats in the tenth row. It might not have a been a bird's eye view like the booth, but they were still extremely good seats.

"Would you like a drink, or do you want dinner now?" Mark wasn't sure if she wanted to see the beginning of the show or if she wanted to make sure they got food first. The rodeos in Beacon Creek always started with mutton busting, which was one of Mark's favorite events. Although, he'd never admit to it.

"Can we watch the mutton busting first, then get dinner?" Leah looked hopefully out at the kids who had gathered in the ring for their chance at riding sheep. The boys all had on blue or black helmets, and the girls—which there were a surprising number of—had on pink or purple helmets.

He chuckled and realized he really had made the right call. Any woman who'd choose mutton busting over food was a keeper. "Sure, we can watch the kids fall off sheep."

"Hey, I happen to know for a fact that a certain Manning boy used to get all excited whenever he got his turn at riding sheep." She looked at him from the corner of her eyes. "In fact, he got so excited one year that he had a little accident."

"Who was that? Because it certainly wasn't this guy." Mark pointed to himself.

"Mmhm, I believe it was a Mark Manning." She smirked.

"There's no way I had any accident when mutton busting." He turned to look at her with a frown. "And besides, you would have been too young to know that even if I had."

She held her hands up. "I didn't say I witnessed it, but I can say that a little birdie told me."

"Ah, I think I understand. Luke told you it was me?"

"Maybe."

With a shake of his head and a deep chuckle, Mark slapped his thigh. "Well, I'll be. Luke's got some explaining to do." He looked around and lowered his voice. "I promised I'd never tell, but since he lied about me, you should know it was actually Luke who had the accident when he wasn't even five years old."

"Get out of town!" Leah exclaimed.

"No, I'm serious. Ask my mom." Mark was preparing a way to get his brother back for the lie. He wasn't sure why Luke would have told Leah this tall tale, but he'd be sure he had the last laugh.

Leah held her hands up. "No judgments here."

He saw the sparkle in her eyes and knew she was trying to hold back laughter. It was on.

Both Mark and Leah thoroughly enjoyed the kids doing their mutton busting. Most of them stayed on, but a couple fell and fell hard. One was barely hanging on sideways until the sheep ran into the rest of its compatriots. Then the little boy fell off and landed at the foot of the smallest mutton in the lot. The boy stood up, lifted his arms in the air, and bellowed, "I did it!" The entire stadium applauded his effort. The way that little boy walked away, one would have thought he had just won the PBR finals in Vegas.

While the organizers set up for the next event, Mark led Leah up for dinner. There was a crush of people all around them and Mark took Leah's hand.

She looked down at his hand and almost smiled when he opened his mouth and ruined it.

Mark held their hands up and looked at Leah while they waited to get through a small group of kids. "Just to make sure I don't lose you."

"Uh-huh. It's more likely I'll lose you in the crowd." Then Leah mumbled low enough so he couldn't hear her, "Just like a little kid."

He furrowed his brows. "What was that?"

She nodded and looked forward. "Looks like we've got a path now." Leah knew not to put too much into his treating her like a kid. It really was crowded; holding hands was smart. She just wanted it to be for more than safety reasons. She wanted Mark to *want* to hold her hand.

Just then, a group of teens smashed between them and Leah was knocked off-kilter and let go of Mark's hand accidentally.

"Leah!" Mark looked around, frantic for her, and then saw her leaning up against the wall shaking her hand. "Are you alright?" he asked when he got close enough for her to hear him.

"Yeah, some kid wrenched my hand when he yanked me away from you." She scowled in the direction of the teens who had already moved on. "Group of kids who are up to no good. Mark my words."

Mark laughed. "I seem to remember a time when most people said the same thing about me and my brothers." He puffed out his chest. "Now look at us."

"Yeah, still a group of kids up to no good." Leah smiled and rubbed her wrist.

"Here, let me take a look." Mark took her injured hand and lightly felt along the wrist and down her hand.

She winced when he touched the part of her wrist that was sore, but it was nothing an ice pack wouldn't help.

"Hmm, I think we might need to amputate. It's a lost cause." Mark tsk'd and threaded his fingers through hers before winking.

"Well Doctor, if you think it's a lost cause maybe we should just get some food and head back to our seats. No need missing out on the rest of the rodeo if there's nothing to be done." This time, Leah sidled up so close to Mark there was zero space between them for kids to break them apart again.

Without her saying a thing, Mark asked for a bag with ice for her wrist. Once they were back at their seats with sodas, steak sandwiches, and garbage fries to share, he put her hand on his thigh and then placed the ice pack on her wrist.

"Thank goodness it was my left hand." She picked up the sandwich and took a huge bite, not noticing that she dripped cheese and sauce into the box holding their fries.

"Yum. More sauce." Mark set his sandwich down and picked up one of the fries from the box on Leah's lap.

When she noticed it, she sighed. "I'm such a mess."

"I wouldn't say that. I think it's smart to eat your sandwich over the fries. This way there's no waste." He winked and took another couple of fries and stuffed them in his mouth. When he got sauce on his chin, Leah laughed.

The two of them tried to eat their food without making a mess, and Leah ended up needing her left hand. But once they finished the food, Mark took the trash away and Leah iced her wrist again.

"Do you think John misses the rodeo?" Leah asked while they watched the bull riders.

Mark nodded. "I do. I think that's part of his problem."

"I was wondering the same thing." Leah turned to Mark. "And if he left a woman behind. Or if a woman left him behind."

"Nah. I don't think John was ever serious with anyone on the circuit."

"How do you know? Did he tell you that?" Leah turned her attention back to the arena when the horn blared and the rider jumped off the bull after doing his seven seconds very successfully.

"No, but he also never said he was into anyone special. If John had a special girl, he would have told one of us. And he didn't."

"Well, I think he looks like a man haunted." Leah turned back to look at Mark again. She loved the way his chin dimpled when he focused hard on something.

It wasn't a sight she saw often. Mark was too much of a joker to look very serious. But right then, as he seemed to be thinking about what she'd said, she got a rare glimpse of his adorable chin dimple.

With a shake of his head, the dimple disappeared and his smile came back. "I'd more believe that John broke a woman's heart than one broke his."

They focused back on the rodeo and didn't talk about anything more serious than when a rider fell off a bull and the clown had to distract the bull before the rider could get back up.

"That was exciting! And no major injuries." Leah smiled.

Mark stood up, and she followed him up the stairs to the exit. He held her hand and they discussed the carnival. "Care to take a ride on the Ferris wheel with me?"

"I'd love to."

They made their way to the midway section of the carnival where Mark purchased tickets for the giant Ferris wheel. Once they were seated and strapped in, he turned to her. "Do you know why it's called a Ferris wheel?"

"Actually, I do. The Ferris wheel is one of those things I've always loved." She smiled out at the sight of the carnival below them. "A man with the last name of Ferris invented the giant wheel back in 1892 for the 1893 World's Columbian Exposition in Chicago."

Leah motioned to the wheel they were currently riding. "But today's Ferris wheel is nothing like the original one. The London Eye is more like the original Ferris wheel. It could hold over two thousand people." Her eyes widened and her smile broadened. "Instead of buckets like what we're in, it had enclosed booths that held up to sixty people each. I've seen pictures of it. It was fantastic."

"Wow, I had no idea. I'd always wondered about the name. I figured it had to be named after the guy who built it, or something like that." He looked out and around at the structure they were on. "What happened to the original Ferris wheel?"

"Well, it was moved around a couple of times. The last place it sat was at the World's Fair in St. Louis in the early nineteen-hundreds. Then they demolished it." She shrugged. "It's sad, really. Something so phenomenal at the time, and they didn't see what they had. I wish it would have made it to some sort of museum so we could still see it today."

"Yeah, there's a lot of history that would be cool to see today." He grinned at her. "What do you say we invent the time machine and go back and see everything we've ever dreamed of?"

"Oh, I like it. Let's start with the Chicago fair and be one of the first to ride the original Ferris wheel. And I want to take pictures of everything." She squeezed his hand.

"But you know, our phones won't work in the past."

"But the camera functions will. As long as we take power chargers with us, we won't have any problems." Leah smirked. She'd find a way to ensure they could take plenty of pictures on their cellphones when they traveled back in time.

"If only time travel were possible." Mark sighed.

She considered for a moment. "It may not be possible for us, but I don't doubt that someday, someone will come up with the ability. We're only stopped by the lack of knowledge, as long as we continue to believe in the impossible."

"Very wise words." Mark nodded and sighed when their ride ended.

"Okay, what's next?" Leah asked after they had disembarked from their journey.

They spent the rest of the night going on rides and playing games. Leah's arms were full of stuffed animals that Mark and she had both won all night long.

"If we win any more, we're gonna have to hire a cart to carry them all back to your truck," Leah joked.

"Then let's go and put what we have in my truck and get a coffee and do some people watching." Mark loved to watch people and make up stories about their lives.

"Oh, I bet we can spy the person who'll come up with plans for our time travel machine."

"As long as it's not a hot tub time machine, I'm fine with whatever they devise." Mark gave her a stern look before busting up laughing.

"Personally, I liked the phone booth time machine." Leah winked. She had a longstanding crush on Keanu Reeves and had seen his time travel movie too many times to count.

They laughed as they headed toward the exit. They weren't alone in exiting the carnival; it was late, and a lot of families were leaving. One moment Mark had a hold on her arm, and the next she was nowhere in sight.

"Leah?" he called out.

Somewhere to his left he heard her voice. "Mark, where'd you go?"

Leah looked around her and her eyes widened when a face appeared around the giant teddy bear, way too close for comfort. "Rocko."

Chapter 13

Mark yelled her name out and looked everywhere for the stack of giant bears she had been carrying. He knew he should have carried them for her, but she insisted she could carry them. He doubted she could see over the heads of the bears, so she must have gotten lost when someone bumped into them and he lost his hold on her. "Leah, where are you?" he called again.

The locals looked at him funny, and he began asking anyone he knew if they had seen Leah. When he came upon someone he didn't recognize, he explained to them what Leah looked like and how many giant bears she was carrying.

Finally, one man nodded and told her he had seen a woman carrying three giant bears and pointed to the side. Mark followed the direction and saw one of Leah's bears on the ground. He picked it up. Knowing she had dropped a bear and left it on the ground worried him. If she was dropping bears, something was wrong.

He asked another person, and they pointed in one direction and he followed the path toward one of the parking lots. That wasn't the lot where they had parked, so he wondered what she was up to. When he found another dropped bear, he knew she was leaving him breadcrumbs and worried about why she'd had to do this.

With both bears in his arms, he headed out to the parking lot. When he heard what sounded like a cry of pain, he dropped the bears and ran as fast as he could.

Leah wasn't sure what to do. Rocko had grabbed her by the arm and was guiding her in the opposite direction of where she knew Mark was. If he didn't have a knife jabbing her in the ribs, she would have yelled out for help.

As she passed by people, she silently willed them to see she was in distress. But with the bears covering most of her body up, she doubted anyone was looking at her, or even at the big bad wolf who held her hostage.

When she passed a larger man, she dropped one of her bears and stared at him, but he was oblivious to her situation. He didn't even notice she had dropped a giant bear, for Pete's sake. But Rocko hadn't noticed, either. Or if he did, he didn't care.

When she turned to look back at her dropped bear, Rocko hissed, "Look forward."

So he had noticed, he just didn't care. She complied and racked her brain for any tips she had picked up from Sophia in a situation like this. All she knew was that if he got her in his vehicle, she was done for. She had to figure out a way to get out of his control before they reached his car or van.

He probably had a van, if he came here expecting to kidnap her. Which meant he had been watching her. He knew where she was and had waited for her to leave the carnival tonight.

What about Mark? Was he safe? Did they hurt him, or leave him alone? Leah doubted they would have been able to get him to go with them. Even if it meant he was stabbed, she doubted he would have been easy to take.

If she ever got out of this, she'd go back to Sophia's gym for more self-defense lessons. Leah was strong and knew how to fight, somewhat. She wasn't as good as Elizabeth and Chloe because she had only grown up with one brother who never beat up on her. He tried once, and after he was taken to the woodshed he'd never been harsh with her again.

They had fought, but only verbally. If Rocko would engage in a fight of words, that she might have a chance of winning. But with his massive muscles, she wasn't sure what she could do against him. However, her first concern was getting that knife out of his hands. She wouldn't be able to do anything as long as he held that knife to her side.

It was time to get rid of another bear. They had just turned a corner, and if Mark was following he'd see which direction they went. Plus, it might help to uncover the knife against her side. Or at the very least, someone might notice the way Rocko was holding her arm.

When she noticed a man admiring her bears, that's when she dropped it. She hoped it would catch his attention, which it did.

"Miss, you dropped your bear," he called out.

Rocko looked over his shoulder. "It has a funky smell."

He scrunched his nose and walked away from the bear.

"It did not," Leah huffed out in indignation.

"Shut up." Rocko pushed the knife against her side, and she yelled out in pain.

Leah wasn't sure, but she thought she felt her skin break. It was either that or her shirt was cut with the tip of his blade.

"What did I say?" He turned her around and brandished the knife in her face.

"You stabbed me!" Leah knew this was her chance. The knife was far enough away that if she could get out of his grip, she could get away from him.

"That was nothing, little girl," he growled.

She had one giant bear left in her grip. And she knew exactly how to use it.

God, I need your help right now. Actually, Leah needs you. Please protect her. If I can't get to her in time, please have someone else intervene and protect her. Mark had heard that cry of pain. He wasn't sure if it was Leah or someone else. But he did know something was wrong. His gut was never wrong, and it was screaming at him that Leah was in danger.

Up ahead, he saw a few people running away from something.

Then a bear's head poked up and went back down. "Leah!" He ran toward the commotion, but as people ran away from it they slowed him down.

When he did finally get to whatever was going on, he froze.

Standing in front of him was Leah with her shirt ripped on the side, standing over a man on the ground in the fetal position. His hand covered his bloody face, and his other covered his groin.

"Leah!" Mark yelled, and ran to her side.

Her hair was a mess and she was breathing hard, but other than that she looked like she was alright.

"What happened? Are you alright?" He put a hand out to touch her, and she shied away. "Leah, it's me, Mark."

She turned frantic eyes to him and then the tears that were pooling in her eyes began to flow and she dropped into his arms. "Leah, darlin', what happened? Did he hurt you?" Mark ran his hands down her back and then her side.

Leah flinched when Mark's hand touched the spot where her shirt was ripped.

"Are you bleeding?" He softly put his hand back on the area. When he pulled it back, there was a small spot of red. "You are. What did he do to you? I'll kill him!"

She sobbed into Mark's chest and couldn't talk.

A witness came up and told Mark what she'd seen. "Your girlfriend is awesome. She disarmed that criminal with her bear and then went to town on him." The woman looked to Leah and back at the man on the ground. "I don't think he's going to be getting up any time soon."

Leah sniffed and wiped her face. "He'll be singing soprano for a while, thanks to Sophia's lessons."

Another person walked up. "I just called the cops. I would have helped, but by the time I realized what was going on she had the crook on the ground." He smiled at her and shook his head. "Wow, you must have some serious training."

Mark pulled Leah away just enough to look into her face. "Darlin', tell me what happened."

Leah sniffed some more and took a deep, cleansing breath. "It was Rocko. He took me from you with a knife to my side."

"Is that what caused the tear and the blood?" Mark asked.

She nodded. "I didn't know what to do." A shudder shook her body, and Mark held her tight.

"Shh, it's alright. I've got you now."

"I knew that if he got me into his van, I was done for. I figured I would rather die fighting than as a whimpering prisoner." Leah pulled back and wiped her face again.

"When I was down to one bear, he pulled the knife away from me. I used the bear as a cushion between us, and when he went after me with the knife I pushed the bear at him while I kicked him in the groin."

"Good job. Sophia taught you well." Mark beamed with pride at his girl.

"Then when he bent over, I dropped the bear and shoved my knee into his face hard enough to break his nose. After that, he fell back." She looked into Mark's face. "Then you showed up."

"I'm so sorry I wasn't here to protect you. Never in a million years did I think Bart or any of his crew would go after you in such a public place." He ran a comforting hand down her back, but kept away from the spot where the knife had pricked her skin.

Sirens could be heard approaching the carnival, and people moved away when security showed up.

After Leah and Mark told their story, the ambulance took off with Rocko handcuffed to the gurney. A police cruiser accompanied them to the hospital.

The local medic who had been on site checked Leah out and cautioned that she should see her doctor if she didn't want to go to the hospital, or even the local clinic. She might need a dose of antibiotics since she was technically stabbed.

"I have no idea if that knife wound will get infected, but you need to at least clean and apply sterile bandages twice a day for the next few days. And I would get a dose of broad-spectrum antibiotics, just in case. You have no idea where that knife has been," the medic cautioned.

"You're right. I'll take her to the clinic." Mark bit his cheek. "They didn't by chance take Rocko to the local clinic, did they?"

The police officer who'd stayed behind shook his head. "No, his injuries are going to require more than the local clinic can handle." He grinned at Leah. "Good job, by the way. I wish more women could handle themselves like you can."

She pursed her lips. "I wish I didn't have to be able to do that."

The cop's smile vanished. "Yeah, that would be better."

"I'll take her to the clinic now. I know they were going to be staffed twenty-four seven throughout the entire rodeo." Mark put an arm around Leah and led her over to where he had moved his truck while she was being examined by the medic.

After receiving a prescription for the antibiotic and an order to stay down for a few days, Leah was discharged and Mark took her home. Since it was so late, he hadn't called her family, or even his. So no one knew what she had gone through. He worried how her parents were going to react, and he hoped that her dad's heart would be able to handle the shock of it all. "Should I call Logan first?"

Leah shook her head. "No, let him sleep. I don't want to disturb him. Not yet, anyway. He's going to have to get up soon to open the store. I'll text him to come over before work."

Mark escorted her inside and refused to leave when she tried to say goodnight. "Your parents are asleep. No one knows what happened to you. I think I should stay right here until someone gets up. Besides, I don't think I can sleep. I'm too wired and upset."

"I don't know if I'll be able to sleep, either. Coffee?" Leah headed to the kitchen and set the coffee maker to working.

Mark stood next to her at the kitchen counter. "I can't tell you how sorry I am that I let Rocko take you from my side. I should have been paying more attention. It's all my fault."

"No, it's not your fault. It's his and Bart's." Leah squared her shoulders and narrowed her eyes. "I hope now the cops can arrest Bart."

"Who's Bart?" Leah's dad asked as he walked into the kitchen.

Leah turned around wide-eyed. "Dad! What are you doing up so early?"

Mr. Hayes looked between the two and noticed they were both still wearing their clothes from last night. "I think the better question is, what are you two still doing up?"

Mark took a step forward. "Mr. Hayes, it's all my fault. I'm so sorry, I should have paid more attention to those around us."

Leah put her arm in front of Mark. "No, it's not. Stop this."

"What happened to your shirt?" Mr. Hayes pointed to Leah's side.

"You better take a seat. Can I get you some tea?" Leah bit her lower lip and winced. This was what she had hoped to avoid.

Once she had tea for her dad, the coffee was ready and they all sat down at the kitchen table. Leah slowly told her dad about what happened, and both she and Mark kept a close eye on him to make sure he wasn't about to have another heart attack.

"You should have called us right away." Mr. Hayes turned hard eyes on Mark.

"I know. And I'm sorry." Mark hung his head.

"Daddy, I told him not to call anyone. And when we got home, again he wanted to wake you up as well as call Logan. But I asked him not to." Leah looked sheepishly at her dad, hoping his heart could take this all in.

"Honey, you need to stop treating me like I'm sick. It's been almost two years since my attack and I'm just fine now." Mr. Hayes sipped his tea. Since his heart attack, coffee was a thing of the past. He now drank mostly herbal tea.

"What's everyone doing here so early?" Mrs. Hayes wiped the sleep from her eyes before tightening her robe.

"Um, we just got here." Leah stood up and poured her mother a cup of coffee and fixed it the way her mom liked. "Sit down, and I'll explain what happened last night." Leah finally noticed the clock and took in a breath when she saw it was already past five in the morning.

Mark noticed and winced. "I better call home. They'll worry when they notice my truck's missing." He stood up and left the room to call home while Leah explained everything to her mom.

Once he was done, Mark bowed his head and prayed. *God, thank you so much for protecting Leah last night. I don't know what I would have done if Rocko had taken her, or worse. This situation is in your hands now. I'll do whatever you want, but please ensure that Bart, or any of the others, can't get to Leah again.*

With a peace filling his entire being, Mark headed back into the kitchen to accept whatever censure the Hayes family had for him.

Chapter 14

L eah woke up later in the day, surprised she had slept so long. Even though the doctor had said no work for her, she still got up and got ready to head into the store. Her mother, however, had other plans for her.

"Leah, please take a seat." Mrs. Hayes gestured for Leah to sit at the kitchen table after she made herself a cup of coffee. "Your brother and dad are going to hire another man to help out at the store for a while. They've needed it for some time now."

"Please tell me this isn't because of me?" Leah's shoulders drooped, and she prayed that they'd be able to afford this. They had only recently been able to get out of the hot water that her dad had gotten them into before his heart attack.

"No, it's not. You know as well as I do that spring is the busiest time for the store." She smiled. "And besides, we all agree that you need more time off. This working sixty hours a week isn't right for a young lady who's being courted."

Leah spluttered and almost spilled her coffee "Wh...what are you talking about?"

"I saw the way Mark looked at you this morning. The young man's besotted with you."

"It was our first date, Mom. Please don't tell me you're already planning for me to leave the house?" The last thing Leah needed was her parents putting pressure on Mark to propose. She wasn't opposed to it, but it was way too soon.

"But you've known him almost your entire life." Mrs. Hayes sat down at the table with her daughter and smiled. "Your father and I had always hoped that Luke Manning would be the one you marry, but Mark is also a great catch. He's just a few years older than you. But that might be better, anyways." She patted Leah's hand when her daughter rolled her eyes.

"Ma, you know that Luke and I were never anything more than friends." Leah shook her head. "As for Mark, please promise me you won't say anything to him."

"Oh, sweetie. You have nothing to worry about."

Leah slumped in her chair. Her mother hadn't exactly said she wouldn't say anything to Mark, but hopefully her statement did mean she wouldn't say a word. After their disastrous first date, she doubted Mark would want to take her out again.

Her mother did her best to keep her inside all day, but around three in the afternoon Leah escaped her mother's eagle eye and headed to the store.

"Leah? What are you doing here?" Logan asked when she entered the store.

"You know how mom gets. I needed some air." Leah looked around and noted they had quite a few people in the store. Her brother, father, and even Stevie were all helping people. She went to the cash register and started to ring up people who had been waiting.

Two hours later, after they had closed the store, Leah's dad approached her. "Honey, you can't be working right now. I know we needed your help, but I did hire someone today who's going to start tomorrow morning."

Leah furrowed a brow. "Who?"

"Shawn Stallings," Logan answered for his dad.

"Shawn? Are you kidding me?" Leah shook her head. He was a nice kid, but lazy.

"I think he just needs to find what makes him happy. Working on a ranch obviously isn't for him. Maybe helping out here in the store will be what he needs." Logan walked past Leah to begin the closing procedures. "If you're gonna stay here, you need to go sit down. I don't want the doctor to get mad at us for working you when you're supposed to be resting."

"What he said," Mark said when he walked through the door. He pursed his lips and stared at Leah. "What are you doing here? I thought you were supposed to take it easy for a few days?"

"What? I got bored." She shrugged her shoulders.

"Mark. Good. Can you please take Leah home?" Mr. Hayes smiled and reached out to shake Mark's hand.

"Of course. How about I take you over to Rosie's for dinner first? If you have enough energy to stay out a bit longer?" Mark raised expectant eyebrows.

"Sounds perfect." Leah smiled at Mark before grabbing her purse and coat and following him out the door. Once they were outside, she said, "Thank you for rescuing me from a night of boredom."

"How are you feeling? I mean, really feeling?" Mark opened the truck door for her and stood next to her as he waited for her reply.

"I'm fine. Like I said before, I was bored."

"How long were you here at the store?"

"Not long. Maybe two hours?" Leah got into the truck.

Mark closed the door and went around to get into the driver's seat. Once they were on the road, it only took them a few minutes to get to Rosie's parking lot. He put his truck in park and turned to her. "Please, be honest with me."

Leah sighed. "I'm a little tired, but we were out all night long. I'm not used to staying up until the cows come home." She chuckled at her own joke.

"Leah, I'm serious. You were abducted at knifepoint last night. Then stabbed with said knife." He turned in his seat and took her hand.

"Mark, thank you, but I'm fine. Really, I am." She tilted her head. "I'm sorry if I worried you."

"You have nothing to apologize for. But I worry that last night will take a toll on you, and"—he sighed and ran a hand through his hair—"I don't know. I'm just worried about you."

"Hey, I'm fine. Really, I am." She squeezed his hand. "Let's try to forget about last night for a little while and go inside and eat. I'm starving."

Mark smiled. "Deal."

They should have been prepared for the gossip, but they weren't. Both of them regretted going in the moment they sat down. All eyes turned to them, and snippets of whispered gossip enveloped them.

"I'd say we should take our food to go, but that would only fuel the gossip." Leah sighed. "What do you say we ignore everyone and just enjoy the food?"

Mark tried, he really did. But having all eyes on him and knowing that they were gossiping about him and his lack of ability to protect Leah really irked him. He knew that he was a failure, he didn't need the entire town telling him so.

Leah noticed his anguish and decided to forgo dessert at the diner. "Let's get out of here. I'm sure my mom made something delicious."

Mark paid their bill and they left, not holding hands as Leah had hoped they would.

When they pulled up into her driveway, she turned in the seat to face him. "Mark, you have to ignore everyone. You know as well as I do how gossip works. Tomorrow they'll have something else to focus on and we'll be forgotten."

He released a deep sigh. "I know, it's just tough hearing them talk about how I let you down last night."

Leah put a hand on his shoulder. "Hey now, you didn't let me down. Even the sheriff said he was surprised that

Rocko made a move in a crowd like that. If the sheriff couldn't have foreseen it, how could you?"

He nodded.

"Come on, let's see what my mom made for dessert. I'm sure it's fantastic. Better than anything Rosie could have made." Leah wasn't sure she was being completely accurate, but her mom did make great pies and cakes.

Her mom didn't let her down; she'd made a chocolate cream pie. One of Mark's favorites, if memory served. Leah smiled and dug into the creamy goodness. By the time they were done, Mark was smiling again.

He also reached out for her hand when she walked him to the front door at nine o'clock.

"I'm sorry, but I really do think I need to get some sleep tonight." Mark covered his yawn with the back of his free hand. "Sorry."

Leah followed suit and yawned. "Don't worry. I think I need more sleep, too."

"Will I see you at church in the morning?" Mark looked hopeful.

She nodded. "As long as I can wake up in time." Leah covered another yawn.

Mark laughed when he caught the yawning bug. "Okay, I think if I don't leave now we'll just keep making each other yawn the rest of the night."

"Thank you for checking in on me tonight. And for dinner." Leah hating mentioning the diner, but she was grateful for the time they'd spent together.

Mark leaned in and kissed her cheek. "I'm just glad you're doing so well, and you let me spend the evening in your company."

"Any time, Mark."

Chapter 15

Leah was stressed. She had woken up later than she wanted. If she didn't hurry up, she'd miss church. No one would begrudge her a day in bed, but she had zero desire to miss church. Not today.

As she snuck in the back, the choir was just finishing their special. When the music director asked everyone to bow their heads for prayer, Leah used that time to sneak down to her family pew. She was seated with head bowed before the prayer was over.

Logan nudged her shoulder after the director started the next hymn. "You're late."

"Shhh, we're in church." Leah put a finger to her lips.

Logan smirked at his little sister and focused back on the service.

Leah wondered if the pastor had created that sermon just for her. It was all about faith in God and ensuring that we trust in Him for our protection and not in man. While

Leah knew she didn't need to have faith in Mark, she did. But more importantly, she had faith in God. While she was going through everything Friday night, she knew she could trust God to protect her, and He did.

If it was her time to go, she knew she couldn't stop it from happening. But something inside her told her to fight, so she did. It just meant that it wasn't her time to go. She still had a lot she wanted to accomplish in this life before God took her home to be with Him.

One of those things she wanted to accomplish was getting married. And the person she hoped God had in mind for her sat in a pew within spitting distance of her.

When services were over, Mark made his way to her side. "Hey there, sleepyhead."

She nudged him with her elbow. "Hey now, I have a great excuse."

"I'm sure you do, but you were still late. I hope all is well?" Mark had worried about her all weekend, even when he was with her. Would she have nightmares over the incident, or would she be able to process it all easily? Or at least, easier than he could.

He had suffered nightmares last night, but thankfully they hadn't kept him awake too long. Once he realized what they were, he prayed and gave the issues over to God and he slept peacefully the rest of the night.

One thing was for certain, Mark's faith was growing throughout all of these trials.

She smiled up at him. "I did, thank you. Did you get the edict for Sunday supper at the ranch today?"

Mark chuckled. "Yup. And I heard your whole family will be there as well. Who's watching the store today?"

"Dad opened along with Stevie and the new guy, Shawn. He's going to head over to the ranch once he feels Shawn's got a handle on it. But I doubt he'll be too far from his phone today." Leah took Mark's hand. "Come on, you can drive me. Mom's waiting for Dad to join her."

Everyone had been called to have dinner at the Triple J Ranch, including the Hayes family. The only one missing was Chloe Manning, but she was planning a trip to visit the family soon with her new boyfriend.

When Leah and Mark entered the house, the Mannings all turned concerned gazes to her. She gulped and pulled at the collar of her shirt. Since she had been running late, she picked the first dress she saw in her closet—a high-necked, green-and-white long-sleeved dress that she rarely wore. Right then and there, she remembered why she didn't usually wear it. The neck was way too tight and it was currently making it tough for her to breath.

Callie walked up to her and gave her a tight hug, causing even more breathing problems for Leah. "I'm so glad you're safe. When I heard what happened I just about blew a gasket." The town's newest sheriff's deputy pulled back and looked Leah in the eyes. "Now tell me. How are you doing, really?"

"I'm fine." Leah looked to everyone in the room. "Really y'all, I'm just fine. The doctor checked me out and he gave me antibiotics just as a precaution. I didn't even need pain meds. I'm taking over-the-counter Tylenol. And not even all the time."

Judith Manning walked over and gave Leah a hug as well. "I'm just so grateful that the Lord protected you."

"It was Sophia's self-defense classes," Roman added.

Mark frowned at his brother. "It was God. He provided the training she was going to need to protect herself from an attacker."

"Hey," Leah called out. "God did protect me, and he put Sophia in my life for a reason. But"—she turned her gaze to Mark and smirked—"I think He also allowed us to win so many of those giant teddy bears just so I would have one to use as a bodyguard."

Both she and Mark laughed at the memory of the torn teddy bear that had taken the brunt of Rocko's knife. It was much easier to deal with those memories if she joked about it. When Leah thought too much and too seriously about it all, sadness overtook her.

"It's just too bad little Teddy didn't make it." Mark looked sad. "But the doctor said he didn't feel any pain."

Leah added, "He fought valiantly. Teddy will never be forgotten." She put a hand over her heart.

The room chuckled, and everyone congratulated Leah on thinking so quickly on her feet and using whatever she had with her to help fend off the attack.

Judith led everyone into the dining room.

A cacophony of sounds emanated from the overly packed dining room. When the Manning family all came together, they couldn't help but be loud and rambunctious. Mark was being his normal self and causing problems. His youngest brother, Roman, was in town for the Spring Fling opening weekend, and Mark was going to take full advantage of the time he had missed messing with his little brother.

Even though the room was crazy loud, when Roman sat down everyone's head turned toward the youngest cowboy in the room. If Leah didn't know better, she would have thought someone had made a raspberry on a baby's belly. However, there were no babies in the family. Then it dawned on her what was going on and she laughed. A full, belly wrenching laugh.

The family moaned and looked to Mark.

A giant smiled crossed Roman's face and he put a hand to his heart. "Mark, I must say, I've missed your childish ways. Since I've been away, I don't think anyone's pulled such fantastic pranks on me." He reached under the padding covering the wooden dining room chair and pulled out a pinkish whoopee cushion. Roman looked from the offending device to his brother. "Really? I thought you were supposed to be older than this."

The room erupted in guffaws and pats on Mark's back from his brothers. Even John laughed, which was unusual for the quiet brother.

"Welcome home, Roman." Caleb smiled at his youngest son. Then turned to Mark. "But I think we should be done with fart pranks. What do you say? Act a bit more your age while we have company?"

Mark turned a sheepish grin to Leah and her parents, who had just joined them. "Sorry." He shrugged, not really sorry. Just more embarrassed that Leah had seen his prank. "It's just something brothers do to each other."

"Uh-huh. Just remember, sisters don't appreciate those types of jokes." Leah raised a brow.

"But, I thought you weren't my sister?" It had been a while since Mark had thought of Leah as his sister. In fact, he'd realized lately what a beautiful woman she had become. And the last thing he wanted was to be her brother.

She crossed her arms over her chest. "I'm not, but you seem to think I am."

"Not anymore," he said under his breath.

Leah arched a brow. "Since when?"

He hadn't realized she had such great hearing. "Well, you have been beating me over the head lately with your *I'm not your sister* comments." And he was very glad she wasn't his sister. Any woman who looked that good in a pair of Wranglers couldn't be his sister. He wasn't sure yet what she was to him, but sister was *not* a descriptor he was going to use.

She tapped his chest. "And don't you forget it." Leah turned and walked to the other end of the dinner table and took a seat next to Elizabeth.

"Looks like she told you." Luke snorted and punched his brother's arm before taking a seat next to his wife.

The seat Mark took was down the table from Leah, but he could still see her if he leaned forward, something he caught himself doing multiple times during the afternoon meal.

After dessert, they all went outside to the firepit. The sun was low on the horizon, just barely hanging above the Rocky Mountains surrounding the western side of the state. The sky was dotted with wisps of clouds here and there, and the orange of the setting sun had begun to turn various shades of orange, yellow, and burnt sienna. Soon there would be purples and deep blues added to the majesty of God's canvas.

Leah loved sunsets in spring. Well, she loved all sunsets. But most especially when she was surrounded by family and friends.

Roman took a seat next to Mark. "So, how long have the two of you been dating?"

"Who?" With furrowed brows, Mark looked at his youngest brother.

Roman chuckled. "Come on, man. You know exactly who I'm talking about. I think it's time you started to grow up and settle down."

"Roman, I have no idea what you're talking about." Mark straightened his shoulders and took on an air of superiority. "I'm very grown up and settled in my work."

"You keep telling yourself that, big brother." He patted Mark's shoulder and reached over for a marshmallow and fork to roast it.

As he stared into the flames, Mark thought about what Roman had said. The warmth of the flames licked at his face and he relaxed into his chair. Images of Leah flashed through the flames. Her as a little girl with pigtails, chasing after him and his brothers. Then her in high school, wearing tight jeans at a football game.

But mostly, images of the woman she'd become lately danced across the flames and jumped into his heart.

He didn't know when she'd moved from pesky little girl to beautiful woman, but he found he liked the warmth that spread through his bones as he thought of the pretty woman sitting across the fire from him.

After their first date went awry, he wasn't sure if he was going to ask her out again. Dinner at Rosie's the night after the attack wasn't really a date. That was more him taking out a friend who'd been injured and just checking she was alright. But now? He knew what he wanted.

Without thinking, he stood and walked over to where she was sitting, laughing with Callie and Elizabeth.

"Hey, cowboy." Leah smiled up at him.

Mark put his hands in his front pockets and lifted his shoulders. "Hey, cowgirl. Are you having fun?"

"I am. I'm glad our families can do this on occasion." Leah nibbled on her lower lip. "I wish we could do it more often."

With joy filling his heart, Mark took a seat next to the prettiest cowgirl he knew. "Me, too."

"Here." Leah handed him a long fork with a marshmallow on a tine, all ready for him to roast it.

"Thanks." Mark put the gooey dessert into the flame and watched as the fire licked the outside of the white puff. He pulled it up a little bit higher so it wouldn't be too blackened when he pulled it out of the fire.

"Any word on Bart?" Leah hated to break the peace that surrounded them, but she'd worried about the criminal and how many times his men had been spotted in town. Especially since Friday when she was attacked.

"No, nothing new..." Mark was interrupted by his sister.

Elizabeth stood up and walked to the middle of the group. "So, we have some news." Elizabeth stood in front of the entire family with her husband standing behind her. Logan had wrapped her tightly in his arms. She put a hand on her stomach.

Leah sucked in a breath, as did Callie beside her.

Nodding, Elizabeth smiled at her sisters-in-law.

Claire stood up from across the fire and clapped her hands. "Really?"

"Yes, we're pregnant!" Elizabeth exclaimed.

"Four months along now," Logan added.

"Oh, this is fantastic!" Judith stood and covered her mouth with both hands and tears of joy spilled down her face.

"This is going to be my first grandchild." Caleb patted Logan on the back. "Is it a boy or a girl?"

Elizabeth laughed. "Dad, it's too soon to know the sex."

"Are you going to find out, or let it be a surprise?" Leah asked.

"Oh, we're gonna find out," Logan exclaimed with a huge grin.

Laughing, Elizabeth turned her head and kissed her husband's cheek. "He's made a bet that it's going to be a girl."

"We're gonna have a little princess." Logan stared out, smiling as though he had already gotten his wish. He put a soft hand on his wife's belly and kissed her neck.

"I'm gonna be an uncle." Mark sat down heavily and stared into the fire, wondering what kind of uncle he would be.

Leah laughed. "I bet you're gonna be the one the kids climb all over and who will spoil them rotten."

"And you're gonna be the uncle who teaches the boys how to pull a girl's pigtails and how to set up the best pranks." Luke laughed and then looked to his wife with longing in his eyes.

"Ah, I see someone else is hoping to be a daddy soon." With a huge grin, Mark slapped his thigh.

Callie looked between the two. "Ah, give us a little bit of time to be married before we start having kids."

"What about you, Claire?" Leah turned to the other new Manning wife. She and Matthew had been married long enough that they could have some news of their own soon.

Claire held up her hands. "Oh, no. Not yet. Matthew and I still have a few things to do before we start our family."

Matthew walked over to his wife and pulled her into his arms. "Oh, I don't know. I think we could still manage everything if a baby came along soon." He leaned down and whispered something in his wife's ear that no one could hear.

When pink tinged Claire's cheeks, Mark laughed. "Sounds like someone wants to start his family sooner rather than later."

A chill crept over Leah, and all of a sudden the hairs on the back of her neck stood on end. She looked around, wondering if someone was watching them.

Mark noticed and asked her, "What's wrong?"

She continued to look around and swallowed hard. "Do you feel it?"

"Feel what?"

"Eyes on us?" Leah looked Mark in the eyes, and she felt a little bit of tension leave her body. She didn't know how he did it, but whenever he was around, she felt...safe. Even after he'd lost her at the rodeo on Friday, he still made her feel safe in his presence.

He scootched closer to her on the bench and put an arm around her. "Hey, you're safe here. You know that, right?"

Leah leaned into his warmth. "Yes. I know I am. I'm just sick and tired of Bart's crew trying to scare me. I wish they'd knock it off."

"I know, darlin'. Me too." He kissed the top of her head.

Leah sighed.

Roman snickered. "It's about time."

The mood had been broken, and Leah pulled away.

Mark stood up and punched his brother's shoulder. "Now who's being immature?"

Roman held up his hands. "Hey now, it's payback time."

The two brothers wrestled until Mark had Roman pinned.

Mark whispered into Roman's ear. "Dude, we've been on one date. Give me a break here."

"Uncle," Roman cried out.

Mark stood up and held a hand out to his brother and smirked. The moment Roman grabbed his hand, the thought crossed his mind to let go and watch his brother fall back on his butt, but when he caught Leah watching them from the corner of his eye he thought better of it.

"Can you believe we're gonna be uncles soon?" Roman shook off the dirt from his clothes and chuckled.

Leah walked up. "Well, something tells me you're going to have to get used to being dirty."

Mark grinned. "I don't know, Elizabeth is pretty clean. I doubt she'll let her kids be dirty."

"Ha, you definitely haven't been around babies lately." Leah laughed and couldn't wait to see how they reacted the first time their little niece or nephew spit up on them.

"Do you think Elizabeth is going to have strange cravings?" Leah mused aloud.

Claire had walked up to the trio and chuckled. "I just hope she doesn't go wanting pickles and ice cream." She made a disgusted face. "Blech!"

"What's wrong with pickles and ice cream?" Elizabeth walked up and looked at the foursome who had been talking about her.

Mark and Roman laughed.

"She's always liked pickles and ice cream," John said when he joined the group.

"Nuh-uh. You're joking, right?" Claire asked.

Elizabeth laughed. "Nope, he's right."

Leah and Claire both looked at Elizabeth as though she had lost her mind.

"When we were kids, we watched a show." Elizabeth narrowed her eyes. "You know, I can't remember the name of it now."

"Yeah, and Matthew dared you to eat pickles and ice cream when it was over." Mark smiled, remembering the way they all teased and egged one another on to do crazy stuff when they were kids.

"And I did," Elizabeth confessed. "It was really good, too. Dill pickles and vanilla ice cream."

Matthew joined them. "I didn't believe you for a long time. I could have sworn you were just trying to get me to eat something gross."

"And then Dad tried it, and when he liked it the rest of you sissies decided to try it," Elizabeth teased.

Matthew ran a hand down his face. "It was gross. I don't care that you and Dad actually liked it, the rest of us all agreed not to try it again. Even Chloe, your twin, thought it was disgusting."

A look of longing crossed Elizabeth's face before she caught herself. "Yeah, those were the days. When we were all living here together."

"You miss her, don't you?" Logan came up and wrapped his wife in his arms.

A sniffle and an errant tear were all that came from Elizabeth.

"Alright, I say it's time for more s'mores. Who's with me?" Mark asked the group, knowing his sister didn't want any more attention on her at that moment.

Lizzie and Logan walked to the back of the grassy area, and he held her tightly.

Leah looked away from them and hoped that one day she would have a husband who loved her as much as Logan loved Elizabeth.

Chapter 16

The rodeo was over and the site cleared out as though no one had even been there. Leah had driven by the fairgrounds Tuesday afternoon on her way to make a delivery. She was surprised that the entire event had been cleared away so quickly.

After she made the delivery, she had to go to the sheriff's office and sign her statement regarding the attack from Rocko. She wasn't looking forward to seeing the brute. She had heard from Logan that he had been treated at the Bozeman hospital, but Sheriff Roscoe wanted him to come back to the Beacon Creek jail to await his hearing.

The Bozeman sheriff had offered to jail him there, but Roscoe wouldn't hear it. Leah wondered if it was because her sheriff didn't trust the Bozeman one. She didn't trust him. Since he hadn't done anything to stop Bart and his gang, she wasn't sure if the Bozeman sheriff wasn't on the take, or maybe one of his deputies was. Either way, she was glad that Rocko was in the Beacon Creek jail. He would not get out unless it was ordered by a judge.

However, that didn't mean she wanted to see the guy, even if he was behind bars and hopefully wearing an orange jumpsuit.

The Beacon Creek jail was small. In fact, they only had two cells, both of which were visible when she entered the building.

"You think you've won, but you've just made things more difficult for yourself," Rocko sneered when Leah entered the jail.

"Shut up!" one of the deputies called out.

Not wanting to show any weakness at all, she ignored the man. Instead, Leah walked directly to the sheriff's tiny office and entered when he motioned for her to. She closed the door behind her so she wouldn't have to hear Rocko's voice. He couldn't see the inside of Roscoe's office from where he sat, but if he was loud enough Leah would be able to hear him.

"Leah, how are you feeling?" the sheriff asked.

She took a seat across from him and smiled. "I'm much better, thank you."

"I just need to go through your statement again, and then you can sign it." The sheriff pulled out a few pages.

With a sigh, she read what she had told the sheriff over the weekend. "Do you think he'll get bail while he waits for a court date?"

Roscoe shook his head. "Very doubtful. Rocko's got a violent past, and with all of the witnesses to your attack, and the video of Stevie's, I don't think the judge will be willing to let him out."

Leah nodded. "Good. That's one less problem." After she signed her statement, she looked at the sheriff. "But what about Bart? Will he come after me now? Or Georgia?"

Pink tinged the sheriff's cheeks. "I don't think you need to worry about Georgia. I've got an eye on her."

Leah raised her brows. "Oh, really?" She had wondered where Georgia was on Sunday afternoon when the family met up, but she just figured the woman was in one of the cabins the Mannings had built for the homeless women. "She wasn't with you Sunday afternoon by chance, was she?"

Roscoe cleared his throat. "I may have been keeping an eye on her while the family was meeting."

"Just keeping an eye on her? Or spending time with the pretty lady?" Leah teased.

"Doing my job, that's all." Roscoe's voice turned gruff, and Leah figured she better not tease the sheriff any more than she already had.

"Right, of course." Leah straightened the papers and handed them back to the sheriff when she stood. "Do you need anything else from me?"

Sheriff Roscoe stood when Leah did. "Just promise me you and your friends won't go anywhere near Bart or the homeless until this situation is taken care of."

Leah held her hands up. "Don't worry, we've all been told by our family that we aren't to go anywhere near Bozeman without an escort. And none of the guys want to get near Bart right now, either." She frowned. "It's just sad. The poor people are being treated so horribly by Bart, and now we can't even give them a sandwich or let them know how much God loves them. It's not fair."

"Life's not fair, Leah." The sheriff ran a hand over the back of his neck. "All you can do right now is pray for them. Let God take care of them right now while you can't."

"You're right, Sheriff. Thanks." When Leah had entered the sheriff's station her heart was heavy, now it was just a little bit lighter knowing that God was in control. Not her, and certainly not Bart or any of his goons.

The entire drive back to her store, which wasn't far, she prayed and thanked God for taking such great care of her, and asked for protection for those in Bart's control.

When she got back to the store, her spirits soared when she saw the old coots setting up for another checkers tournament. Leah loved it when they had their tournaments at her shop. Not only did they get a lot of people coming in to check on the progress of the game, but those same people usually shopped.

It also meant more people that she knew and trusted would be around her store. And that would help Mark and Logan to stop fretting so much over her safety. She appreciated their support, but it was getting a little bit stifling lately. And Logan needed to be spending more time with Elizabeth. She was having morning sickness at the oddest hours, and Leah knew that having Logan around more would comfort Elizabeth.

"Hey ya, Mr. Macon and Mr. Addison," Leah called when she entered the store.

"Leah, it's about time someone pretty came in." Mr. Macon was always a little bit of a flirt.

Leah looked around for any signs that Ms. Barton was in the store. Mr. Macon usually only flirted with Leah when his girlfriend wasn't around, but she wanted to be sure. "Where's Ms. Barton?"

"Oh, she'll be here. She just had to stop in at the post office first." Mr. Macon made his way to the register to pay for his soda before he sat himself down to play his game.

They kept a small refrigerator in the store and stocked it with water and Coke products, just the way the locals preferred. They also had snacks that everyone could purchase. When Logan came home and noticed how many people stopped in to see the checkers and chess tournaments, he started stocking more and more snacks and drinks. Which turned a tidy profit. They didn't sell them for as much as the convenience store down the street, but they did still have a nice markup. The sales from snacks weren't going to keep them in the black, but they usually kept people around long enough for them to see other things they needed and then buy.

Leah spent the next hour selling drinks, snacks, and even a few high-ticket items as people came and went to watch the tournament. She loved these days, as they always went so quickly. And a lot of her friends came into the store.

When Sophia entered, Leah jumped up from her perch and went to her friend. "Sophia, so good to see you. I'd been meaning to come to your gym, but my schedule has been a bit crazy."

"Leah, I'm sorry I didn't stop by sooner. How are you?" Concern etched her friend's face.

Leah waved a hand in front of her face. "I'm fine. And I wanted to thank you for teaching me everything you have so far. If it hadn't been for your self-defense classes, I have no idea what would have happened." She shivered when the idea of being forced into Rocko's vehicle entered her mind.

"That's part of why I'm here. I was thinking about setting up more self-defense classes for women. Going a bit further than the free classes I already offer."

"Count me in," said one woman who had overheard the conversation. "And I know my sisters are gonna want to come as well."

Another woman—Leah thought her name was Natalie—raised a hand. "Oh, me too. And my sister-in-law wants to join."

Leah smiled and patted her friend's shoulder. "Looks like you're going to have a full house without any advertising. You might want to set up an online registration form to make sure you don't get too many people showing up."

"Wow, that's a great idea. Thanks." Sophia looked to the two women. "I'd love to have you all join." She told them the cost and what night it would be on. Both women didn't seem to mind the cost. They just wanted to be able to defend themselves like Leah had done.

"Ladies, you should know that I've taken a lot of classes from Sophia. So don't think that you'll be able to defend against an attacker after just one class." Leah had actually attended most of the self-defense classes Sophia held over the past three years.

"We know. Word has spread, and I think you're going to have quite a few women who'll sign up. The Diner Divas have been talking up your classes. I actually came to town to find out more, but stopped in here first to pick up an order." Natalie looked to Leah and held out her printout with the order details.

"Right, I'll go grab this now. It's in the back room." Leah took the paper with her and went to the online order storeroom to grab the boxes.

Once the order had been double-checked and loaded into Natalie's truck, the woman had already given her information to Sophia to sign her up for the classes that would start the following week.

After both ladies had gone, Sophia walked up to Leah and gave her a hug. "You are going to be the best advertising for my classes. I might have to do two classes a week if they're right about the divas spreading the word." She shook her head. "I hadn't even said a word to anyone about starting the classes up again. Well, I think I did say something to Rosie the other day about thinking about the classes."

"That's all it takes. Shoot, I wouldn't be surprised if the divas have listening devices set up all over town. I honestly don't know how they always know the gossip before anyone else does." Leah shook her head and pursed her lips. Most of the time their gossiping ways were a burden on the town, but maybe this time they would actually do some good.

"Hmm, you might be right." Sophia waved a hand in front of her. "Not about the listening devices, but they do tend to know more than anyone else. I think I'll have to say something in front of them to make sure they keep spreading the word." A devious smile crossed her face.

Leah laughed. "I love it! Use their loose lips to make sure you get a ton of free advertising. Great idea." She put a finger to her chin and tapped it. "Hmm, I might have to do that the next time we need to sell a few larger ticket items."

"Well, I had come in here to see if you could help me get the word out about my classes, but it sounds as though it's already out."

"I'll still help, and make sure to keep a space for me. Especially if you're going to do an advanced class. I would love to learn more techniques, like how to disarm a man who's got a knife up against your side." Leah rubbed the spot where Rocko had slashed her. It was healing up nicely and she no longer had to put on clean bandages, but it did still ache.

"The key is to keep an attacker from getting that close to begin with. What you did, that was ingenious. And I think I'm going to have to include the giant teddy bear in my training classes from here on out." Sophia grinned.

"Ha, ha. Make fun of me. I see how it is." Leah feigned hurt feelings, but couldn't stop herself from laughing.

"I'll catch you later. And Leah, you've always got a spot in any of my classes." Sophia hugged her friend goodbye and left to finish running her errands.

Before her shift ended, Mark came in.

Chapter 17

Leah's heart fluttered when she saw Mark come in. She had seen him almost every day for the past week, but she still got nervous whenever he visited her. "Hey ya, cowboy."

"Hey ya, darlin'." Mark had started calling her *darlin'* lately, and Leah liked it.

He looked around and smiled at the old coots up in the front corner of the store. "So, who's winning so far today?"

"Well, it looks like Mr. Cannon is winning this round. Mr. Addison won the last round, but I think it's only because Ms. Barton came in and distracted Mr. Macon. He was ahead until his girlfriend showed up." Leah chuckled.

"Poor Mr. Walters. He must hate that Mr. Cannon is winning." Mark grinned.

A customer came up to the counter, so Leah had to go help him. Mark continued watching the game until she was done. Even though Mark had come into the store just about every night that Leah closed, he was nervous this time. They hadn't been out on another date yet, but not because he didn't want to; Leah had been busy and closed most nights this week.

Mark would have asked her out to lunch, but his work on the ranch kept him busy all day long. However, he was here to ask her out for a proper date on her next day off.

The moment Leah was done and Mark saw the customer leave out of the corner of his eye, he headed toward her. He knew she was busy, but he hoped he could get enough of her time to ask her out before the next customer stole her away.

"So, Leah. I've come in here to see when your next day off is." His palms were sweaty, and he was unsure how she'd respond. They'd had a lot of fun, if you took out the attempted kidnapping and attack. But up until that point they'd had a fun night. And she'd been really nice every time he'd seen her since then. She didn't even blame him for what happened after the rodeo.

"Oh." Leah looked confused. "Um."

Mark wondered if he'd said something wrong. Was she already moving on to someone else? "What's wrong?"

"Well, I thought you came in to keep an eye on me tonight."

He chuckled. "That too. But I wanted to take you riding on your next day off. On our property. I figured that would be a safe date, and Bart couldn't get to you on Triple J land."

Leah nodded. "Yeah, your fences are pretty tight. And I doubt any of Bart's crew can ride a horse."

"So, is that a yes?"

"Yes, I'd like that. I have Friday off, and then again on Sunday. But on Friday late morning I do have a follow-up doctor's appointment." Leah knew she had nothing wrong, but the doctor did want to double-check her wound and make sure everything was healing up right.

Mark mentally went over the rest of the week in his mind. "I can come into town Friday afternoon and pick you up. Then after we're done riding, we could go out for dinner somewhere?"

"Anywhere but Bozeman." Leah had zero desire to head into that city unless she had no other options. She didn't know all of Bart's men on sight, and who knew how many of them were on the lookout for her? Especially after Rocko's botched attempt at her kidnapping. For all she knew, she was public enemy number one to those guys.

"Agreed. But I don't want to do dinner here in town, either." Mark thought about it. "We could go to the Cattleman's Association over in Four Corners."

Leah frowned. "They've got great steak, but so do you. Plus, the women there always wear dresses for dinner."

Mark smirked. "That's right, you don't wear dresses except for church and special occasions."

She shrugged.

He crossed his arms. "What, a date with me isn't special enough?"

She chuckled. "That's not it. I'd have to bring clothes to change into after our ride, and I'd need a shower. That's too much. What do you say we just grill up steaks at your ranch? I love your dad's barbecue sauce. No one does better steaks than you guys."

He puffed his chest out. "We do make the best grilled anything around."

She slapped his arm. "Don't go gettin' a big head or anything. I said your *dad* makes the best sauce." Leah arched a brow.

He held up his hands. "Fine, fine. Dad makes the best sauce. But I'll have you know that last time you came over for grilled steaks, I made the sauce."

"Oh, that explains it." She winked.

"Hey, what's that supposed to mean?"

Leah smirked. "Nothing at all. Just make sure your dad makes the sauce on Friday and not you, alright?"

Before he could answer, Leah was called away and Mark chuckled as he turned back to watch the rest of the checkers game. He was beginning to enjoy their banter and looked forward to their next round.

Friday came way too quickly for Leah. After her doctor's appointment, which went exactly as she'd expected, she went home to change her clothes for a ride and dinner at the ranch. She was glad she asked to do dinner there instead of going out. It wasn't that she didn't like going out, because she did. However, she was tired from all of the hours lately and the stress of wondering if

Bart or one of his goons was going to be waiting for her around the corner.

Since she was going to be riding for the next couple hours, she decided to wear comfortable Wranglers, her riding boots, and one of her favorite western shirts. She wasn't trying to be cover-model ready; she wanted to look nice, but she also wanted to make sure she was comfortable. She also brought one of her favorite denim jackets that was lined with Sherpa and flannel. It would keep her plenty warm for the cool night ahead.

Mark was right on time and waiting for her downstairs, talking to her mother, when Leah came down.

"I hope you're ready for a long ride. I was thinking we could ride back to those old caves we used to explore as kids." Mark's eyes twinkled when he mentioned the old days.

Leah felt her cheeks heat as she remembered how she'd follow her brother and the Manning boys when they left her all alone. She knew they knew she was following them, but they didn't seem to mind having her trail behind them. Once in a while, Lizzie and Chloe would also go with them. Especially when Logan hit high school and started dating Lizzie. Then she was almost always with them. Leah, however, was never invited unless it was by Chloe or Lizzie.

"That sounds great." She picked up her purse and jacket and said goodbye to her mom.

On the drive out, they both began to reminisce about their childhood.

"You guys always knew I was following, didn't you?" she asked once they cleared town.

Mark kept his eyes on the road, but smiled. "Yeah, we did. The first time, your brother was worried we'd lose you and he kept telling us to slow it down. At first we didn't know why. But when Luke looked back, he saw you."

"I'm surprised Luke didn't try to talk y'all into losing me." Leah chuckled.

"He did."

"Really? Did my brother stick up for me?" Leah turned in her seat to look at the handsome cowboy. He had always been good looking; even when he was a pesky teenager he was cute.

Mark glanced at her before answering, "Actually, it was me. When Luke said we should lose you in the trees, I said that wasn't the cowboy way."

"Really? You did?" Leah sounded amazed that he would stick up for her back then.

"Of course. Do you know what our dad would have done to us all of us if he knew that we'd tried to lose you in the woods?" He laughed and shook his head. "I doubt we would have been able to sit down for a month after he was done with us."

"Ouch." Leah flinched.

Mark waved a hand. "No, not really. But we would have been in a heap of trouble. And I doubt we would have been able to ride the rest of the summer. Our dad always drove home the importance of taking care of the girls in our lives."

"So that's why I never lost you in the woods. Or I guess *you* never lost *me*." She was starting to feel as though he'd been there for her her entire life.

"When Bobby Myers started teasing me in junior high, was that you who gave him the black eye?" Leah knew someone had threatened Bobby, and when he refused to leave her alone, the person didn't back down. Bobby had been the biggest bully at school. No one ever stood up to him except for one person. She had suspected it was Matthew Manning. No one ever told her who, except to say it was one of the Manning brothers.

Mark didn't say anything, he only smiled.

"You know, after that incident boys left me alone. No one ever teased me again." Leah pursed her lips. "Except for you guys and my brother."

"Even back then I knew you were one of us. And us Mannings always take care of our own." Mark winked at her.

In the past when he referred to her as family, it was in the sisterly sort of way. But this time it didn't feel like he was calling her his sister. And that knowledge caused butterflies to take flight throughout her entire being.

Mark took hold of her hand and squeezed it. But instead of letting it go, he held it the rest of the way to his ranch.

Leah hated when he had to let go so they could get out of the truck, but she took it as a good sign that he even wanted to hold her hand that long. Maybe he would again. And maybe, just maybe, if she was lucky, he'd give her a kiss goodnight. And not the peck on the cheek or kiss on top of the head kind of thing her brother did once in a while. She wanted a full-blown, lip-on-lip action that would send shivers down her spine.

"Leah, what on Earth convinced you to go riding with my brother today?" Luke Manning sauntered down the front steps of the ranch house. While he'd recently moved to town with his new wife, he did still work the ranch with his family. Since his wife was a sheriff's deputy, they needed to live closer to town. But Leah knew he wanted to build a house on the family ranch and live there. She suspected one day he would.

"Well"—Leah grinned—"your brother promised to show me the caves. And you know how much I've always wanted a guided tour of those things." She hugged her old friend before heading inside to greet Mrs. Manning.

Luke chuckled. "Just be careful, I hear there's bears in those caves now."

Leah turned worried eyes on Mark, who shook his head and rolled his eyes.

"My brother thinks he's a comedian, folks." Mark slapped his brother's back and followed Leah inside.

Mark had set everything out for their ride before he left for town, so when he and Leah headed to the barn it didn't take them long to saddle up the horses and attach their gear. Mark always carried a shotgun and bear spray with him. He also gave the same to Leah. As all cowgirls were, she was proficient with multiple weapons and obviously had her own bear spray that she carried. But Mark wanted to make sure she had enough. The spray worked on plenty of wildlife as well as goons.

He wished she would have carried her spray into the rodeo so she could have stopped Rocko sooner, but it did work out in the end.

Once they were on their horses and heading out, Mark thought it was a good time to tell her the latest about Bart. "So, I heard from the sheriff earlier today." He cringed.

Leah accidentally pulled back the reins and her mount stopped. "What's happened?"

It wasn't terror that Mark heard in her voice, but there was definitely worry and maybe apprehension? He needed to make sure she didn't worry, but still kept an eye out. "Rocko isn't getting bail. The judge denied it. But he somehow retained the services of a good lawyer. An expensive one."

She clicked her tongue and nudged her horse forward. They were taking this trip at a slow, leisurely pace to start since there were too many barriers where they were. She knew from experience that once they were out in the open fields, they'd be able to let the horses have their head.

Before she responded to what Mark said, she took a moment to think about it. "How could a homeless thug afford an expensive attorney?"

"That's what the sheriff wants to know. He thinks there might be some sort of organized crime behind what Bart and his goons are doing. And that's why the

Bozeman sheriff hasn't been able to get anything on them."

She sighed. "That would make a lot of sense. At first I thought that sheriff might be involved somehow. But if it's organized crime, then maybe he isn't involved."

"He could be getting pressured, or threatened." Mark looked around all of a sudden.

The hair on Leah's neck pricked, and she looked, too. "Are we being watched?"

"Might be." He winced. "I'm sorry, but I think we should turn around. I don't know if there's danger, but with both of us feeling as though we're being watched, it's most likely the case."

"I swear, if I ever get a chance I'm going to bop Bart right in the nose. He's done nothing but ruin every date we've had so far." Leah turned her horse around and narrowed her gaze into the trees in the distance.

Mark pulled out his cellphone. "I'm calling the sheriff."

The phone rang only once before he picked up. "Mark, what can I do for ya?"

"I'm out in the back forty with Leah, and we think someone's out here watching us."

"That's what I was afraid of." The sigh that came over the phone was loud and heavy. "I'm here at your ranch. Come back home and I'll go out and check things with your brothers."

"I can stay here and wait for you." Mark didn't like the idea of not being a part of a posse on his own ranch.

Besides, he knew exactly where it all went down, not his brothers.

"But you need to keep an eye out for Leah. She needs to come back now. They're probably after her."

Mark looked at Leah, who couldn't hear what the sheriff was saying. "Of course, you're right. Be right there." He felt like a cad. Leah should be his top priority, not his ego.

"What's going on?" Leah asked.

"We need to head back, now. The sheriff is already here for some reason." He gave her a pointed look. If Mark wasn't mistaken, the sheriff knew something was going down and he had come to help them.

"Do you think he followed Bart or one of his other goons here?" Leah kicked the sides of her horse to get her to go faster, and let more of the reins loose.

Even with the gates and cattle around, they needed to hurry up. When they got to the first gate that should have been closed and noted it was open, Mark almost cursed. "Someone's definitely following us." He dismounted, pulled the gate closed behind them, and fastened the latch once they were both through.

Leah looked around and pulled the shotgun out of its holster on the horse. "Can you lock the gate so they can't open it again?"

Mark shook his head. "No, I'll need to get some locks and come back out here. We've never needed to lock the fields before. But we do have enough locks to keep our cattle in, at least." He started to get back on his horse when the sound of a horse approaching reached his ears.

"Good, I'll come back with you." Leah turned, aiming the gun toward the sound. A feeling of unease spread throughout her entire body. She'd never shot a person before, but if Mark was in danger, she would protect him.

Chapter 18

"Whoa, it's just me." Matthew held his hands in the air.

Mark frowned. "Were you following us?"

"No, I was out checking the fence lines and I noted a lone rider going this way." Matthew pointed toward where they had been going originally.

"We were being followed," Mark stated. "Did you get a good look at the guy?"

Matthew shook his head.

"The sheriff's here. We need to head back and join him in the search." Mark led them back home, but all three were vigilant and had their weapons out, just in case.

When they entered the paddock, the sheriff was already on a horse along with Caleb and Luke.

"Good, Matthew's with you. John is inside with your mom and the other girls." Caleb pointed to the house.

"Mark, I need you to stay behind and help protect the women."

Leah raised a brow, but didn't say anything. She was perfectly capable of taking care of herself and the other women in the house. Besides, she knew that Judith was also a very capable woman. And with John there, they didn't need anyone else.

"But Dad, I can help," Mark complained.

"Son, I know you can. But I need you here protecting your mom and the rest of the family."

"Mark," the sheriff interrupted, "I've got a couple of deputies coming. When they get here, can you join them in the hunt?"

He nodded. "Of course, Sheriff."

"And Leah, I need you to keep all of the windows and doors locked." The sheriff looked at how she held the shotgun over her shoulder. "You know how to use that thing?"

Leah's brows furrowed. "Of course I do."

"Good, don't hesitate to shoot unless it's one of us," the sheriff ordered.

Mark and Leah headed inside once Mark had tethered the horses inside the barn. Since the deputies were coming, he needed to keep the horses ready to go.

"Do you think it's one of Bart's goons?" Leah asked when they entered the mud room and removed their boots.

"Most likely. But there is the possibility it could be a poacher or a cattle rustler." He grinned at Leah. "It wouldn't be the first time."

"True, I just hope this time none of you Mannings get shot."

Mark wiped the grin from his face. "So do I. So. Do. I." The memory of Luke and Callie being shot played in his mind like a movie. He grimaced, but sent up a quick prayer for protection. Protection for everyone in the house, but also for those trailing the culprit.

"You know, we have a large selection of locks and chains you could use to make it more difficult to open the gates. They don't require keys or codes, just are more complicated to open. It might help to slow down any rustlers, if that's what's going on here." Leah prayed it was something as simple as cattle rustlers. Not that cattle rustlers were simple, but it was better than Bart's goons going after them like this.

"Did you see the man trailing you?" Georgia asked when they came out of the mud room. She had wrapped her arms around her middle and wore a frown.

Leah shook her head. "No, we didn't. But Matthew said he saw a lone rider."

"Bart?" Fear filled Georgia's eyes, and she began to shake.

"Shh, don't worry. The sheriff will take care of it all." Judith wrapped a comforting arm around her charge.

"How'd the sheriff know there would be trouble here?" Mark asked, looking between his mother and Georgia.

"Uh, he didn't." Judith smiled at Georgia, who blushed in response.

Leah chuckled. "I had wondered. He's seemed much happier lately, and has been over here a lot."

Their sheriff had been divorced for quite some time. But he was also a little bit older than Georgia. Leah wasn't sure, but she though the woman was at least forty, maybe a bit older. And she knew the sheriff was in his mid-fifties. However, with her background Georgia just might need a strong, older man who could protect her. Someone who was grounded and dependable. The sheriff would do just that.

"What?" Mark's confused gaze swiveled from one woman to the next.

Leah patted his shoulder. "I'll explain later, Mark." She turned to look at Judith. "Men can be so clueless sometimes."

Both Georgia and Judith laughed at that.

"Very true." Judith gave a pointed look to both of her sons, who stood nearby. John had been standing close by, but was quiet as usual.

Leah knew something had gone wrong with John, but no one seemed to know what it was. Maybe she could get him to open up to her. Other than his actual sisters, she was the closest woman to him. In town, anyways. Leah did suspect John's attitude was because a woman had broken his heart, so he might not want to talk to his brothers about it. Maybe a woman's ear was exactly what he needed. And no man his age wanted to discuss women with their mothers.

Although, Leah wondered why he hadn't spoken to Elizabeth yet. Or, she thought, maybe he had and Lizzie was staying mum on the entire situation. That thought made her wonder if she shouldn't just keep her nose out of it.

Leah was shocked out of her reverie when John spoke up.

"Georgia, Roscoe is a nice guy. He deserves a nice woman. So please, don't lead him on if you aren't sure about your feelings for him." That was the most John had said in front of Leah since he'd come home.

And the topic, along with the longing look in his eyes, only confirmed her suspicions—John had his heart broken, big time.

Thirty minutes later the doorbell rang, causing Georgia to jump. Judith put an arm around the woman and comforted her. Leah knew that Georgia had had a rough time of it, but she didn't realize the woman was so skittish. Could the man on the property be here for the formerly homeless woman and not Leah?

Mark answered the door and came back with two deputies, Callie being one of them. Leah rolled her eyes. So it was alright for a woman to answer a dangerous call, but it wasn't alright for Leah to help?

"Mark, can you take us out to where you were when you saw the man?" Callie asked.

"I can take you," Leah offered.

Callie looked between Mark and her partner.

Mark shook his head. "No, Leah. If that guy is here for you, I'd much rather you stay in the house with everyone else."

Leah put a hand on her hip and pursed her lips. "You know I can take care of myself, right?"

Callie put her hands in the air. "Hey, no one is doubting that one bit. But the house is a more defensible position. And there are other people here who could benefit from your protection." She looked to Georgia and John.

Leah felt like a heel. She hadn't even considered whether or not anyone else could take care of themselves. Or even if they needed help. No matter why the guy was on the Triple J land, those in the house did need a capable protector. And Callie was right, the house was more defensible than being out in the open. "You're right. I didn't even think about anyone else. I'll stay here and help."

Judith put a hand on Leah's shoulder. "Thank you, Leah. I appreciate your help."

Mark pulled Leah in for a hug and whispered in her ear, "I really need you to protect my family. Thank you."

She hugged him back and sighed. He felt so good and smelled even better. His usual scent of pine and spice was overshadowed by his leather scent and something else. He wasn't on the horse long enough for that scent, but there was something earthy and all man about him. She took in a long sniff and hoped no one noticed.

"Be careful." Leah pulled back and looked into his eyes. "I want a do-over date. Got it?" She smirked.

His little chin dimple showed up when he gazed into her eyes. "Most definitely." Then he kissed the top of her head.

Since there were three of them, Mark had to take time to saddle up another horse. He knew John wouldn't mind if the deputy rode his horse. Callie was going to ride Whiskers, which was the horse he had saddled up for Leah to begin with.

Callie rubbed Whiskers' neck and spoke in low tones to her. The horse nudged her shoulder and seemed happy to see her old friend. Since joining the force, Callie hadn't been out to ride nearly enough. But there did always seem to be women enough to ride Whiskers, thankfully.

Once everyone was on a horse, they took off at a gallop, each taking turns opening and closing the gates they had to go through.

While Mark did worry about Leah's safety, he knew she'd be safer at home. And he was also glad that she would be looking after his mom and Georgia. John could take care of himself. The four of them would be just fine. So instead, he turned his attention to the task at hand, finding the lone rider and sussing out his intentions.

When they caught up to the sheriff, Mark expected to find a goon or a rustler. What he saw instead surprised him.

Chapter 19

Mark had never thought to see this person again. He couldn't even remember the last time he saw the man. Had it actually been over a decade?

Mr. Johnson's wayward son Cal, whom Mark hadn't seen in forever, was sitting astride a horse and smiling. Was this the person who had been following them earlier?

"Cal? Cal Johnson? Is that you?" Mark inched closer, unsure if his eyes weren't lying to him.

"Mark, good to see you again. It's been ages." Cal smiled and waved.

"Where've ya been?"

"Oh, here and there." Cal turned back to Matthew. "Sorry if I startled any of you. I was just out for a ride, and honestly, I didn't think anyone would mind if I rode through your land."

"We don't mind. Just do us a favor and close the gates behind you. We've had a few issues over the years and need to keep the gates closed. Especially when cattle are in the fields." Sitting atop his horse, Matthew looked out over the land.

Mark scanned the horizon for anyone else. He wondered if it was Cal that Matthew saw earlier. Unless they continued looking around their property, they wouldn't have any way of knowing if someone else was there or not.

Cal's brows furrowed. "Is it dangerous around here now?"

"Not normally." Matthew rubbed the back of his neck. "But for now, you might not want to wander alone on our land. We've angered someone and we're not yet sure how he's going to respond."

Well, that was one way of putting it. Mark might have phrased it a bit different, but really, Call didn't need to know exactly what was going on.

"Oh, alright. Then I'll head back to our land. I was just heading out to the caves. Curious to see if they're still like they used to be when we were kids." Cal chuckled.

"Tell ya what, when this situation is cleared up we'll get the guys all together and go spelunking like we used to when we were kids." Mark had missed his old friend and would enjoy catching up over a long ride.

"Sounds great." Cal turned and began his ride home.

The sheriff took off his hat and wiped the sweat from his forehead. "I'm not sure there's anything really going on here other than an old neighbor riding through your land. What do you think?"

Matthew and Mark both shook their heads.

"I think we should head back home and let everyone know that Cal's home." Mark headed back. He wanted to check in on Leah and make sure she was alright. And he hoped it wasn't too late to have a nice barbecue dinner with his date.

What Mark had hoped would be a nice, quiet dinner with him and Leah turned into a full-blown neighborhood event. The moment his mom heard Cal was back, she called Mr. Johnson and invited them both over for dinner. And of course, the sheriff and both of his deputies were invited to stay.

Then Matthew called Logan and Elizabeth, so the entire Manning family was there. Well, minus Chloe. But she was supposed to come next weekend, so there would be another big family barbecue then as well. And now that spring had sprung they would have the Sunday supper barbecue every week, as long as it didn't rain.

Mark loved his family, and he really did enjoy the giant barbecues. The more the merrier, he always said. But for this one night, he had hoped it would have been just him and Leah.

Once the food was prepared on the table outside, a mass of people converged and it was utter chaos. Fun family chaos, but still crazy. Mark didn't have any opportunities to speak with Leah, just the two of them. He hoped they would have some time to talk when he took her home.

Since such a large group wasn't expected, dessert had to be s'mores. Judith didn't have time to make more pies. No one complained when the fire was started and everyone gathered around with their marshmallows.

"So, looks like an old friend is finally back in town," Leah said when she sat next to Mark on a log near the fire. "I always wondered what happened to Cal when he left."

"Me, too." Mark pulled his flaming marshmallow out of the fire and blew on it. "I never would have guessed that he'd end up on a Texas oil rig."

"I know, right? He always seemed like a slacker. Don't those oil fellows work hard?" Leah put her marshmallow on her graham cracker and put a piece of chocolate and graham cracker on top to make a s'more sandwich.

"They do. Almost as hard as us ranchers." Mark chuckled and handed Leah a napkin to wipe her face. She had left a trail of chocolatey marshmallow all along her chin. For just one second he wondered what it would be like to kiss it off her face.

Leah licked her lips and her tongue darted out toward her chin.

Mark watched with fascination and desire. He lost all train of thought and stared at her lips. Would he ever get a chance to kiss the cowgirl? Or was he forever doomed to disastrous dates that had to be cancelled midstride?

So far, both dates had started out fantastic only to end with disaster. But this time, at least, no one was hurt—so far. He'd have to wait and see how the night ended when he took her home.

"Why do you think Cal stayed away for so long without a single visit?" Leah leaned over and whispered after she'd cleaned her face up.

"Have you met old Mr. Johnson?" Mark had known the curmudgeon his entire life. He was worse than the grinch. His dad had hounded Cal his entire life. It was no surprise when he up and left the day after high school. Even his older brother Steven hardly came by for a visit.

Leah nodded. "True. I'd run away if he was my dad, too."

Mark stared at Cal across the fire. "But, I guess Cal heard about his dad and has come home to set things right before it's too late."

"Yeah, these things will do that to a family." Leah lowered her eyes to the fire and thanked God He gave her a wonderful dad, and had helped to heal him of his heart disease, too.

When the night finally came to an end, Mark got up to take Leah home and hopefully get a chance to talk to her alone.

Logan put a hand up. "Don't worry, Mark. We'll take Leah home, she's right on our way."

Leah opened her mouth to say something, then closed it. She really didn't know what to say. Her brother was right: he drove right past her house on his way home, and it didn't make any sense to have Mark drive into town late on a Friday night.

Mark did get up and walked them out front. "Can I have a moment with Leah before you leave?"

Elizabeth smiled and pulled her husband toward their truck. "Sure, we'll just wait in the truck. Take your time."

"Thanks." He waved to his sister and her husband and watched until they were inside the truck and it was just him and Leah outside. "So, it looks like another date ruined. I'm really sorry about today."

She waved a hand in the air. "Don't worry about it. There wasn't anything either of us could have done about Cal coming home when he did."

Mark took her hands in his. "I want to try this again, but don't know how."

"Hmm, what do you say just you and I go out to supper on Sunday after church?" Leah gave him a saucy smile.

"And what if someone interrupts us again?"

"We should go elsewhere. Maybe try the Cattleman's Association like you suggested before?" Leah did like that place, and if it gave them some time alone then dressing up wouldn't be so bad.

"It's a date. Do you want to leave from church? Or should I give you time to change after service?" Mark would go to service dressed for Sunday supper at the Cattleman's. But he could wait for Leah to change if she needed.

"No need. I can wear a dress to church that will work for supper as well. See you Sunday." She stood there for just a second, hoping he'd kiss her but knowing he wouldn't. Not with Lizzie and Logan waiting, and most likely watching them.

Mark leaned in when he felt the pull toward the pretty cowgirl, but stopped himself. He didn't want their first kiss to be with an audience, and after the day they'd had. He wanted it to be romantic, something she'd remember for a long time to come. Shoot, he wanted a kiss he'd remember. "Goodnight." He cleared his hoarse voice and tried again. "Goodnight, Leah. See you soon."

She smiled and walked to her brother's truck. When she was about to get inside, she turned and waved. Leah couldn't wait for their Sunday supper. She only hoped and prayed that nothing and no *one* would interrupt it.

Chapter 20

The next day came early, and Mark moaned when he heard their rooster outside his window. "Not today, you big turkey." He turned over and covered his head with his covers.

The rooster kept crowing.

Mark didn't know how, but it seemed their rooster was more intelligent than the average fowl. If it wasn't so old and beloved by the family, he'd go out and serve it up for dinner that night.

Stan the rooster always seemed to know when someone was trying to sleep later than they ought to. And the rooster would cock and crow outside their window until they were up and at 'em. The entire family had commented on this one bird and his antics.

"Fine, Stan. Go round up the hens and make sure they're laying plenty of eggs today." Mark sat up in bed and ran a hand down his face. "And stop bugging me." The sound of Stan's crowing could still be heard.

"Alright, alright. I get it." Mark got out of bed and went to his window. Once he opened the shades, Stan shut his beak and strutted away to where his ladies awaited him.

It was still dark out, but the sun's light was just beginning to peek above the eastern horizon. A pinch of orange light could be seen, and Mark shook his head. "Dumb bird, he probably wouldn't even taste good."

After Mark had dressed, he headed out for a cup of coffee and realized he was the last one up. "Well, I'll be." He shook his head and figured Stan just might know what he was doing after all.

"Hey, sleepyhead." Matthew handed him a cup of coffee and grinned.

"Sorry, I couldn't get to sleep last night." Mark had tossed and turned for a couple of hours. He couldn't get his mind to shut off. He even got up and read his Bible for a little while, hoping it would calm his brain down. Nothing helped. Then a little after midnight, he finally drifted off with thoughts of a pretty cowgirl on his mind.

"I had a few of those when I first met Claire." Matthew looked into the distance and sighed.

"When did they stop?" Mark frowned, afraid of the answer.

With a dreamy look, Matthew turned back to him. "Hm?" He shook himself. "Oh, yes. I don't think I had a good night's sleep until I married Claire."

Mark waved his hands in the air. "No, no. Don't tell me that. I'm not ready to even *think* about that."

"Then what are you doing with Leah? She's not someone you can just date and move on from without some serious issues." Matthew's happy face turned stern, and he pursed his lips. "Her brother is our brother-in-law. We'll see her a lot for the rest of our lives. If you aren't sure about her, then you shouldn't be dating her."

"But..." He ran a hand through his hair. "How will I know unless I date her?"

With a heavy sigh, Matthew took a seat at the kitchen table. "Look, I can see that you care for her. Shoot, everyone can see it."

Mark sat at the table and took a long drink of his coffee. "But if I don't see it, then what?"

"Then you let her know how you feel, and hopefully you can still be friends."

"And what if I think I want more?" Mark looked down at his coffee mug, unsure how this conversation had started and why he was opening up to Matthew about a woman like he never had.

After taking a long drink, Matthew eyed his brother. "I think you need to spend some time thinking about how you feel. Can you see yourself with Leah a year from now? How about five years from now? Or twenty? You've known her almost her entire life. When you think about the future and her, what do you see?"

Mark shrugged. "I don't know. That's the problem. Right now, I like her and want more than friendship. But a future? I don't know that I'm ready for that with anyone yet."

"Then I think that's your answer." Matthew stood up and drank the last of his coffee. "Come on, we have to ride the fences today. I want to make sure Cal was the only one who went through our land yesterday."

"Good idea." Mark stood and finished off his coffee, then went to fill a thermos with more hot coffee for the ride. He was going to need it. Such serious thoughts so early in the morning were going to give him a headache.

After about an hour of riding along the lines, only discussing areas of the fencing that could use some shoring up, Mark started to think back on the day before and his time with Leah. They'd had a lot of fun before their time was interrupted. Were those interruptions signs from God that he needed to keep things casual with her? Or was it just bad luck?

"Mark, what do you think?" Matthew pointed in the distance.

Mark brough himself out of his thoughts and looked to where his brother was pointing. "I'd bet it's the Johnson bull again. He hasn't been allowed into the pasture for a while and my bet is that he's ticked." He chuckled when he noticed some broken fencing in the distance.

Matthew took his hat off and ran a hand through his dark locks. "I don't know." He galloped toward the line, and Mark followed.

They both stopped far enough from the fence line to check for hoofprints.

"Look, right there." Mark pointed.

"Looks more like horse prints than a bull's." Matthew nodded. "Someone broke this line down on purpose."

"But was it Bart? That's the question rolling around in your head right now, isn't it?" Mark was asking himself the same thing. If Bart and his gang were messing with them, this was one way to do it.

Nodding, his older brother looked out in the pasture from the Johnson farm and then scanned the Triple J land. "I don't see anything else out here. Our cattle aren't even in this pasture right now. They're almost fifty acres away from here. Why break the lines here?"

"To distract us? Or to mess with Mr. Johnson? Where's his cattle?" Mark looked over the land on the Johnson side, but couldn't see any signs of recent cattle movement.

Matthew pulled out his cell and began taking pictures of everything. "I'm going to call Mr. Johnson and see if there's anything happening on his side of things." He narrowed his eyes and looked at his brother. "Do you think Cal's coming home was just coincidence? Or is he involved in all of this?"

Mark shook his head. "Don't go there, brother. We were having trouble before he came home. I think it's just all bad timing for him."

"You're right. I know you are. It's just, well, with every-thing going on I guess I just don't trust anything right now." Matthew put his hat back on and dialed their neighbor.

Mark watched the area as Matthew called Mr. John-son, who answered his phone. Luckily they all had de-cent cell coverage on most of their property. There were bad spots, but most were in patches they didn't use much anyway. As he watched the land, he didn't notice anything out of the ordinary other than the horse hoofprints around the downed fence. If it weren't for the evidence of horseshoes, Mark would have thought the cattle, or old bull, did it.

"Well"—Matthew hung up his call—"Mr. Johnson hasn't noticed anyone or anything out of the ordinary lately. He's gonna send Cal over here to look at the fence before we fix it."

"This doesn't necessarily mean that Bart or his goons have been here. But, it is suspicious." Mark led them toward the next section they were going to check.

The two brothers spent the rest of the morning checking lines as well as gates. There wasn't any evidence of other issues anywhere near the Johnson ranch. Lunch was approaching, but they still had a lot of lines to inspect as well as gates.

"Come on, let's head back this way." Mark motioned with his arm in a direction that would take them down the middle of their land. "We can check the mid-gates and see if anyone's been through them lately. Then after lunch we can check the lines on the other side of our lands."

On their other side they butted up next to a small ranch, as well as open country that the Bureau of Land Management never sold. The government had set that aside as wild country, and it was where the caves were located.

"Sounds good. We should probably check the caves, too. Just to make sure no one's there." Matthew followed his brother, who picked up his pace the closer they got to home, and food.

After a home-cooked lunch of hot, open-faced roast beef sandwiches and homemade potato salad with their mother's homemade pickles, Matthew suggested they pack a bag with water and beef jerky.

"Ma, we might be a little late since we're heading all the way back to the caves. So don't worry if we aren't back in time for dinner." Matthew packed his bag, and Judith handed him a bag of chips to add to the snacks.

"Thanks, Ma." Mark bussed his mom on her cheek before they left the house.

"Don't forget coats, just in case," Judith called out as they left the mud room.

Matthew turned back and grabbed the coats his mother held out for him while Mark went to get the horses from the barn.

Chapter 21

To say that Leah was distracted was an understatement. She opened that day and would be working right until just before closing. Her brother and Stevie would close. Saturdays were busy days, but they did close earlier than normal. Most folks in the area didn't shop past six at night at their store. One of the changes Logan had made when he returned home was to shorten their Saturday hours. And it worked nicely.

Except for today. They were swamped and it was already afternoon. Leah should have restocked the clothes already, but every time she went to the back to get a box she ended up daydreaming about a certain cowboy. It took multiple calls from her brother to get her back on task.

"Leah, I need you to focus and watch the front. I'm meeting Lizzie for a late lunch at Rosie's. It's the first day this week that she's felt like going out to eat. I don't want to miss my window." He chuckled. His wife's pregnancy had hit her hard lately, and her *morning* sickness wasn't just confined to mornings. She was one of the *lucky* ones and had it all day long.

Leah shooed him out the door. "Go, go and enjoy time with your wife. Stevie and I will be just fine." She turned to the kid. "Won't we?"

"Sure, but I could use some food, too." He put a hand over his grumbling tummy.

Leah laughed. "Why don't you go pick us up sandwiches from Rosie's and I'll keep an eye on the counter."

"Thanks, boss." Stevie grinned and ran out the door.

Leah had an account at Rosie's, and she texted the restaurant owner and asked that she put her and Stevie's order on her account. The kid had been working a lot of hours lately, and had been very helpful. She also felt bad about his injuries. She would breathe a whole lot easier once all of Bart's goons were arrested and put behind bars, where they all belonged.

Traffic in her store had died down, as usual for this time, and she started straightening the racks. Once she had the clothes looking good again, she went to the first aisle and began to take note of what needed restocking. As soon as Stevie was back, she'd begin bringing out the items they needed before she took off for the night.

The bell above the door rang as someone opened it, and she figured it was Stevie back with their late lunch. "It's about time. I thought maybe you had gone all the way to Bozeman for..." She halted the moment she turned and saw who came through the door.

Bart stood next to the closed door, eyeing her. "Leah Hayes. All alone in the store." He looked at her and licked his lips as though he was about to eat her up.

"Hannibal—I mean Bart." She sneered and put her hands on her hips. She knew Stevie would be here soon. If he saw Bart in the doorway, surely he'd know who it was and call the sheriff before coming in. All she had to do was stall and the sheriff would get his man. "What do you want?"

Besides, their busy day couldn't already be over. Even though it was late afternoon, there would have to be more customers coming in shortly. And, one of the local ranchers had called in an order and said he would be by this afternoon to get it. So surely she wouldn't be all alone with the wannabe Hannibal Lecter for long.

"I just wanted to stop in and say hello to one of the prettiest cowgirls in the county." He winked at Leah.

She just barely held back an eye roll. "Did you need to buy something, or is this just a social call?" She was torn. On the one hand, she wanted him out of there right away. But on the other, she hoped Stevie would call the sheriff and he'd show up and arrest the snake on the spot.

"Oh, it's purely social." He winked again.

This time Leah about puked. She couldn't hold back the eye roll.

Bart laughed. "Oh, come now. We're friends, aren't we?" He held his hands out and took two steps away from the door.

She shook her head. "No. I'm not friends with anyone who hurts women and young men for pleasure."

"I assure you, I don't hurt anyone for pleasure." He tsk'd. "I hate it when someone needs to be taught a lesson." He inched closer to her.

"No, you don't." Leah shook her head and slowly looked around for a weapon, just in case she needed to fend off the creep. "I know you enjoy hurting others."

"Now, Leah. I didn't come here to argue with you." Bart's condescending voice said otherwise. "I came to say hi to a friend and make sure you were alright."

Leah had had enough of him, and as he inched closer to her, the hairs on her arms began to stand on end. It was time to get rid of the trash.

She pointed out the door. "Bart, you need to leave, now."

"That's no way to talk to a friend." He narrowed his eyes.

"You aren't my friend. How many times do I need to tell you this?" Leah started doing some inching of her own. She knew one aisle over was where they kept the crowbars. If he got too close, she could use one to defend herself and keep him at bay while she screamed at the top of her lungs for help.

"Trust me, you want to be my friend." His menacing voice was laced with plenty of meaning.

She had to get him out of there and call the sheriff. Something bad must have happened to Stevie, again, to keep him away this long. Leah wasn't sure what Bart did to the poor guy, but somehow he must have gotten to Stevie before the kid could get back to the store.

"Bart, I'm warning you. If you don't leave now, I will have no choice but to defend myself against your threats." She was now at the top of the aisle that held the crowbars.

"I'm here offering you my friendship, and you're threatening me?" He wagged his finger back and forth. "That's not very nice, or smart."

"You aren't here offering friendship, you're here to do something bad. I don't know what you've got planned, but I won't be cowed. And you won't get away with this." She took a few steps back and stopped next to the spot where the crowbars were stored. Leah knew the store like the back of her hand. She could have easily maneuvered through the place and picked up anything while blindfolded.

Just as she was about to reach for the crowbar, her brother walked in with Stevie and one of the deputies.

"Bart, you aren't welcome in our store, or our town," Logan practically spat out at the sorry excuse for a man.

Leah had never been so happy to see her brother, or a deputy.

The creep sneered at Leah and turned around. "I was only stopping in to say hi since I was in town to see someone else."

"Bart, I need you to come with me back to the station. We've got some questions for you." Deputy Deacon motioned for the criminal to go with him.

"Deputy, am I under arrest?" Bart's incredulity dripped with sarcasm.

"Not at the moment, unless Miss Hayes wishes to file a complaint?" Chris looked at Leah with expectant eyes.

"As long as he leaves, I don't have any reason to file a complaint. But you should know, he refused to leave when I asked him to." Leah crossed her arms over her chest and glared at Bart.

Stevie walked in looking sheepish. "Sorry I took so long."

Bart laughed, which was more like a cackle, and walked out with Deputy Deacon.

"Tell Leah what you were doing." Logan handed the bag with a cold sandwich in it to his sister.

"A hot woman was talking to me. I couldn't just leave her, could I?" Stevie looked down at the floor.

"It was one of Bart's girls." Logan shook his head.

"Oh, Stevie. Come on, you've got work to do." Leah tried to hide her laugh behind a cough, but it didn't work too well.

"How was I to know she was only messing with me?" Stevie's shoulders sagged, and he went to the back to clock back in.

"Is Lizzie alright?" Leah worried about her sister-in-law being pregnant and left alone somewhere.

"She's fine. Mr. Miller said he'd bring her here once she was ready to leave. Harper and Sophia came in while we were eating, and she's gonna hang out with them for a while." Logan picked up a box from behind the counter and went to restock a shelf of flashlights.

"That's good. I'm glad she's gonna be safe." Leah eyed the bag in her hand. "And now I think I'm going to the office to eat."

When Leah sat at the desk, she bowed her head to pray. *Lord, how has it come to this? All we tried to do was help a group of women living on the streets. Why are we being attacked as we are? Will it ever be safe to go back to Bozeman? Will those women be safe from Bart and his gang?* Leah finished her prayer, but didn't feel the peace she normally did after speaking to her Lord. Instead, she felt as though the worst was yet to come.

Chapter 22

"Looks like it's gonna rain later tonight." Mark looked up at the darkening sky and noticed the storm clouds in the distance.

"Do you think we'll make it to the cave and back before it does?" Matthew took his hat off and looked up. Above him, the sky was blue with a smattering of white dots. But in the north, dark clouds moved along the winds toward them.

"Hard to say. But either way, we need to pick up the pace."

"Agreed. Hya." Matthew urged his horse forward.

Mark followed, and they picked up their pace. So far there were no signs of anyone on their property lately. Until they hit the back fence, where they found a section down.

Matthew pulled out his cellphone and snapped more pictures. "I don't know who's done this, but I don't think it's Bart and his crew. This looks more like kids who have no clue what they're doing."

"Agreed. It looks to me like someone is crossing through and doesn't know where the gates are, so they're just smashing through the fence line." Mark shook his head. "I feel for their poor horses. I hope they aren't injured."

Matthew looked around. "I don't see signs of horse-hair or blood." He scratched his neck. "Could be they're just kicking the posts down and then guiding their horses through the downed fence?"

"Could be." Mark dismounted, and with his horse's reins in his hand he looked around at the ground in front of the posts. "Look." He pointed to boot prints. "Two sets of boots on the ground here. You might be right."

Matthew rode down the line a few feet and looked on the other side of the fence. "Mark, come over here." He pointed to the other side, near the tree line next to the creek that ran along the back of their property.

After getting back on his horse, Mark rode through the downed fence and over to where his brother pointed. His shoulders drooped and he got down off his horse again. An animal's mutilated carcass was lying on the ground next to a tree. After inspecting the tag in the ear, he moved away from the body and closer to his brother.

"Looks like someone stole one of Mr. Johnson's cows and tried to butcher it here. They made a mess. But it's also pretty fresh." Mark hated that someone had stolen the cow and didn't even know how to butcher the thing properly. Most of the meat was left on the cow to rot. Or attract animals.

"We're gonna need to bury it, or burn it. We don't need any bears catching the scent and heading our way." Mark shook his head.

"I'll come join you." Matthew went to where the fence was busted and then joined his brother. "Yeah, it looks like some kids might have done this."

"Runaways?" Mark hoped not. Nothing good would come to kids who didn't know enough to at least bury a dead animal.

Matthew headed to some bushes nearby and dismounted. He inspected the leaves and looked at what was left of the berries. "Huckleberry bush. But they didn't do a good job of cleaning the vines. There's still enough here to warrant coming back."

"You don't think they left the cow here with the intention to come back and cut more meat off to cook, do you?" Mark looked back at the carcass with disgust. Even if the cow had been killed the day before, it was still too late to eat anything off of it. Bugs had already discovered the meat and were making a meal out of it.

Mark didn't think anyone could be that stupid. But if it was a small group of kids, who knew what they were up to or what they thought they could do.

"We need to go check the caves before heading home." Matthew looked at the clouds coming in too fast. "And we need to call the sheriff. He's gonna need to keep an eye out for whoever this is. But you're right, this isn't

Bart or any of his goons. They would know better than this."

"Do you think it's possible some of the homeless got away from him and are trying to go home?" Mark doubted they'd be out this far, but that could explain why Bart's men were in town, if not to just mess with them.

Matthew shook his head. "Doubtful. Those guys and gals should know enough to stay away from here. I bet if anyone wanted to get away from Bart, they'd just go to a shelter and ask for help there."

"Or a church," Mark added.

Both cowboys set to work lighting the cow on fire. With a storm coming, it was safer to go ahead and burn the carcass. And it would be faster than trying to bury a one-thousand-pound cow.

"While we wait, we really should head to the caves and check them out. Then come back here to wait for the fire to go out." Matthew got back on his horse.

Mark had tied his horse to a nearby tree and untied the reins before getting on his horse. "I just pray we can do all of this before it rains. I really don't want to be out when it pours."

Both cowboys set off at a quick pace. They knew exactly where to go, and without fences to slow them down they made it quickly to the entrance of the cave system. Most caves were too short or too shallow to have anything other than spiders and rodents, but there were a couple of caves that could easily house people.

When the boys were teens, they kept a trunk here with a couple of old horse blankets and some matches. It was more in case they ever got stuck out here, but Mark couldn't remember if they ever brought the trunk home or not. "Hey, is our old trunk still out here?"

Matthew chuckled. "You know what, I think it might be. I was supposed to get it a couple years back, but I got busy and just forgot."

"Well, that'll be one way to tell if anyone's been out here or not." Mark led the way to the cave that held their old trunk.

"I hope our stuff is still here." Matthew dismounted and tied his horse to a tree right at the mouth of the cave.

"Are you hoping to use it for your future kids?" Mark asked.

That stopped Matthew short before the entrance to the cave. "You know, I hadn't really thought about it. But yeah, I guess when my kids get old enough I'd like to show them this place and tell them about how we used to fish in that stream and then eat our catch here."

"Things sure were simpler when we were kids, weren't they?" Mark mused.

Without another word, both of them went inside the cave, hoping to find a group of runaway teens hiding out. Instead, they found a mess. One that would attract plenty of wildlife if not cleaned up soon.

With no kids in sight, or even adults, Matthew and Mark checked the back of the cave. Whoever had been here wasn't around now. But they had left plenty of debris and signs of recent activity. There were three sleeping bags rolled up inside the trunk.

"So, someone is living here. Most likely three teenaged boys. Girls wouldn't leave this sort of mess and stink." Mark waved a hand in front of his nose.

Matthew chuckled. "Yeah. We should report this to the sheriff and let him deal with it, since it's on BLM land." He patted his brother's back and they headed out.

They made it back to the burning carcass before the flames had completely taken care of the body. Mark watched the sky as they waited for the fire to do its job. If they were lucky they'd get home before the worst of the storm hit, but neither believed they'd make it back dry.

Chapter 23

"I was just about to head out and look for you two." Caleb Manning took the reins of Matthew's horse. John took Mark's horse and handed him a thermos of coffee when he dismounted. "Here, you might want to take a few swigs before getting out of those wet clothes."

"We'll take care of the horses while you two change and warm up," Caleb said. "What took you so long? We expected you at least an hour ago." He handed each of his sons a change of clothes.

"I told Ma we'd probably be late," Matthew called out from behind the tack room door where he and Mark were changing.

"Yes, but we finished dinner almost two hours ago. What happened?" John asked.

"It was slow goin' comin' home with the storm. It hit about halfway home." Mark took off his soaking wet shirt and rubbed his upper torso off with a towel his brother had given him.

Matthew then used the towel on his body. "We stopped under the large oak hoping to wait it out, or at least the worst of it. But..."—he chuckled—"the storm just got worse, so we decided to come home instead of being swept away by the water."

"Was it that bad out there?" John asked.

Mark looked to Matthew. "Yes," both brothers said in unison.

"Well, we weren't going to be swept away by a flood or anything like that, but it sure is coming down out there." Matthew put on his clean shirt.

John laughed. "Better you than me. I would have come home sooner if I had been out there."

"We wanted to come back sooner, but we found something that needed to be dealt with." Mark went on to tell his dad and brother what they'd found, and how they handled it.

While they were telling their tale, Caleb and John took care of the horses. They unsaddled them, gave them extra feed, and took brushes to their coats, getting them cleaned off. Then once they were all brushed down, they put warm horse blankets on both animals before closing them in their stalls for the night.

Once both men were fully dressed and dried off as good as they were gonna get, they all headed back inside.

Sunday morning dawned with a bright blue sky, no clouds in sight. Leah was grateful for that. She had to deal with wet customers once Bart left, and thanks to all the restocking needs she ended up staying at work until close. When her brother escorted her home, she was glad for his company.

Today she was escorted to church by her parents, as normal. "So, you've got a date this afternoon with Mark Manning?" her mother asked with a smile.

"You look beautiful, Leah." Her dad hugged her, and if she wasn't mistaken he got all teary-eyed on her.

Her tough-as-nails father, who she had never seen cry, looked as though he was about to get all watery on her.

"Dad, are you alright?" She put a hand on his shoulder.

He sniffed. "Of course I am. But I'm gonna miss you when you're gone."

Leah furrowed her brow. "Gone? You're gonna miss me for lunch?"

"No, when you marry Mark." Mr. Hayes wiped the moisture from his eyes.

"Ah, this is only our third date. And the first two didn't end well. I don't think you need to worry about marriage." She shivered and hoped no one else was thinking this about her and Mark. It was way too soon.

Mrs. Hayes waved a hand. "I know, dear. But let's get real. It's your *third* date with a man you've known most of your life. It's got to be serious."

"Ah, no. Let's stop this right here and now." Leah waved both hands in front of her. There was no way

Leah and Mark would survive if people were out planning their wedding so soon. Even though she'd been crushing on him since high school, that didn't mean she was ready for a wedding.

And Mark! Oh, horsefeathers. The man who'd never dated anyone for very long and was always joking around? If he heard this, who knew what he'd do. He'd probably ghost her. And that was the last thing she wanted.

"Well, it's out. The divas have been spreading gossip about you two. There's even a bet going on about when you'll get married." A sparkle entered her dad's eyes, and she hoped he hadn't taken part in any bets on her.

"Please, just stop this talk. You know Mark as well as I do, and he's not the kind who'll settle down easily, or quickly." Worry permeated her being, and she hoped he hadn't heard any rumors yet.

As Leah took her seat, she looked around at the crowd in attendance. There were more people than usual. It was almost like a Christmas service, and she wondered why so many had come to church.

"Ma, is there a special service today?" Leah asked when she opened her bulletin and didn't see anything out of the ordinary.

Her dad cleared his throat. "Honey, I think they're all here for the show." He gave a knowing look at his daughter and then turned to look at Mark.

She smacked her face with her palm and moaned. "No, this is going to ruin everything."

Her mom patted her leg. "Don't worry, dear. If it's meant to be, Mark will take it all in stride."

"And if it's not, it's better to know now before your heart gets broken," her dad added.

Leah's mind kept going to what her parents said during the service, and she missed most of what the pastor said. But one thing did stick out in her mind—don't worry about tomorrow, for tomorrow will worry about itself. As they sang the closing hymns, she mulled that over in her mind.

Did it mean that she shouldn't look to the future? No, she knew it was a good thing to make plans. But worrying about what might or might not happen, that must have been what the pastor was talking about. God was in control. She had to keep reminding herself of that. If she trusted in God, which she did, then she had no business worrying about what might come. Either with Mark, or Bart.

She knew from experience that God did take care of his people. She would rely on that knowledge and do as she felt the Lord leading her.

When the service was over and she met Mark out in the parking lot, she was pleasantly surprised by the look on his face.

"Leah, you're so beautiful." Mark leaned in and kissed her cheek. He wasn't about to give her a full-blown kiss right in front of the entire town and have them spread it all over. He knew the Diner Divas had already started gossiping about them, but he didn't care. Everyone knew they always oversold their stories.

She looked him up and down. He was wearing dark-washed denim jeans with his black boots and black hat. She loved it when he wore his black hat. Even though Mark was a good guy, it gave him just a tiny aura of badness, which turned her on. His button-up blue cowboy shirt matched her dress, which surprised her.

"You don't look so bad yourself, cowboy." Leah appreciated his fresh scent, which always sent shivers down her spine. There was something about the smell of pine mixed with his spice. She didn't know if it was his cologne or his natural scent, but she wanted to spend more time with him to find out. When he took her hand, she also picked up his leather scent. And when all three tied together, it was like the perfect aroma candle lightly filling the air around her and she felt peace envelop her.

When a pink pouf appeared in the corner of her eyes, she mumbled, "Not now."

"What?" Mark turned furrowed brows her way.

"Leah and Mark. What a cute couple you two make." Mrs. Macon's southern voice grated on Mark's nerves.

Mark squeezed Leah's hand in support and turned a forced smile on the intruder. "Mrs. Macon. I hope you enjoyed the Sunday service."

"I'll tell you what I enjoyed most—seeing you two looking so perfect together." Mrs. Macon eyed them both. "And you match. Oh, Leah," she sighed, "your light denim dress is perfect with his blue shirt. Did you two coordinate your outfits?"

Leah looked down at her dress. While it did match his denim shirt, the rest of her did not match him. She had on her red cowgirl boots and a red leather jacket. He was in denim, blue, and black. Although, when she took a second look their colors did blend well together.

Mark's nostrils flared, and he was about to lose his patience with the elderly busybody. This time, it was Leah who squeezed his hand in solidarity. He relaxed his shoulders and counted to five before saying, "No, we just look good together."

"Have a nice day, Mrs. Macon." Leah pulled on Mark's hand and led him to his truck.

Once they were both inside, she busted up laughing. "Please tell me you weren't about to go off on the biggest gossip in town?"

"I'm sorry, but sometimes they just go too far. Maybe we should try and find them husbands." Mark backed out of his parking spot and headed toward the Cattleman's Association.

"Well, Lou Ann Dobbs is married and she still gossips." Leah tried to think of men in town they could set the single divas up with.

"Maybe if they were all married, or at least had men in their lives, they'd settle down and gossip a bit less?" Mark hoped they could find something to keep those busybodies out of their hair. "When there's a big project, they do tend to gossip less. Can we get the town to create a job for them?"

Leah chuckled, and he liked the sound of her voice. It filled him with joy and contentment.

"Let me think about it, and maybe between the both of us we can create a large enough project for them that they stay out of our business, at least for a little while." Leah hoped they would stay away from her and Mark's budding relationship long enough to give them a chance.

It was a short ride to the restaurant, and since Mark had called in reservations earlier, they were seated upon arrival and had sweet tea before either stomach had a chance to grumble.

Leah looked around the room. "You know, I don't think I've been here for a meal in ages. Logan has a membership, as does my dad, but we've never been big on coming here for meals, or even the dances."

"Why is that?" Mark truly wanted to know. The Cattleman's Association was basically the ranchers' version of a country club. This club was only about a forty-five-minute drive from town, and over an hour from his ranch, but it was always worth the drive. Their food, while not the same as the barbecue at his ranch, had always pleased his palate. Mark couldn't ever remember a bad meal, or a bad evening, when he attended their functions.

She shrugged. "I guess I'm just not the fancy dinner kinda gal. I prefer the dances in town to the fancy shindigs they hold here. I went on a date here once a few years back and just felt truly out of place."

"Yeah, I can see that." Mark nodded as he drank his tea and looked over his menu.

"What? You don't think I belong here?" Leah's feathers were ruffled.

He turned large eyes to her. "No, that didn't come out right. Oh, fiddlesticks." He put a hand to the back of his neck. If he wasn't careful, this date would end with food on his head.

"Then what, exactly, did you mean?" Leah folded her arms over her chest and gave him a sour look.

"Leah, you're better than this place." He waved. "Look around, most of these people put on airs. They act as though this is one of those rich country clubs, when in fact most of these people are just like you and me. Trying to get through the year without any issues on their ranch. And hoping the price of beef doesn't go any lower."

She relaxed and put her arms back on the table. After taking a look around her, she looked back at him with softer eyes. "I'm sorry. It's just like you said. They put on airs and I just don't feel comfortable with this. I'm more of the jeans and t-shirt kinda person." Leah sighed. "In fact, I'm happy when it's cold outside and no one cares if I'm wearing jeans and sweaters to church instead of a dress."

"While I wholeheartedly support you in jeans, I gotta say"—he took a breath and looked her in the eyes—"I love it when you wear a dress. Especially the one you've got on now. Is that new?"

She felt her cheeks heat, and she looked down. "Yes, it is. I bought it a while back, not sure when I'd get a chance to wear it."

"Well, I hope to see it again when you feel comfortable wearing a dress." Mark did love her legs in jeans, but there was something about seeing her in a feminine dress that caused his heart to beat extra fast. As it was doing right then.

The waiter interrupted the connection they were making when he walked up and asked what they'd like to order.

Sighing, Mark placed his order after Leah. The rest of the meal their conversation flowed naturally. Talking about their jobs, the food, and oddly enough, the weather. When Mark told her about getting stuck out in the rain on Saturday, Leah took in a breath and covered her mouth.

"And you aren't sick at all?" Worry laced her words as she waited to hear what he said.

"Nope. We get used to it. Spring rains come on like yesterday all the time. While I don't like getting stuck in the rain, it's not uncommon, and my body doesn't give me a hard time as long as I take a long hot shower when I get home and eat plenty of protein." He winked, knowing she would appreciate his desire to eat steak.

"And Ma always makes us a hot pie when it rains. So after we've warmed up, we get a hot meal, hot dessert, and hot tea. Our bodies don't have a chance against that kind of treatment." Mark took a sip of his hot coffee. The Cattleman's Association used coffee from a little shop in Frenchtown called the Frenchtown Roasting Company. His sister was best friends with the shop's owner and always brought them a huge bag of freshly roasted coffee when she visited.

"This coffee reminds me of Chloe. She's coming to town next weekend for a visit. You should come out on Saturday night. We're gonna have a big dinner. The entire family is invited. I think Elizabeth was going to tell your parents today after church." Mark sighed when he took another sip. "And Chloe will be bringing us some of this coffee."

Leah sipped her coffee and smiled. "If you're gonna serve this coffee after dinner, then I'm there. But on one condition." She set her cup down.

"What's that?"

"Your dad has to make his famous barbecue sauce." She smiled.

Mark chuckled. "I don't think you could keep him from making it."

Neither was in any hurry to leave the restaurant. The meal was fantastic, the company superb. But the waiter had come by a couple of times looking to take the check. Mark finally paid and they left hand in hand.

"Thank you for today, this was a wonderful date." Leah beamed as he closed her truck door.

Once he was seated in the driver's seat, he looked to her. "I really had a great time, too. I think getting out of town was exactly what we needed for a great date."

"I agree. I mean, all of that gossip." She sighed.

"Gossip?" Mark turned on the ignition.

"Yeah, about us." She stilled in her seat. Not wanting to look at him, she tentatively asked, "You have heard it, right?"

"Some, but I don't pay the divas any mind." He drove out onto the highway and headed home.

The drive was a quiet affair, but it wasn't awkward. Both of them were stuck in their head. Mark was thinking about what a great time they had and how easy the conversation flowed. He liked Leah, a lot. If they could take things slowly, then maybe it would work.

Leah's mind was also pleasantly engaged with going over their lunch conversation. When they were close to the town, she turned to looked at him. "This was probably the best date I've ever had. Thank you."

He chuckled. "It was definitely our best date so far."

So far. She mulled over that phrase and a slow smile spread across her face. "Does that mean you want to do this again?"

He glanced at her when he stopped at the stop sign before entering the downtown area. "Yes, I think so. Are you open to seeing me again?"

"Well, I'll be seeing you on Saturday from the sounds of it," she teased.

"I wouldn't call a family dinner a date."

She wouldn't either, but she had no desire to push him. Guys like him wouldn't appreciate a girl pushing the relationship. "True, but I'm closing all week. Well, except for Thursday night."

He grinned. "How about dinner and a movie? There's a new action flick playing over in Three Forks."

The idea intrigued her. If they could continue going on dates outside of town, then they might escape some of the worst of the gossip. "Sounds good. See you then."

He pulled up in front of her house and got out to open her truck door for her. Leah smiled and held her dress as she scooted out of the truck. They walked up to the door of her house and stopped just shy of going in.

"I'm really glad we did this." Mark reached up to move a stray hair out of her face.

"So am I. Again, thank you for a wonderful afternoon." Heat infused her entire being when he touched her face. She looked up into his eyes as he leaned in closer to her. A tingling feeling started in her chest and began to move throughout her body. He was going to kiss her. Finally.

Just before his lips could brush hers, the front door opened.

"Oh, sorry. Didn't mean to interrupt," her mom began to prattle on. "Go back to kissing. Don't mind me." She kept talking and didn't move or close the door.

Leah sighed; the tingling feeling stopped dead in its tracks. Knowing that her mom had killed the mood, she pulled back from Mark. His crestfallen face told her he felt exactly the same as she did. Or at least, that's what she chose to take away from his look.

"Um, I guess I'll see you on Thursday?" He took her hand and held it for a moment.

When Leah nodded and smiled, he squeezed her hand and let go. "Good night, Mrs. Hayes. See you later."

"Oh, don't you want to come in and visit for a while?" Leah's mom asked.

He smiled and declined the offer, stating he had to get home and get everything ready for the week ahead.

"Goodnight, Leah." The smoldering look he gave her sent chills down Leah's spine.

"Night," Leah whispered.

Chapter 24

Mark didn't even remember the drive home that evening. He spent the entire time going over his date with Leah and wishing he would have kissed her in the truck before walking her to the door. When he walked inside his house with a giant smile on his face, his dad greeted him.

"Well, I take it things finally went well for your date with Leah?" Caleb closed the door behind his son.

"They did. She's also gonna join us Saturday for the dinner with Chloe." Mark couldn't wipe the smile off his face. His only regret for the day was not getting a chance to kiss his date.

"You won't see her until then?" Caleb frowned.

"Oh, no. I'm gonna take her out Thursday night. It's her only night off this week." He hung his jacket on the hook behind the door where most of them kept at least one jacket.

"Well, be sure to get a good night's sleep tonight. Tomorrow we're meeting with the sheriff to discuss what you and Matthew found out behind our property." His dad took off down the hall, and Mark headed to the kitchen.

The next morning came early, and Mark was up before that blasted rooster could crow outside his window. The plan was to get all the animals fed, come in and shower before breakfast, and then head out to see the sheriff. But Mark was surprised when he got out of his shower and saw the sheriff seated at the table with his family for breakfast.

"Sheriff, it's good to see you." Mark grinned and looked between him and Georgia, whose cheeks began to turn pink. If he wasn't mistaken, there was something going on between the two. He knew they both liked each other, but what he didn't know was if they'd gone out yet or not. He'd have to find out.

Look at him, he was being as much of a gossip as those Diner Divas. Mark shook his head and took his seat, vowing to stay out of their business. If they wanted to date, he would support them and *not* gossip about them.

"So, tell me about the intruders and the cave." Sheriff Roscoe had turned his attention from Georgia to Mark about halfway through his meal.

"We saw evidence of someone starting out on Mr. Johnson's property, and then mowing down fence lines through ours until they got out the back and into the BLM land." Mark finished his egg casserole and began a third cup of coffee.

"Did you see if they started further out, or just saw the fence between your land and the Johnsons' down?" Roscoe narrowed his eyes and took another bite of the fluffy egg casserole filled with sausage, ground beef, vegetables, and cheese.

"We didn't go any farther than our own line, so we can't be sure. But we did call Mr. Johnson and he was going to send Cal out to investigate their property. But, we did find a dead and mutilated steer that had one of the Johnson ranch's tags."

As Mark explained the rest of their story, Judith and Georgia cleared away the plates and set a carafe of fresh coffee in the middle of the table for the men to enjoy.

Once they were done explaining everything they could to the sheriff, he got up to leave. "I'll head over to see the Johnsons and find out if Cal discovered anything yet." The sheriff put his hat on and turned to Caleb. "You mind if I ride out from your property to check on that cave today?"

Caleb shook his head. "Not at all. In fact, I'll saddle up the horses and Mark and Matthew can take you out there when you're ready. Just call me when you leave the Johnson ranch and we'll be ready for ya."

The sheriff tipped his hat and left.

When Roscoe came back almost two hours later, the boys had their horses, as well as an extra one for the sheriff, all saddled and geared up for anything. Judith and Georgia even fixed them a picnic lunch in case they were out there too long.

"Ah, I see you saddled up Chip for me. Thanks." Roscoe smiled and mounted the gelding.

Once they were all ready, Mark took the lead and showed them the first fence that the boys had discovered was broken. "We'll have to come back out tomorrow and fix all the damaged fences. Thankfully, none of us had cattle in the areas where the fences are down."

Then they made their way to the backside of the Manning property to where they'd had to burn the mutilated corpse of a stolen steer.

The sheriff dismounted and looked around the area. "You say you just burned it right where it was?"

Matthew nodded.

"I would say it's either a group of kids or homeless coming through from another area." Roscoe took his hat off and poked around in the trees surrounding the blackened-out area. "Most likely it's a group of runaways, or younger homeless. Or possibly someone who's new to life on the streets. Or in this case, forest."

"Yeah, we thought the same thing. It certainly wasn't anyone from around here. Just about all kids from a young age learn how to butcher cattle, or at the very least know not to leave a partially butchered animal out in the open like this. It only attracts predators." Mark looked around at the trees surrounding the area and realized it was a very remote place, as well as a hidden spot. It would have been tough for anyone to be noticed in this part of the woods. Even if Mark or his brothers had been patrolling the back section of their land.

"It's a good thing you didn't have your cattle in the back forty to pasture." The sheriff put his hat back on and mounted Chip before following Matthew, who led them to the cave.

"Here's the cave system we grew up playing in." Matthew dismounted and tied his horse to a tree. "Mark, you wanna stay out here with the horses?"

"Sure thing. You can deal with the stench of the cave, I'll stay out here in the fresh air." Mark chuckled and stayed atop his horse and looked around to see if he could find any signs of others in the area.

While Matthew and Roscoe went inside the cave, Mark discovered two horses. They were still saddled and the poor animals were in need of a brush down, as well as some hay. He gathered their reins and headed back to where Matthew and Roscoe had tethered their horses, knowing they would find the culprits shortly if they hadn't already.

His ears picked up sounds coming from the cave and he had his shotgun out, just in case it was needed. However, something in his spirit told him all was going to be fine.

"What were we supposed to do? They just turfed us." The voice came from a male who sounded like he was still a kid.

"You should have asked for help," the sheriff responded.

"Pft, yeah right. Like anyone was going to help us," another young voice said.

When Mark got closer to the entrance of the cave, he saw three young men, teenagers most likely, come out of the cave with Matthew and Roscoe right behind them. Their guns weren't out, so Mark put his away. He didn't want to scare the boys.

"We found the culprits. Runaways from a group home," Matthew called out.

The tallest of the three boys, gangly with messy brown hair that looked as though it hadn't seen a cut in months, said, "We were kicked out when we turned eighteen last month." He turned hard eyes to Mark, just daring him to say something.

Mark slowly looked between the boys. "I'm Mark Manning."

No one said anything until the sheriff poked the tallest boy in the back.

"I'm Carter Smith." He turned around and glared at the sheriff.

The kid standing next to Carter waved and gave an impish smile. "I'm Flynn Smith."

The third kid, who looked like he might have grown up on a ranch but could use some more protein, spoke up. "I'm Boone Smith."

"I take it none of you are actually related?" Mark flicked the brim of his hat and gave a bored look at the boys standing in front of him. He could already tell that Carter was the leader and would be a handful.

"You'd be wrong. We're brothers." Carter held his head up high and challenged Mark with his eyes.

"Uh-huh. I'm guessing you boys grew up together in the same situation?" If these boys were from a group home, that meant they were orphans. There wouldn't be anyone to come help them with the mess they'd gotten themselves into.

Flynn winced. "Yeah, we be brothers by choice."

Mark looked between the three of them and over to the two horses. "But you could only get two horses?"

Boone rubbed his arms and looked at the ground.

"I'm guessing these here horses aren't really yours?" Mark raised a brow and looked to the sheriff.

"Horse thieving is a felony around these parts. And it once carried a penalty of hanging. People don't go stealing other people's horses in Montana." The sheriff pushed the boys forward. "I'm gonna have to take you in for questioning."

Carter looked to his two brothers and frowned. "It's all my fault. I took the horses."

"No, we all did it," Flynn confessed.

"It was my idea." Boone stepped forward and looked the sheriff in his eyes. "And I was the one who tried to butcher the cow and made a mess of it." He shook his head but kept his eyes on the sheriff.

"I see. Well, I still need to take y'all in for questioning."

"Does this mean you're gonna arrest us?" Carter stared at the sheriff, incredulity covering his face.

"I don't know yet. But I do know we need to get back. So get on your horses and come with us." The sheriff waited for the boys to mount up before he led the way back.

Mark and Matthew took up the rear.

"And don't go gettin' any ideas of running. We know these parts better than you, and our horses are in much better shape." Matthew eyed the poor horses the boys had and shook his head.

"I think we need to take care of the animals until their owners can be located." Mark immediately thought about what he needed to do in order to care for the poor beasts.

The three boys never tried to run; instead, they kept their mouths shut and did as they were told. When they all stopped for a snack and some water, the boys scarfed the jerky down and Mark handed them the sandwiches his mother had packed that morning. They were close enough that Matthew, Mark, and Roscoe could wait for lunch until they returned to the ranch. Those skinny boys, however, needed to eat as much as they could take in.

Mark took a closer look at Flynn and noticed his bony shoulders and how the boy's clothes hung on him. The boy must have been out on his own for more than a month. Unless that group home was starving the kids. He'd have to ask the sheriff to look into it.

Even the other two boys looked as though they'd been out on their own for longer than a month. Not to mention the fact that they were very ripe. His nose twitched in disgust any time he got near them. And this throat closed up once in protest of the stench that he could actually taste.

Maybe the boys should shower out in one of the bunkhouses before the sheriff took them in? Mark was sure he could find them some clean clothes that would fit. Then he'd add their scraps of cloth to the burn pile. There was no way a stench like theirs would come out in the wash.

When they approached the paddock, Mark pulled up next to the sheriff and asked if he could get them clean before they were questioned.

"I think that'd be a might fine idea. Should we hose them down out back first?" The sheriff chuckled.

Carter grumbled, "You'd stink too if you had to live out in the wild."

Matthew came up as close as his nose would allow. "Actually, we wouldn't. Ranchers like us know how to live off the land without stealing."

"And without stinking to high heaven." Mark waved a hand in front of his nose. "Come on, I've got a place where you can wash up before you leave."

"I'll go and see if we have any clothes in their sizes and let Ma know to add three more plates for a late lunch." Matthew left his horse in the barn and went to the main house.

"Sheriff, if you'll keep an eye on them, I'll take care of the horses," Mark offered.

"Just point me to the bunkhouse you want us to use." Roscoe dismounted and motioned for the three teens to do so as well.

Once the boys were all in the nearest bunkhouse, Mark went to work on getting the stolen horses settled first. They needed the most care, and his horse could wait a little while as he cleaned and fed the visiting horses.

Mark enjoyed the rhythm of brushing a horse down when he was alone. He could escape anything that bothered him, or he could think about anything that wouldn't leave him alone. This time, his thoughts continued to drift toward Leah Hayes. He liked the woman, but everything was getting so serious so soon, with his parents and brothers teasing him about marriage, not to mention the gossip he'd heard.

He knew that Leah had heard it too, but he had tried to play it off as though it were nothing when they spoke about it. However, as he brushed the horses and fed them, he worried that the town would push them into marriage. He wasn't even sure he wanted to marry. Sure, Leah was great. She was easy on the eyes, a lot of fun, and their conversations seemed to never lack. But did that mean he was ready for something more with the pretty cowgirl? He knew he had to think about what he wanted before she got her hopes up. He had to make sure he wasn't leading her on if he wasn't ready for the next step.

Before Mark knew it the sheriff was back with the boys, who smelled like clean boys instead of rotten sewers.

"Hey, Georgia says lunch is hot and waiting for us." The sparkle in the sheriff's eyes was most definitely evident every time he said the woman's name.

Mark wanted to know what was going on, but he also knew it was none of his business. When they were ready to tell everyone they were dating, they would. Until then, Mark was going to stay out of it. He was going to treat them the way he wished the Diner Divas would treat him and Leah.

Shoot, he wished his own family would give him and Leah the space they needed to figure things out before they started picking out wedding cakes, or flowers, or whatever it was that families did when a couple *announced* their engagement.

Mark and Leah certainly hadn't announced anything. They weren't even an official couple, for crying out loud. Mark sighed and put Chip away before joining everyone for a hot lunch.

After Matthew said grace, Caleb walked into the kitchen and grabbed a cup of coffee.

When he sat down at the kitchen table, the sheriff introduced him to the boys.

"And you all came without a fuss?" Caleb eyed each one, waiting to see what they said.

Carter spoke for the group. "We knew we had been discovered." He shrugged. "There was no way to get around it."

"Have you ever fixed a fence?" Caleb took a drink of his hot coffee and waited for the boys as though he were chatting with the guys down at the diner.

Boone swallowed his beef stew. "No, sir. We've never even been near a ranch until recently."

"Ah, well that explains a lot." Mr. Manning looked out the kitchen window, then looked to each boy again. "If the sheriff doesn't arrest you, what do you plan on doing?"

"We'll move on from here and look for work, maybe up in Bozeman." Carter practically guzzled the last of the stew juices in his bowl. "May I have another serving, Mrs. Manning?" He picked up his bowl and looked hopefully at the matriarch of the family.

"Why, of course you may. All of you are welcome to eat until you're full." She smiled at the boys and stood up. "Would you like more biscuits?"

"Yes, ma'am." Flynn smiled at Judith as though the sun shone on her.

She filled their bowls and set two more biscuits down by each of them.

Caleb sent a silent signal to the sheriff, who nodded.

"What do you boys think about working off your debts?" Caleb took a bite of a biscuit his wife set before him and grabbed her hand. She squeezed it in return.

"Debts?" Flynn asked between a mouthful of biscuit with honey and huckleberry jam.

"Of course. You've broken our fence in multiple places, killed a steer from the Johnson ranch, and stolen two horses." Caleb counted off their misdeeds on one hand. "Am I missing anything?"

The boys gave him a sheepish look.

"Ah, there's more. Possibly some stolen pies or groceries?" the sheriff asked.

"We only took what we needed to survive." Carter glared daggers at the sheriff.

Chapter 25

Once lunch was over and the table cleared, Caleb pulled the sheriff to the side. "I'd like to keep the boys. Teach them how to ranch, and how to own up to their mistakes."

"And I'll bet Judith wants to play mother hen." Roscoe smirked, knowing his old friend would want to make sure the boys were healthy and strong.

A slow smile spread across Caleb's face. "I think Judith would have liked more kids." He held his hands up when the sheriff started to guffaw. "I know, I know. We already have seven, but she wanted more. And if I'm being honest, so did I."

The sheriff nodded. "I'm not surprised. You both have so much love in your hearts. The way you take in the homeless women and help them get back up on their feet again, I'm surprised you haven't gone and adopted any kids yet."

"We talked about it once. But"—Caleb shrugged one shoulder—"we're getting older. We agreed that helping those who need it is what God has called us to. And grandkids will be coming soon, so Judith will get her babies that way."

Roscoe looked to where Georgia was washing dishes. "Babies. All women seem to want them, don't they?"

A chuckle escaped Caleb's mouth. "Not all women do. And certainly not middle-aged women." He put a hand on his old friend's shoulder. "I think you should ask her out and then see what happens."

"I'm too old for dating and kids." Roscoe looked away from the beautiful woman and back to his friend.

"No, you're only as old as you think you are. Look around. We're the same age and about to have our first grandkid. We're up for the challenge. And, we want to take in three wayward teenagers. If we can do all that, you can ask a pretty woman out."

Grumbling, the sheriff nodded. "Fine, you can have the boys after I take them in and question them properly. I won't do anything official, but I do want to look up their names and see what's going on with them."

"Of course. That makes sense. And with the women here, and my pregnant daughter coming out here all the time, I know I'd feel better if you double-check their past. But, I gotta tell ya, I got a feelin' about them boys. I think they just need a family supporting them." Caleb ran a hand through his mussed-up hair.

Roscoe took his hat off the peg in the hallway and paused. "You might be right. Come on over in an hour and you can get the boys and bring them back, as long as they don't have warrants out for them."

The next day, Mark took Flynn with him into town to pick up supplies. "Now, you know how to be on your best behavior, right?"

"Yes, sir. I don't touch nothing without your permission. And I stay by your side." Flynn nodded and tapped the brim of his cowboy hat when he got out of Mark's truck.

The Mannings had outfitted all three boys in country wear, including cowboy hats. They weren't in the best shape, but the boys were excited just the same.

"That's right. Be polite, and no cussin'. We may be ranchers, but are also godly men who keep our mouths clean." He looked to the boy. "Understand?"

"Yes, sir. You don't have to worry about me. I'm not a cusser. But"—Flynn looked down and toed his boot in the dirt—"you might want to have a talk with Carter. He was always getting his mouth washed out with soap."

It took all his willpower, but Mark kept his laugh in. "I'll do that. Thanks."

Once they were inside, Flynn's mouth dropped open and he looked around. "A real, honest to goodness western general store. I've never seen one except on TV."

This time, Mark did chuckle. "Yeah, we aren't like those big city box stores. You'll only find items in here that ranchers and farmers actually use." He thought for a minute. "Well, at Christmas they do stock some of the fancy stuff, like lighted caps."

Flynn turned confused eyes to Mark.

"Last Christmas, I saw this skull cap that could be used while hunting in the dark. It had two small LED lights." Mark pointed to a spot above his forehead. "Right here. When you pushed a button, they lit up. And they were bright. But it's really not something we use on a ranch. At least, not regularly."

"Oh, that sounds cool. Did you get one?"

Mark chuckled. "Nope. I almost did, but decided I wouldn't use it. It would only be beneficial in the winter, but it's too cold to wear a polyester beanie. Maybe if they did a wool cap with one, that would be cool."

"Hey, is this one of your new ranch hands?" Leah walked up with a huge grin on her face and held her hand out to Flynn. "I'm Leah Hayes. I reckon I'll see you a lot around the ranch, and town if you stick around."

Flynn's cheeks pinked, and he looked to the ground when he put a hand out. "Flynn Smith. Nice to meet you, ma'am."

She shook it.

"My mom's a ma'am. Please, just call me Leah." She smiled at the boy and then turned to Mark. "So, your order is all packed. If you want to pull around to the back with your truck, it might be easier to load it there."

Just then, the bell over the door dinged.

"Sure thing. Thanks, Leah." He smiled extra-long at her and felt his heart rate jump. She was so beautiful, even after working a long day in the store hauling things around. But could he see a future with her?

"Oh, I knew I saw you come in here, Mark. And to see your sweet Leah." Martha Stanhope beamed and put a hand over her heart.

"Mrs. Stanhope, nice to see you." It wasn't, but Mark was taught to be polite, so he would be.

"When should we expect an announcement and invitation?" Martha waggled her brows and looked between Mark and Leah.

Flynn looked between all three and turned confused eyes on Mark. "Are you getting married?"

"Oh, for the love of..." Mark shut up and put both hands over his face.

Leah squeaked and turned around to mess with something on a shelf.

Without a word or a backward glance, Mark pulled Flynn by his shirt sleeve and exited the store as fast as he could.

"What did I say?" Mrs. Stanhope looked perplexed, and Mark wasn't about to say a thing to the gossipmonger. With his luck, she'd turn it all around and who knew what the next story would be.

When Mark pulled the truck up in the back, his heart sank. Leah was beautiful and outgoing, just the sort of woman he'd do well with. But he knew he wasn't ready for a commitment. If she'd just been a town girl, he might have kept seeing her. But since he knew he wasn't ready for anything long term, he'd have to let her down easily. Especially with all the gossip going around about them.

The ranch needed his attention right now, specifically with these new boys. Flynn was easygoing and not a problem, but that Carter kid was going to be a handful. He had a chip on his shoulder the size of Montana, and it would take a lot of hacking away to get it down to size. Then Boone, the poor kid, he followed Carter in whatever he did.

When Matthew told Carter and Boone they were going out to fix the fences that morning, you'd have thought Matthew was trying to get them to kill someone. Carter threw a fit as though he were only a five-year-old, and Boone wasn't too far behind him.

It took Caleb stepping in and reminding them that they were there to fix their misdeeds, and that the work really wasn't that hard. When Mark offered to take Flynn into town to help with the supply run, Carter seemed to calm down a bit. Not much, but enough that they were able to get the boys up on horses and out to get started on a fence.

Mark's thoughts had turned to that encounter, and he knew he'd have to find out why Carter and Boone calmed down a little bit when he offered to take Flynn into town. Did Flynn need something in town? Or did they know he wouldn't do well with manual labor?

Just looking at the teen, anyone could tell Flynn wasn't built for ranching. In fact, he was the kind of guy who would do well with an indoor job. A thought hit him, and he knew just the thing for Flynn. He'd have to discuss it with his pa later that night first. The boys, all three of them, had some work to do before they could move on to anything else. But he knew his idea would be great.

His dad agreed with him when they were outside checking on the cattle after dinner. They had left the boys inside, moaning and complaining about their muscle aches and pains. They weren't used to manual labor. Matthew laughed and told them to man up.

But his ma gave them some ibuprofen tablets and a tall glass of water. Then sent them off to soak in hot baths with Epsom salt. She said it would fix what ailed them. And it most likely would. Well, that and a good night's sleep.

The next morning over breakfast, Mark decided to test the waters with his idea and see what Flynn thought about it. "Say, Flynn, how are you with numbers?"

The boy shrugged. "I'm alright." He took a bite of his eggs and smiled up at Judith, who filled his coffee mug.

"Once you've all worked off what you owe"—Mark gave them all a knowing look—"how would you feel about a part-time job in the general store?" Mark hadn't spoken to Leah yet about his idea, or the fact that they should probably not date anymore. He'd need to talk to her, but with everyone coming over this weekend for a big family shindig, he wasn't sure he wanted to rock the boat. At least, not yet.

"I'd like that." Flynn's eyes widened, just like when he first entered the store the day before.

Mark thought he just might have found Flynn's calling. Now to get Leah and Logan on board. Logan would probably be easy.

A few minutes later, while he was stuck in his own thoughts, he noticed that everyone was quiet. He looked up and smiled. The sheriff had just walked in, and Georgia brought him a cup of coffee along with a pretty smile. He hoped those two would stop dancing around and go out on a real date. That might get the divas off his trail, too.

"Thank you, pretty lady." Roscoe winked.

The three boys watched the sheriff. Flynn looked as though he was worried they were going to be arrested after all. Boone looked between Carter and the sheriff, while Carter glared daggers at the lawman.

Roscoe took a seat next to Georgia and drank his coffee before he spoke up about why he was there. "I just got through talking to Mr. Johnson." The sheriff looked at all three boys. "He's the one who owned the steer you stole."

Carter sat tall in his chair. "Yeah, what of it?"

"Now, he has every right to press charges, so you better watch your manners." The sheriff glared at Carter, who backed down. "He's agreed to let you work off the cost of the lost cattle along with the cost of fixing the fences you broke."

"More ranch work?" Flynn's crestfallen look made Mark feel for the boy.

"That's right. There's consequences for stealing and breaking things. Weren't you ever taught that?" Mr. Manning asked.

"Yes, sir." Boone looked down at his plate and sighed.

"If you work hard, it shouldn't take too long to pay it off." The sheriff refilled his coffee mug and looked between the boys. "I estimate two months of hard labor and you'll have everyone here paid off."

"What about the owner of the horses they stole? Any word on them yet?" Caleb asked.

"Nothing yet. But I haven't really looked. I've asked Callie to look into that. She should have something later today, or tomorrow."

Flynn licked his lips. "Do you think the owners will press charges?" They had told the sheriff where they'd picked up the horses. While they didn't know the names of the ranches, they knew the general area. Callie would just have to search for missing or stolen horse reports in those areas to find out the names of the owners.

"It's hard to say. If you agree to work for them, you might be able to get away with just a reprimand. The horses will be returned to them, so that will help. And with a little bit of love and feed, they'll be good as new." Roscoe was confident the Mannings would take good care of the horses and nurse them back to health.

"Will they expect us to work for them, too?" Carter's brusque tone said more than his words. He wasn't happy about having to work off his debt.

"Carter"—Mark looked at the boy—"this is good for you. We're going to teach you how to ranch, something you could do for a living if you get your act together."

"Hmph." Carter stood up, and Boone followed. They both went outside and got back to work in the barn, mucking out stalls.

The sheriff followed them outside, along with Caleb and Mark.

Chapter 26

The next few days went by slowly for Mark and the Manning family. The three boys were a handful. Boone took to the work better than anyone expected. Flynn, however, was having a tough time of it. And Caleb, well, he was just being difficult.

Friday came, and so did Chloe.

"Oh Ma, it's so good to see you again. And Elizabeth, congratulations!" Chloe hugged her mother and twin sister for a few beats longer than normal. When she pulled back, tears streaked down her cheeks.

"Mr. Manning, good to see you again." Brandon Beck shook his hand.

"Please, call me Caleb. Now that you're dating my daughter, I think it's fine to be on a first-name basis."

"Thank you, sir." Brandon chuckled. "I mean, Caleb."

"Come on in and close the door, it's cold out there." Judith ushered her daughter and Brandon inside to the warm kitchen where she had hot tea and coffee ready for them.

"I wish the weather would decide what it wants. One day it's hot as an oven, then the next we've got a biting wind." Judith shivered and poured hot tea in a mug for herself after serving hot drinks to everyone at her kitchen table.

"I know, I was just telling Brandon yesterday that I wasn't sure if I should bring a coat for the weekend. But thankfully he suggested I should, and I'm glad for it." Chloe looked lovingly at her new boyfriend. They had dated for a month over a year ago, then Brandon took off for a job, and this past Thanksgiving he came home. They rekindled their relationship, and things had been going very strongly for the two lovebirds.

Brandon winked at Chloe before taking a sip of his hot coffee.

"So, what's on the agenda for this weekend? Besides congratulating my twin for being pregnant?" Chloe had screamed so loudly over the phone when Lizzie told her the good news that her neighbors heard her. in fact, just about all of Frenchtown had heard the good news before the night was out.

The front door closed, and voices could be heard in the hallway.

Leah walked in and practically ran to Chloe and gave her a long hug. "I've missed you. You have to come back and visit more often."

"Thanks, Leah. I miss all of you, too. But you do know that you can come and visit me any time you want, right?" Chloe had asked Leah to come for a weekend this past Christmas, but with the store, she couldn't get away for even a day.

"If we ever get any more help, I'd love to come and visit one weekend." Leah looked at Mark and pink tinged her cheeks. She had spent that past week thinking about what was going on with the cowboy. He hadn't called or texted since she saw him in the store, and she was glad for the break.

After the gossip burning its way through town reached her ears, she wasn't sure she wanted to see Mark any time soon. If it weren't for the family gathering this weekend to see Chloe and her boyfriend, she wouldn't come within three miles of the Triple J Ranch.

She and Mark had to do something to calm it all down. While she did find him extremely good looking, and they had a lot of fun together, she wasn't sure she was ready for things to escalate this quickly. If rumors were to be believed, she and Mark were getting married within the month. It was too much.

Too much pressure.

Too much intensity.

Too much stress.

Too much gossip.

It all had to stop, and now. There was only one way to stop it, but she wasn't sure she wanted to do something so drastic.

However, with his radio silence, she worried he might actually be on the same wavelength as her. Wait, wasn't that a good thing? If so, then why did she worry about it? She was confused. And the one thing she knew about confusion was that this was the wrong time to make any major decisions.

So, Leah was going to enjoy the weekend with family and friends. See who these new young guys were, and what their stories were all about. Maybe she could do something to help them. Yes, that would get her mind off of Mark and the blasted rumors about her upcoming wedding.

Focusing on someone else and what they needed was always a great way to get out of one's head, and away from her own problems. Leah knew this from experience. She also knew that if she focused elsewhere, her current problems would take care of themselves eventually.

She wasn't running from her problems.

Shoot, she wasn't even hiding.

She was looking to help someone else.

Yup, that was it. At least, that was the story she was going with.

"Hiya, cowgirl." Mark's sexy voice hit her heart, and she just about crumbled.

Her willpower was shot to high heaven. If he asked her out then and there, she'd not be able to say no.

"Heya, cowboy. Are you excited to see your sister?" Leah bit her lower lip and prayed that they'd be able to have a civil conversation about nothing important.

"Actually"—he looked to where his sister stood in the corner of the kitchen, filling up a plate of treats for her and Brandon—"I am glad to see her. It's been too long."

"What? Since Christmas?" Leah knew that Chloe hadn't been home for the past few months, and she didn't think Mark had left town, either.

Mark looked up at the ceiling and thought for a moment. "You know, I think you're right. We were all supposed to meet up in February, but that big storm hit and no one could get out of town, so we never did. My parents went to visit them right after Christmas, but I think they're the only ones who've made it to see Chloe since Christmas."

"Well, I for one am glad she and Brandon are here this weekend. I'd heard a lot about him and was curious. I can understand why she was so deliriously happy at Christmas, and wanted to go home so soon." Leah chuckled, thinking back to Christmas and the sparkle that filled Chloe's eyes for the few days she was home.

"You do?" Mark scrunched his nose. "You don't think he's a bit scrawny?" He flexed his biceps, not sure if he should be jealous.

Leah laughed. "Alright, alright." She held her hands up. "He's not as built as you are."

Mark nodded. "Got that right." It was amazing how quickly they could go from unsure to bantering back and forth. He liked Leah, he really did. But if she expected him to propose any time soon, she was going to be in for a huge heartbreak.

What was he to do? Should he keep going out with her, or break up with her? Well, it wouldn't exactly be breaking up with her—they weren't truly a couple. Unless you believed the gossip. *Oh, pork rinds. Does she believe the gossip?*

Leah watched Mark's face turn from a joking demeanor to one of serious contemplation. But what really caught her attention was his lack of chin dimple. Normally when he was being serious, the totally adorable dimple popped up on his chin, but this time his chin looked smooth. Well, a few little lines around his mouth, but maybe that was a downturned look? She wasn't sure, but she didn't like what she saw on his face.

"What do you say we go for a walk?" Leah blurted.

"Huh?" Mark shook his head and then looked outside when he realized what she had said.

"I think we should talk."

He hated when a woman said that. But this was Leah. Maybe she had something serious she needed to discuss? He wanted to talk to her about Flynn, so maybe this was his chance. Or Flynn's chance?

"Sure, but it's cold out there, so you better bundle up." Mark walked to the entryway and took his coat and scarf off the peg and watched as Leah put her outerwear back on.

Once they were outside and alone, neither said a word for a while.

Then Mark got up the courage and began, "So, you met Flynn?"

She nodded.

"I was wondering if you still needed a part-time hand at the store? I noticed that even after the Three Forks general store opened up, you still had some lines out your doors." Mark kept moving and didn't look at Leah. He wanted to, though. He also wanted to kiss her.

Leah stopped. "You want me to hire a guy who broke your fences and stole a cow from Mr. Johnson? Not to mention that group of boys took off with two horses, and who knows what else." She shook her head. "I don't think so."

Mark held up a hand. "Now wait a minute. Do you know their story?"

She frowned. "Not really, just that you found them poachers in your caves after they made a mess."

"There's a lot more to it." Mark began by telling her they were orphans who had been kicked out of their group home after turning eighteen. They didn't even get to finish high school. Nor were they given any assistance in finding employment, or housing, or anything else.

They were turfed, as Carter called it. Kicked to the curb, as Boone said one night after supper. Flynn, he was quiet about it all. But that didn't mean Mark hadn't noticed the look of pain that crossed the sad boy's eyes.

Leah felt her nose prick and tears form. Before they fell, she sniffled and rubbed her eyes. The last thing she wanted was to cry in front of Mark, even if it was for a good reason. "I see. Of course, I'll help them however I can. Do you think Flynn has ever worked a job?"

He shook his head. "No, I don't think they were allowed to work, which is really sad. If they had gotten jobs after school, they would have had some skills. We're working with them and teaching 'em how to ranch and farm. But, Flynn." Mark rubbed a hand over his face.

"He's not really a rancher. Or a farmer. I think he might do well in the store though. You should have seen his face when we walked in your store earlier this week. It was as though he was in heaven."

"Really? I hadn't noticed." If she was honest with herself, that day her attention was all on Mark. She noticed the kid, but didn't really *see* him. And that was a failing on her part. She should have paid more attention to the boy. "I'll talk with Logan and see if we can't give him some hours. When will he be done working off his debt here?"

"Um, it's gonna be a while. But if you can give me a day here or there, I'm sure we can work around his schedule."

"What about the other boys? If you get Flynn a job, you're gonna have to get them ones, too. We can't hire all three. Even just the one is going to be tight." It wasn't that she didn't want the other boys working with her—she did. She had noticed how strong Boone looked. It would be nice to have a delivery boy, or someone who could do all the heavy lifting for her when Logan wasn't around. Maybe they could hire a delivery boy as well?

"I think we'll get them jobs on ranches in the area. Dad spoke with Mr. Johnson, and he's looking forward to having some more help. If they do a good job paying him back, he might hire one of them. And if that's the case, we can probably hire the other one. Dad's already said they can stay in one of the bunkhouses if they get jobs in the area. They could help us out with odd jobs, after they pay back what they owe, in exchange for room and board."

Leah nodded. "That's a great idea. But how will Flynn get into town?"

They spoke about their ideas and various scenarios for the next hour, not realizing that they had basically run off from the family.

"Mark? Leah? You guys around here anywhere?" Matthew called out.

"Over here." Mark waved from the barn. They had sought shelter inside the barn when their noses started to freeze off after one of the more blistering gusts of wind came through.

"What are you doing out here all alone?" He grinned and waggled his brows.

One more person who thought more was going on than what really was. Mark wasn't sure how to deal with this, so he ignored the insinuation. "We're talking about Flynn and the guys. I'm trying to get Leah to hire at least one of them."

Matthew's eyes widened. "Oh, that's a great idea. I wish I would have thought of it."

"That's because it takes an actual brain to think of something this great." Mark laughed and patted his older brother on the back. The two of them joked around and pretended to fight on the walk back to the house.

Leah trailed behind with a genuine smile crossing her features. It really was a good idea. They wouldn't need Flynn much, but if they ended up having a good summer, they could offer him more hours once he had worked off his debt. She had planned on telling him she didn't think they should date anymore, but this was a much better conversation.

She'd have to find time to tell him what she was thinking, but for tonight she'd just enjoy the time with their family and friends. She really didn't want to put a damper on Chloe's weekend home, anyways. It would be better to wait until Chloe and Brandon left, then tell Mark what she'd decided. Besides, with the couple here visiting, Leah doubted Mark would have time for a date.

With all of the attention on Chloe and Brandon that night, Leah was caught off guard the next afternoon when she came out after her shift for dinner with the family.

Chapter 27

M r. Hayes offered to close up the store Saturday night so Leah could head out for the big barbecue supper the Mannings had planned.

Leah never turned down a Manning barbecue if she could help it. So when her dad told her to head out early, she didn't complain.

But when she arrived at the Triple J Ranch, she wished she would have.

"Leah, I'm so glad you were able to come early. Come and help me carry these plates outside." Judith led Leah to the kitchen, where three large platters waited to go out to the table. "We got lucky that the windstorm left and warm air was behind it."

The weather was a balmy fifty-three degrees, and the sun hadn't quite set yet. It filled the skies with shades of oranges, reds, and a dash of purple. Leah loved it when the skies were colorful like that.

Before they headed outside, Judith stopped Leah. "I hear you're getting pretty serious with my boy. Is it true?"

The platter in Leah's hands shook, and she almost dropped it. Since she was close to the counter, she stopped and put it on the sideboard. "I'm not sure what Mark thinks, but this isn't serious. We've only gone out a few times." She shook her head. "And most of our dates ended in disaster." She almost added, *And so far, no kisses*. But she kept that to herself.

Judith pursed her lips. "That's what I was afraid of." When Leah's brows furrowed, Judith continued, "The rumor mill is on fire about you and Mark. I was approached earlier today by someone I barely even know asking about your wedding to my son." She arched a brow.

"No, no. This can't be happening." Leah leaned against the counter, put her hand on her forehead, and sighed. "Why can't those stupid nosy bodies keep their blasted noses out of my business?"

Judith put a comforting arm around Leah's shoulders. "Leah, dear. I hope you know that we love you and support you and Mark, no matter what you decide. You'll always be a part of this family."

Tears welled in Leah's eyes. "Thank you, Judith. I really appreciate your support." She wiped her eyes. "You won't be upset if Mark and I don't keep seeing each other?" Leah knew that both families liked seeing them together. But they couldn't be a couple just because it was something their families wanted. They had to be truly in love with each other. Leah did have strong feelings for Mark, but she doubted he had strong enough feelings for her to weather this storm.

Once the pressure got to him, she knew he'd turn tail and run. He'd hurt her if this *relationship* went on much longer. Mark wasn't the fall-in-love kinda guy. She knew that. She had seen his patterns over the years. He dated someone for a little while, usually less than a month, and then he ended things when the girl started getting designs on him and a future.

Or when the rumor mill started up. She knew several girls from high school who had wanted things to progress with Mark, but instead had their hearts broken when the divas began wagging their tongues. She wouldn't be another notch on his heartbreaker belt.

And, she really hated being the topic of conversation around town. It was too much pressure for anyone. Leah had no idea how Logan and Lizzie dealt with it, or even the other Manning brothers who'd recently married.

For weeks on end, she was constantly chiding people around town for spreading gossip that she was certain came from the Diner Divas. One of these days, someone was going to have to get them to stop their gossiping ways for good. Hopefully sooner rather than later.

"Sweetheart, no matter what you two decide, Caleb and I will support you." Judith hesitated a moment. "But, I must say, that I enjoy seeing you both together. You're a calming soul for my son. And yet, you also share his sense of humor." She held her hands up when Leah was about to interject. "But, that doesn't mean you have to be a couple. Do whatever you feel God leading you to do."

Tears welled up in Leah's eyes and she swiped at them.

"Just do me one favor." Judith put a calming hand on Leah's shoulder. "Please pray about your decision before making it."

Leah nodded. She had been praying, so that was an easy thing to agree to.

Once she had her emotions under control, Leah and Judith made their way outside with the platters of food.

And the only open seat was next to Mark. *Of course.*

He gave her a sheepish look and shrugged his shoulders.

She sighed and resigned herself to a night next to Mark. Which, if she was being honest with herself, was just plain confusing. She thought that with their long-standing friendship they could at least have a fun night with the family and not have things be so awkward, but every time she leaned over him to get something, he backed up so they didn't touch. It was as though just the idea of her touch grossed Mark out.

Normally she was pretty confident in herself, but with the way Mark was reacting to her she had to wonder if she stank, or if it was something worse. At one point, she even tried to secretly sniff her armpits. Nothing smelled off. Well, not that she could tell anyway.

As the night progressed, Leah was more convinced that everything was wrong with Mark. She no longer got butterflies in her stomach when she took in his manly scent. The leather-and-spices combo with pine actually turned her off. Even the food tasted all wrong. She *never* had a problem with the taste of the Manning spreads. But her stomach refused to accept much, and what she did get down tasted more like cardboard.

For a little while she worried she was getting sick. But when John got close and his masculine scent wafted her way, it didn't bother her at all. It didn't turn her head, either.

It was then that she realized it was Mark who was making her sick to her stomach.

The uncertainty of what was going on, and the pressure of the town, was too much for her. She was about to burst at the seams, it was so overwhelming. She couldn't let this simmer; she had to do something about it right away. Even though she had decided to wait until after Chloe left, she knew she couldn't.

It wouldn't be fair to her to keep feeling so awful. And it wouldn't be fair to Mark to keep letting him think things were okay.

They most certainly weren't okay. And if she was being honest, she knew Mark felt the same way. He was probably wondering how to get out of it all as well.

If things didn't get settled, she would make herself sick. And she had no time for illness. Not with how busy the store was, and the prospect of training another new guy. Shawn was working out great and his training so far had been a breeze, but this wasn't his first job.

Flynn had never worked a job in his life. Leah hoped he would at least have a decent work ethic. But the boy had never worked a cash register, never had to deal with customers who could at times be difficult. The boy would have to learn that the customer was always right, even when they weren't. And then learn how to correct the customer's thinking when they were wrong so that they would actually be in the right. It could be daunting.

The real question was *when*. Not when in the future, but when *tonight*. Should she go up to him right then or wait until the end of the night, right before leaving?

Mark was miserable. Normally he loved the family gatherings, but tonight it was all wrong. Chloe was great, as was Brandon, but the way everyone looked at Mark and then over to Leah made his stomach churn. Even though the spring evenings were still cool, he felt sweat beading across his forehead. At one point he even felt drops of perspiration rolling down his back. Was he getting sick? Did he have a fever?

Whenever he'd walk away from Leah, he would start to feel better. But each time he was next to her again, anxiety welled within him. This was all wrong. He never should have asked her out to begin with. She was his little sister in a roundabout way, but still, they were related by marriage and that was that.

The divas had been going on and on about him and Leah all week long. It was as though the outside world didn't even exist, it was all about Mark and Leah, two little lovebirds...and all that. He could never escape the attention no matter how much he tried to hide his face when in town all week.

He'd had enough. This had to end. But he didn't want to hurt her feelings. That was the last thing Mark wanted to do. Then the guilt started rolling in, and he wondered if he could keep seeing her a little bit longer. Would she decide to end things on her own? That would make it so much better for him. And for her, too. If Leah ended it, she wouldn't be heartbroken, would she?

The idea of ghosting her was preposterous. He'd known guys who'd done that, and it only hurt the girl in the end. He was more man than that. But was he man enough to end this on his own? No, he needed help.

God, I don't know what to do. Leah is such a great gal, but I don't think she's for me. You know I'm not big on the idea of being with one woman for the rest of my life, I'm just not ready for it. And Leah is the sort that a man marries. She's not the date-a-few-times-and-leave-her kinda gal. Help me figure out how best to get out of this without hurting her.

When a sense of peace had enveloped him, it burst the moment Matthew came over and put a hand on his shoulder.

"So, I hear you and Leah are getting serious." Matthew grinned.

Mark moaned. "Not you, too."

"Then the rumors are false?"

"Of course they are." Mark rubbed his face. "How do I get out of this?"

"Just be honest with her. She deserves that much." Matthew grimaced and walked back to his wife.

Mark watched as Matthew held Chloe tight and whispered in her ear. When she looked to Leah, he knew his brother had spilled the beans. He'd have to talk to Leah tonight, before she left. His brother was right: Leah deserved the truth, and this was something that should be done in person. Not over the phone or via text.

The moment the party decided to head back inside after all the s'mores were gone, Mark took a leap of faith and searched out Leah. It was the perfect time to have a private conversation with her.

"Leah, can we talk?" Mark's smile didn't quite reach his eyes, but he still tried. A tingling sensation went down his spine, and not the good kind.

She took in a deep breath and slowly let it out. "Sure."

As they walked toward a more private area, he worried he was about to break her heart. But he reasoned with himself that the sooner he did this, the better.

Once they were out of earshot of the others who still mingled about outside, Leah put a hand on his arm. "Mark, I'm glad you wanted to talk. There's something I really need to say."

He furrowed his brow and hoped she wasn't about to pledge her undying love. But he knew that wasn't it when she looked up at him with worry in her eyes.

"Of course. You know you can talk to me about anything." For a moment he worried it might have been something to do with Big Bart, but he'd have heard sooner if the goon or any of his gang had said or done something to upset her.

She rubbed her forehead and winced. "Have you heard the rumors spreading around town faster than a wildfire in summer?"

He nodded and grimaced. So she'd heard them. too. Mark should have known she would be bothered by them. Even if she was really into their new relationship, the rumors would have to bother her, at least somewhat.

"Well, um." She fidgeted with her hands in front of her. "I don't know...I mean... The pressure is too much. I wonder if we shouldn't cool things down." She looked up at him. "Ya know?"

He sighed and felt the weight of the world release from his shoulders. "Yes, I do know." A genuine smile spread across his features. "I wanted to say the same exact thing to you. I don't see how any couple could survive a full-court press from the Diner Divas."

"So, friends?" She turned hopeful eyes to him.

"The best." He opened his arms, and she walked into his embrace.

Mark sighed, happier than he'd been in over a week. Maybe these feelings he had for her were a passing fancy. Maybe now they could settle in to being the best of friends, no strings attached. And no Diner Divas gossiping about them.

But when she pulled away and said goodnight, his chest tightened and ached. Why, if he'd gotten exactly what he wanted, did his heart hurt?

Chapter 28

That wasn't so bad. Leah walked away from Mark thinking she'd done the right thing. Her mind told her it was the right move. But her gut told her she'd just made a huge mistake. She shook her head and told her stomach to get in line with her head and heart. Her heart was in line, wasn't it? Or was her heart in line with her gut? She sighed and figured that her mixed emotions would probably fade overnight.

When she walked inside, she felt suffocated. The expectant looks on everyone's faces were too much. She'd tell her family about the breakup in the morning and let Mark tell his family when he was ready. She didn't want to stick around in case he might want to tell them that night.

"I'm beat. If I want to pay attention in church tomorrow, I need to head home for sleep." Leah thanked the Mannings for a fantastic meal and drove herself home.

As she drove home she second-guessed herself, and third, and then fourth-guessed. Had she made the right decision? Mark seemed very happy with it. But when they hugged, that wasn't the hug of friends saying goodnight. It was too warm, and too...something. She couldn't put her finger on it, but there was something there. Could it be just residual emotions from their dates? She prayed that was all it was.

Now that she'd broken it off with Mark there would be no going back, and she knew it.

Leah didn't know how gossip spread so quickly, but when she walked into church the next morning, everyone already knew. The whispers made their way to her ears, and whenever she got close enough, the gossips stopped talking and gave her sad, pitiful looks. As though she had been dumped by Mark. Humph, she was the one who did the dumping, thank you very much.

However, if it got the gossips to stop then she'd deal with one or two days of sad eyes and hugs from the townswomen.

She took her seat in her family pew next to her mother and focused on the preacher. His sermon focused on 2 Corinthians 10:5—*Casting down imaginations, and every high thing that exalteth itself against the knowledge of God, and bringing into captivity every thought to the obedience of Christ.*

Leah really thought about what the Bible was trying to tell her. She needed to keep her thoughts focused on God, not on herself or anything else. That wasn't easy to do. But if she did, then maybe some of the anxiety she'd felt lately would melt away.

If she focused her thoughts on God, instead of say the gossip, would things have gone differently with Mark? Would they be together, moving forward? Instead of in this weird place?

When she came into church that morning, she did instinctively look for the cute cowboy. When she saw him, she made sure not to look too long or walk near him. In time they would be friends again, she was confident of that. But right then and there, her emotions were too raw and unsure.

How was one supposed to act around the man you just broke up with?

Okay, she thought, this was exactly why God wanted us to focus on Him instead of ourselves. She felt herself spiral down a dark path if she thought too much about Mark and everything. But when she thought about God, her spirits lifted and she felt peace.

That was exactly what she needed, peace.

Instead of hanging around after services and fellowshipping with friends and family, Leah left to fellowship with the Lord. Time alone with God in prayer was what she needed to get her head on straight.

As she walked along the footpath running parallel with the little river that flowed on the outskirts of town, she prayed and asked God for his comfort and direction.

But every time she started to get into her conversation with God, other thoughts interrupted her mind. She was bombarded by thoughts and ideas. Some good, others not so good. One that kept coming up, which she had a hard time dispelling, was how easy it was to break up with Mark. He was obviously relieved when she said she wanted to go back to being friends.

What was wrong with her that Mark didn't want her? And she would spiral down, and insecurities about other things would pop up. But the moment she stopped her negative thoughts and refocused on God, peace would start to envelop her. But then another insignificant thought would pop up, and she'd begin the cycle all over again.

After about an hour of walking and beating herself up, only to let it go and feel God's peace, and then start the cycle all over again, she sat down and cleared her mind. After taking a few breaths, she focused her energy on the sermon and the pastor's words. Then she thought about God, and Paul. And how Paul struggled with this as well.

Finally, after close to three hours of prayer, she got herself out of her own head and back on track. As she walked home the enemy tried to assault her with her insecurities again, but she pushed them out and began to hum hymns praising God. When she arrived at home, she was enveloped with a sense of peace she couldn't remember feeling in a very long time.

Once those negative thoughts had been banished, she felt true joy. Leah had made the right decision about Mark. Maybe one day they would end up together, but for now they were better off as friends.

The next few days went by so fast, Leah didn't even realize when it was Wednesday. She had spoken to her brother and father about bringing Flynn on board, and Logan arranged it all. Someone from the Triple J would bring Flynn into town and he'd begin working at 10 a.m. every day for the rest of the week. He'd work until someone from the ranch could get him and bring him home.

So when Caleb came inside with Flynn right behind him, Leah was surprised. "It's Wednesday already?"

Caleb chuckled. "Yes, it is. And Flynn here"—he put his hand on the teen's shoulder—"is ready to start."

"Great, the first thing we need to do is get his employment papers all situated. As discussed, he'll start out making minimum wage." Leah walked around the counter and smiled at the shy young man. "Come on, follow me."

"Wait." Caleb put up a hand. "We discussed it, and the sheriff agrees. There will be no wages for Flynn here until all three boys have worked off what they owe."

Leah's brow furrowed. "But none of them took anything from us."

"True, but the owners of the horses that these boys"—he cleared his throat—"*borrowed* think they need to work off more. But since the owners are more than half a day's drive from here, they agreed we would tack on the amount that everyone agreed was fair for renting the horses." Caleb eyed Flynn, who ducked his head.

"Ah, I see. So we should keep track of his hours, but he won't actually draw a check until all three boys have paid back what they owe everyone?" It was a great idea.

One that Leah totally agreed with. This would teach the boys responsibility as well as consequence. They hadn't really thought through what they did, not realizing that once they were caught there would be consequences.

Living in a group home with at least a dozen other boys during their formative years probably made it difficult for them to learn important lessons such as these. Leah could get behind the idea of teaching these boys how to make it in society without getting into trouble. And she'd feel good about helping them out this way.

With Flynn being such a quiet kid, she figured she'd be getting the easy part of it all.

"Okay, I still need to get some papers filled out for our insurance, and for once he starts drawing a check. Then we'll get him trained up for how to service customers in a general store." Leah looked to Flynn and tilted her head. "Do you think you'll enjoy working with customers? Answering questions, loading their vehicles with their purchases, and even restocking the shelves?"

Flynn's smile was sweet and his cheeks pinked. "Yes, Miss Leah. I do believe I'll like this work." Then under his breath, he added, "Much more than ranching."

She chuckled. "Good enough. Come on with me to the back and we'll get you going." Before they entered the back room area, Leah turned around to Caleb. "What time do you think someone'll be by tonight to get Flynn?"

"Elizabeth and Logan will be coming out for dinner tonight, so they'll stop on by before four to get him." Caleb waved at Leah and left.

Leah wasn't sure what she thought it would be like to train a guy who'd never worked a day in his life, but she wasn't prepared for all of Flynn's questions and uncertainty. They boy suffered from major self-doubt. It was no wonder he was so quiet.

"Flynn"—Leah looked around to make sure no one was close by—"I think you could do really well at this if you believed in yourself."

He shook his head in disbelief.

"You're a nice kid. Respectful, and I think if you give yourself a chance, you'll see that you're quite smart, too." Leah had been impressed with how quickly he learned the layout of the store, and how well he restocked.

Flynn didn't ask any questions about the restocking process, or where something was. She'd give him a box and he'd get right to it. He was fast and efficient. Every time she went and checked his work, it was good. He even straightened the items next to what he was re-stocking. While he wasn't ready yet to interact with cus-tomers, she did sense that he would do well.

Only time would tell if he was good at customer ser-vice, but if nothing else Flynn would be perfect for a position as stock boy. That would free up her time to spend with customers and looking up new products to try selling. She was always trying to find the next great thing a rancher or farmer would need. And that research took time.

"Leah, hi there." Lizzie hugged her sister-in-law when she entered the store at four o'clock that afternoon.

"Lizzie, you're looking much better. Not so green around the gills." Leah giggled. She knew Elizabeth had been having a tough time with morning sickness at all hours of the day, but the past two days when she'd seen her friend, she looked much better.

"Thank you. I don't know if I'm past the worst of it or if little baby Hayes has just given me a reprieve for the week." She put a protective hand across her belly. "But I'll take it either way."

"Let's pray you're past the worst of it." Leah winked and turned around. Then she called out, "Flynn, your ride's here."

Flynn came out from the back and smiled. "Already? That was a fast six hours."

Leah chuckled. "Much better than mucking out stalls?"

He nodded. "I'll say." Flynn took off the apron he wore to denote his position as stock boy and handed it to Leah. "I'll see you tomorrow morning."

"Yup, have a good night." She took the apron and went to put it in the back room. She also pulled her phone out of her apron and texted her dad, who was supposed to already be there to help her close the store.

Her mom called her back within only a few minutes. "I'm so sorry, dear, but your dad's not feeling so well."

Panic immediately took over. "Oh, no! Is it his heart?" The only thing she could think of was him having another heart attack. When he had his first one she had been manning the store by herself, like now. And she'd closed up shop right away and met them at the local medical clinic, where he was then taken via ambulance to a Bozeman hospital.

"No, sweetie, thank goodness. I think he might be coming down with a cold. That's all. But since we don't know for sure, he's gonna stay home for the night and rest."

"Did you take him to see the doctor today?"

"No, we had a video call. And the doctor said to take it easy and drink plenty of liquids. But now you're at the store all alone. Logan's at his in-laws' for dinner. What about Stevie?" The worry in her mom's voice came through loud and clear.

"Don't worry, Mom. I'll call one of my friends to come by. I'll be fine." A week ago, Leah would have called Mark. Now? She'd have to call Sophia.

"Alright, but be safe." Her mom hung up the phone.

When she dialed Sophia, she felt odd. Here she was, a grown woman needing a babysitter. But if she was honest with herself, it was a smart to have another person here with her. Even if they couldn't stop Bart or one of his goons, a friend would be able to call the sheriff and let them know right away what had happened.

"Hiya, Leah. What's up?" The perky gym owner had been a friend to Leah for many years and was probably the toughest person Leah knew, male or female.

"Hey there. I was just wondering if you were busy tonight?" Leah bit her lip, waiting for a response.

"Oh, sorry. Tonight is the beginners' self-defense class. I had to reschedule it from Monday night because

we had a pipe burst in the gym and water got everywhere."

"Yeah, that's right. I heard about it from one of the
divas who came in Monday evening. Is it all cleaned up
now?" Leah had meant to go over and ask Sophia if she
needed help, but this week was crazy. Between training
Flynn and all the orders they had from local farmers and
some of the ranchers, too, she'd run out of energy before
the day was even over with.

"We're just fine over here. Don't you go worrying
about me. What's up with you? Did you want someone
to join you for dinner?" Sophia asked.

"Ah..." Leah hemmed and hawed before coming
clean. It wasn't that she didn't want Sophia to know
what was going on, it was that she didn't want Sophia
to worry about her. But maybe Sophia could help find
someone? "I'm alone at the store now. My dad's not
feeling well, and he was supposed to help close. Do you
know someone who could come babysit me?"

Sophia chuckled. "It's not babysitting. We're just helping to make sure you're safe. That's all." She paused a
moment, then continued, "I don't know who can come
over. Let me check and see who's still here. Maybe
someone can come by on their way home? I'll check and
text you."

"Thanks, Soph. I appreciate it." When Leah hung up,
she sighed. She knew she wasn't being a pain by asking
for help. It was important to ask for help when it was
needed, and she rarely asked. But she was an independent woman, for Pete's sake. Why couldn't she close up

shop alone? Rocko was in jail. Bart wouldn't dare come to town and do his own dirty work. The rest of the guys on Bart's team were chumps. She could easily take them down. Couldn't she?

Not ten minutes later, one of her friends walked through the door with a huge smile on her face. "Leah, it's been ages. I'm so glad I was in the gym when Sophia got your call."

"Harper Bensen. Thank you for coming by." Leah beamed at her friend. They spent most of the evening chatting and catching up on everything.

Harper was one of the town's nurses, and a good friend to Leah as well as Elizabeth. She was also one of the original cowgirls to work with Elizabeth on the homeless project in Bozeman. She had a heart of gold, as most nurses do, and loved helping people in need. Leah couldn't help but be buoyed by her friend's visit.

"See, I told you I would be fine." Leah locked the door to the general store and noted that not one bad thing had happened all night. And neither of them noticed any strangers or lurkers. Not one hair on Leah's body stood at attention during the evening, or even then while they were out in the open.

"That doesn't mean you would have been safe. It just means that no one bothered to come in while I was there." Harper raised her chin. "I am pretty tough and mean. No one messes with Nurse Harper."

"You got that right." Leah chuckled, and they walked to the parking lot and said goodnight. "Thank you, though. Seriously. I'm grateful you were able to spend the whole evening with me. And it was fun catching up."

"Yes, it was. We need to get together again soon." Harper waved as she got into her truck.

They made plans to meet up for lunch at Rosie's Diner on Saturday.

Chapter 29

The week went by quickly, with Leah closing most nights and not alone. When Saturday rolled around, she was excited for her lunch date with Harper. Life had been so crazy that she'd never even had a chance to gush over the dates with Mark to any of her friends, and then commiserate over the breakup. It all just happened, and Leah looked back as she walked to the diner from the general store and wondered how she'd gotten to that day. Spring was already half over and she'd barely seen her friends.

Something had to be done. She couldn't keep living life in a vacuum of all work and no play. Sure, the family business was important, but Logan made time for his wife. Why couldn't Leah make time for her friends?

Well, this was just the first step. She had yet to make it to one of Sophia's classes. Leah was going to have a chat with her brother about the schedule so that she didn't close so much. Now that Elizabeth was doing better, Logan needed to close more. And once her father was better, maybe he could take one night a week and close.

Eventually their two new hires could help Stevie close, and that would make it so much easier on her entire family. She already felt lighter. Things were looking up.

Even more so when she walked in and saw Elizabeth and Sophia had joined Harper at a large table in the back corner. "Ladies! It's so good to see you all."

"Leah!" All three women laughed, and everyone hugged and started getting all caught up on each other's lives.

When her long lunch was over, Leah got up feeling so much better about where she was. They even discussed what had happened with Mark. Not in too much detail, but enough that she felt she had made the right decision, even though she missed the handsome cowboy.

"If it's meant to be, he'll come and ask you out again in God's timing." Harper hugged Leah when they left the diner and went their separate ways.

Logan had asked that she bring him back a sandwich which was in the brown bag in her hands. She walked down the street toward the general store, saying hi and waving to those she knew along the way. Until a hand grabbed her and pulled her into an alley.

"Whatcha got for me, little lady?" Rocko's sneering voice sent chills down Leah's spine.

"Get lost," she scoffed, and tried to pull away from him. His grip was too tight, and his fingers only dug in more to her arm.

"Give me your wallet," he demanded.

"How about I give you a black eye?" She narrowed her eyes at the criminal.

He tightened his grip on her arm even more. "You better do as I say." The pain shot through her arm, but she made sure he didn't see her wince.

"Alright, then how about a fat lip?" She was feeling brave. It was broad daylight and someone would come by and help her. She just knew it. Plus, someone had to have seen him take her off the street. This was Beacon Creek, not Bozeman. Everyone watched what everyone was doing around these parts. Especially the Diner Divas.

"You better watch that tongue of yours, little girl," he sneered, and pulled her closer to him.

Leah finally pulled her arm out of his grip and got into a fighting stance. "How about I give you a broken nose?" She put her fists up in front of her face, ready to fight back if he tried anything. She did her best to ignore the pain flaring up in her arm from the way he'd held her like a vise grip.

From behind her, Leah heard the voice of an angel. "How about you leave the lady alone?"

A shot of adrenaline raced up her spine. Mark had come to her rescue. Not that she needed it, but she felt much better knowing she had backup now.

"Oh, if it isn't the boyfriend." Rocko waved off Mark and looked back at Leah. "You better tell your boyfriend to back off if he wants to walk away."

Ignoring his jab, she asked, "Did you escape from jail?" Leah hadn't heard that he was released, but she wouldn't be surprised if he did escape. That was probably why he wanted her money.

"I've got connections." He leered at her. "So, like I said, give me your money."

"Not a chance." Leah wasn't going to be cowed by this overly large goon. She'd let him scare her before, but not this time.

"Rocko, if you know what's good for you"—Mark stepped between Leah and Big Bart's main goon—"you'll leave town and not come back."

Rocko chortled. "I think you have it backwards, little boy."

"Like the man said, Rocko, you should leave town and not come back." Logan entered the alley and walked up next to Mark, forming a wall of muscle between Rocko and Leah.

"You think the two of you can take me down?" He laughed. "It'll take more than you two to do anything." Rocko swung out at Logan and hit his stomach.

Logan bent over, coughing.

Mark swung and missed.

Rocko jabbed at Mark, but he was ready and jumped back, out of the reach of the man's beefy fist.

Leah ran around behind Rocko.

Mark swung out at Rocko and clipped his jaw. His *rock-solid* jaw. He shook his hand out, and Rocko took advantage and got in a right hook to Mark's face.

Leah kicked at the back of Rocko's knee, causing him to fall down. While he was down, she kicked him between the legs.

Logan pulled her off him just as the sheriff entered the alley.

"Alright, back away." Sheriff Roscoe looked between everyone. "What happened here?"

"That creep"—Leah motioned to Rocko—"pulled me off the street and demanded I give him my money. He also hurt me." Leah looked at her arm. While it was covered by her shirt, the material was torn from his manhandling. She pulled back the ripped sleeve; large fingerprints were already beginning to show up on her arm. "This is going to bruise, badly."

The sheriff shook his head. "Rocko, you were warned to leave town. Even your own attorney said to go home. Looks like I have to arrest you again." The sheriff recited him his Miranda rights and cuffed him.

Leah began to shake, and Mark put his arms around her. "Hey, are you alright?"

She nodded. "Just the adrenaline leaving my system."

"Why don't you take her home? I'll take care of the store." Logan hugged Leah, but looked at Mark.

"Of course. I'll be happy to make sure she gets home safely." Mark put an arm around her shoulder and walked her back to his truck. "I'll get your brother to bring your truck by your house later."

She nodded and got into the truck. Leah had no idea what had just happened. It seemed everything was going by so quickly she didn't have time to process any of it.

"Did we just stand up to Rocko and win?" she asked when they left the parking lot.

"Yes, we did. Good job, by the way." Mark looked out of the corner of his eye at Leah and held her hand.

"What about Bart? Was he anywhere near?" Leah's mind whirled around all the possibilities. Could they get Bart now, too? Or would he be smarter than that?

Mark shook his head. "No, I didn't see him anywhere. But I'll ask the sheriff if he knows anything."

The drive to her house was quick, and when she exited the truck Mark was right there next to her.

"Come on, I'll walk you in and help you tell your parents what happened." Mark took her hand and they walked in together.

Mark was still reeling from the experience. Who knew what would have happened if he hadn't been in town to pick up Flynn after his shift at the store? When he saw Leah being yanked into that alley, he'd yelled to Flynn to get help and he ran after the woman who had occupied a lot of time in his mind and heart lately.

All he could think of was what if he couldn't help her, again. He wasn't about to leave her in the clutches of that psycho. Not if he could help it. There was an outlet to that alley, but it was full of trash cans. He'd hoped Leah could use those to distract or deter Rocko while Mark ran toward them. He'd prayed as he ran that he'd be in time.

All he had at that moment was his faith in God.

Now that they were at her house, he thanked God for protecting Leah and bringing the sheriff so quickly. All he could think about was Leah, and how he could have lost her. When he sat down on the sofa next to Leah, he let go of a deep sigh and rubbed his face. When he touched the spot where Rocko had hit him, he winced.

"Oh, you're hurt, too." Leah fussed over him and looked closely at his face. "That's gonna be great shiner." She stood. "I'll get us both some ice for our bruises."

"No, sit back down. I'll get you ice." Mrs. Hayes left them alone in the living room.

Leah sat back down next to Mark. "Thank you for coming to my rescue."

He held up his hands. "What do you mean? I think you rescued us."

A chuckle escaped her lips. "No, I think it was more of a team effort."

"Maybe." Mark nodded. "Logan and I distracted Rocko while you took him down. That was some fancy footwork there. Where'd you learn that?"

"From Sophia."

"Of course."

"Here you are. Two ice packs for the conquering heroes." Mrs. Hayes came in and handed Leah an ice pack for her arm. One that would wrap around. "Lay back, Mark. I've got a bag of frozen peas for your eyes."

"That's better than a steak on my eye." He chuckled and did exactly as Leah's mom directed. "Oh, that feels good. Thank you, Mrs. Hayes."

When the doorbell rang, Leah jumped.

"Are you alright?" Mark had noticed the movement, but more importantly the look of worry that crossed her face when the loud noise rang.

Leah winced and looked down at her arm. "I'll be fine."

The sheriff walked in and looked at them both. "How are you two holding up?"

"I'll be fine. Just a bruise." Leah pointed to the ice pack on her arm.

Mark grinned. "I'm gonna have a nice shiner." He looked at Leah, and they both shared a smile.

"What about Logan?" The sheriff looked around the room.

"He stayed at the store, but he's probably just gonna have a sore stomach." Leah furrowed her brow. "It wasn't much of a fight with all three of us."

The sheriff chuckled. "Really? Rocko's gonna need medical attention on his knee. Whoever kicked it out did a real number on it."

Leah beamed with pride. "That was me."

With a smile still on his face, the sheriff pulled out his notepad. "Alright, tell me what happened starting with you, Leah."

She went through her story, and Mark sat there listening to her melodic voice. Leah was one tough cowgirl. He had always appreciated how fierce she could be. And independent. He supposed that happened when there were just two kids growing up in a house.

All week long, he'd second-guessed his decision to call things off with Leah. Then he'd remember she was the one who actually said the words first. He agreed with her, and he had planned on saying the exact same words. But she'd beaten him to the punch. At the time he was glad she was the one who had done the ending, and not him.

The gossip mill went into overdrive the second they got wind of what had happened. But it had died down the past two days. Now they were focused on Cal Johnson. It seemed when romance was on the vine, no one cared about the prodigal son returning. Now it was all anyone could talk about. Poor Cal.

But, better him than Mark.

What would happen if Mark and Leah tried to make a go of it again? Would the pressure get to them? Did she even want to make a go of it with him?

Her hand reached out across the sofa cushions and took hold of his. Leah squeezed his hand.

Mark realized that the sheriff had asked him to tell his story, but he'd been thinking about Leah instead. He cleared his throat. "Right. Well, Leah pretty much said it all."

When the sheriff's gaze meandered between the two and then landed on their joined hands, Mark sat up straight. "I mean..." He told his story, and eventually the heat in his cheeks went away and anger replaced the embarrassment.

"Alright, I've got Rocko handcuffed to his gurney and on his way to Missoula. I figure if he's in a Missoula hospital, the sheriff there can keep a good eye on him."

"You still don't trust the law in Bozeman?" Leah asked.

Roscoe scratched his chin. "Well, it's not that I *don't* trust him. It's more that I'm not sure he's really in control there. At least when it comes to Big Bart and his gang."

Mark had wondered the same thing. Most likely Bart was putting pressure on the Bozeman sheriff, or maybe it was the organized crime boss who seemed to be pulling Bart's strings. They weren't sure about that part, but if Mark were a betting man he'd bet an entire barbecue dinner on it.

However, his main concern now was ensuring that Leah, and his entire town, were safe from Bart and whoever he was connected to. "Do you think Leah will be safe now?"

The sheriff's brow furrowed. "I can't really be certain." He looked at Leah. "I'd suggest you don't go anywhere by yourself anymore. At least not until this situation is taken care of. I think you all should employ the buddy system."

Leah deflated. "Great, just what I need." She threw her hands in the air and her ice pack dropped to the sofa. She picked it up and put it back on her arm.

"I'm sorry, Leah. I know this sucks. I'll help however I can." And Mark would. He'd be there every night she closed if that was what it took to keep her safe.

"All of my deputies know to drive by your store and house as much as they can, all day and night." Roscoe furrowed his brow. "I'll head down to Missoula tomorrow and speak with the judge about this. Hopefully he's not in cahoots with Bart's gang. If I have to, I'll even send him to the capital."

"Do you think it's any different in Helena?" Mark couldn't imagine the leader of a crime syndicate *not* having his claws in the politicians of their state. From what he'd heard, if this crime boss was actually calling the shots then he'd own people everywhere in this state. It was just a matter of finding out who wasn't afraid of the mobster.

"Who is this guy everyone keeps referring to but never names?" Leah pursed her lips.

Roscoe rubbed the back of his neck. "Well, we aren't sure Bart is associated with the local crime boss, but it's a possibility that they are friends, at the very least."

"Okay, so who is this mobster? I've never heard of any mob boss coming to Montana. Why would he? We're a small state, population-wise."

Mark looked at the sheriff and shrugged.

"Well, his name is Mickie 'The Shiv' Solomon," Roscoe replied. "He's originally from Kansas City. From what I can tell, he's a younger brother in a crime family who wanted to run his own crew and moved here."

Leah nodded. "So while he's a big gun, he's not the biggest. Most likely he reports back to his family in Kansas City, who are probably pretty big."

"Looks that way. My guess is that Bart seeds Mickie's gang with some of his better homeless guys. He trains them up on the streets, and when they're ready for the big time they move over to the Solomon syndicate." The sheriff raised a finger. "But, that's just speculation at this point. There's no proof. One of Bart's guys did move over to work for Mickie, but we don't know why. It just could have been the natural progression of a criminal."

"A criminal looking for more advancement?" Mark shook his head. "I guess everyone wants to advance in their *careers*. It takes all types, right?"

"Oh, brother. The more I see of the outside world, the more I just want to stay here in our small little town and keep everyone else away." Leah scoffed. "it's no wonder so many small towns aren't very welcoming."

"Well, this small town still welcomes strangers, as long as they follow the law." Sheriff Roscoe put his hat on and said his goodbyes before heading out.

Chapter 30

The next few days saw Leah working the early shifts while Logan closed. The rest of the guys took turns closing or opening. But Leah wasn't happy with making Logan take all the closing shifts. "Logan, your wife's pregnant. She works all day long, and I can't believe she wants to spend her evenings here in the store while you're working."

"She's fine. Lizzie understands what's happening right now. Plus, she's enjoying getting a good look at what's coming down the pipeline." Logan chuckled and threw a magazine that had been dogeared by his wife down on the desk in front of Leah.

Leah and Logan were working on placing orders for the upcoming Christmas season. Even though it was still months away, if a store wanted the best assortment of decorations then they had to order early. Last year, the big deal was the little red trucks with the Christmas trees in the back. Leah was sure they would still be a hit, but she also thought the gnomes would be quite popular this year.

"Go home. I'll stay for the closing shift, too. Both Stevie and Flynn are here tonight, which means someone from the Triple J will be by later on. We'll be fine." Leah picked up the magazine. "And I'll go through and see what Lizzie's marked off in this book. It'll be interesting to see if she and I agree on what's going to be huge this year." Leah chuckled and fanned through the magazine.

"How about I bring you back dinner, then I'll go home?" Logan offered.

"Sounds good, thanks! I'll text my order to Rosie."

Leah had to do a double-take when the first page she opened to had a male model wearing a funny Christmas t-shirt of a Santa toting a large hunting rifle who looked identical to Mark Manning. "No way. I would have known if he did any modeling."

She pulled the page closer and then was able to pick out the minute differences between the cowboys. For one, the model had perfect hair. Mark did not. Although, Leah thought his hair pretty perfect as it was. He was almost always in need a of trim, but she liked that he wore it a bit longer. The model had shorter hair. Leah knew that Mark would never crop his hair so short or have that kind of style, the one where hair product was obviously used.

If Mark ever put a styling gel or mousse in his hair, his brothers would rib him without end. And the smile wasn't right, either. But this could have easily been a Mark Manning twin. Maybe he was Mark's doppelgänger? She laughed at the idea and set the magazine down. "Oh, I'm in trouble if every model I see that looks anywhere near Mark makes me think of the cowboy." Frustration bubbled up, and she worried that she'd made a mistake in breaking it off with him.

When Mark came to her rescue the other day, she had been elated to see him. And not just because she had someone to help her. She was truly glad it was Mark who showed up first. Then, when he held her hand and wrapped her in a warm hug, she sighed. The constant rehashing of what he smelled like and how it felt to be in his arms was doing her no good.

Sure, Mark had called every day since Rocko attacked her, checking in on her. But she hadn't seen him yet. Leah kept reminding herself that if Mark truly cared for her in a romantic way, he wouldn't have been so easy to break up with. He would have argued for them to stay together. Instead, he was just as eager as she was to get the gossiping grandmothers off their tails.

But a nagging thought in the back of her mind wouldn't leave her alone. Why did he keep calling her? Why did he hold her hand so long that day? And why was he walking into her office right then and there?

"Mark?" Leah stood, baffled as to why he was in the office.

The handsome cowboy smiled and held up a brown bag from Rosie's Diner. "Did someone order a chicken salad?"

She pointed at the bag. "Did my brother wrangle you into being his delivery boy?"

"I asked." He grinned. "I wanted to come by and see how you're doing, and when I saw Logan on the sidewalk he told me you were going to close."

"And let me guess, you're gonna be my babysitter?" Leah put her hands on her hips. "What about Flynn and Stevie? They'll both be closing tonight with me."

"Yes, and I'm gonna help." He tried to wink with his black eye and winced. "This will give me a chance to see for myself how Flynn's doing."

"Ouch, that eye doesn't look like it feels very good. You might want to keep the winking to a minimum for now." She chuckled.

He put a hand over the black-and-blue eye and winced again. "Yeah, well." He shrugged. "I got nothing."

They both shared a laugh, and she took the bag from Mark's hands. "Take a load off. Have you had dinner yet?"

"Yup, Flynn and I had both just finished a burger at Rosie's when Logan came in. I thought I'd treat the boy to the diner since he's been working so hard lately."

Leah knew that Flynn was doing well at the store, but she hadn't really spoken to him about the ranch and how that was all going. "How's he doing on the ranch? Is he picking up on the chores?"

Mark looked around and lowered his voice. "I don't think he'll ever be a rancher."

"Well, he's doing really well here with us. I know we want to officially hire him once he's done working off what he owes. I think this might be his calling. He's even starting to chat with the guys before the checkers games." Leah had been impressed when she noticed Flynn laughing with ol' Tom Addison two days earlier. He had yet to joke around with her.

"Good to know. I'll have to have a talk with the ol' coots and see what they have to say." Mark sat there with his hands in his lap, fidgeting. His eyes darted from the desk back to Leah.

"Is everything alright?" She had never seen him so nervous. Not even when he asked her out for the first time on a real date did he seem this nervous.

"Yes." Mark stood up and went to close the door to the office where they sat. "I wanted to talk with you about something."

She pushed the remains of her salad away. "Shoot. What's up?"

He ran his hand over his mouth and down his chin. "When we spoke at the family supper, we were both in agreement that day. But since then...well...I've been thinking."

Leah's stomach did a somersault. Was he getting ready to change things on her? Or was he just going to ask about her decision?

"Do you still feel that was the right choice?" Sweat broke out on his upper lip, and he wiped his face again.

Leah noticed how nervous he was and felt her heartbeat pick up. Did he think it was a wrong choice? "Uh, I think at the time it was. But now?" She shrugged, not wanting to hope he would ask her out again.

"I was thinking that maybe we jumped the gun." He held his hands up. "I know, we both agreed it was for the best. But what if we had handled it all differently? Maybe Rocko wouldn't have had a chance to get to you."

Leah slumped in her chair. "Mark Manning, if you think Rocko would have left me alone if we were still seeing each other, you're dumber than a doorknob!" She jumped up and pointed out the door. "OUT! Now!" Her blood was boiling. *The lily-livered snake actually thought I would have been safer if we were still together?* "Didn't you hear what Rocko said? He called you my boyfriend. He thought we were still together!" Leah stomped from behind the desk. "Apparently the only place the Diner Divas can't penetrate is the town's jail."

"Whoa, little lady. What did I say?" Confusion covered Mark's face as he backed up toward the door.

The door was shoved open and hit Mark in the back. He stumbled forward.

"Hey, what's with all the racket in here?" Flynn looked between the arguing couple.

Leah pointed to Mark. "Doofus here thinks that had he been around, Rocko would have left me alone. Like I need a man just to keep the riff-raff away?" She huffed.

"No, that's not what I meant. Not at all." Mark ran a hand through his already messy hair. "I only meant that, well..." He sighed. "I don't know what I meant."

"Dude," Flynn chuckled, "just tell her how you feel." He looked to Leah. "Be honest about your feelings. Don't use Rocko as an excuse or let him ruin anything you two got going."

"Huh?" Leah furrowed her brows.

"Man, way to go." Mark's cheeks flamed.

Flynn rolled his eyes. "Dude, man up." He turned around and left a confused Leah looking between the two men.

"What is he talking about?" She rubbed her shoulder where Rocko had yanked on her.

"Are you alright?" He motioned toward her arm. "Does it hurt? Do you need a doctor?"

"I'll tell you what I need." She sighed. "I need you to speak plainly with me. What did Flynn mean? And what were you trying to say?"

Mark closed the door again. "Please, take a seat. I'll try this again." He sat across from her and took a deep breath. "I like you, Leah. I never stopped liking you."

She opened her mouth, but nothing came out. She tried again. "You like me?"

"Yes, the way a man should like a woman. We've known each other most of our lives. We've been friends. And we dated." He paused. "To be honest, I miss the dating. I miss holding your hand. I miss holding you."

Hope built in Leah's chest, and she prayed he wasn't going to let her down yet again. "Really?" She felt the beginnings of tears prick her eyes.

Mark stood up and went to her side. "Yes. I want to try this again. And not because you need my protection. I know you're more man than I am." He chuckled.

She frowned. "No woman wants to be told she's more manly than the man she's attracted to."

His eyes rose. "Really? You're attracted to me?"

"That's what you got out of what I said?" Leah scoffed and backed away.

"Sorry. I'm just not good at this couple stuff." He sighed. "What I meant was that you're tougher than I've ever given you credit for. I don't know if it's all those classes you took with Sophia or just your natural talents, but you don't need any man to protect you."

Leah smiled and felt her nose begin to burn. If she wasn't careful, she'd start crying any minute. And she did *not* want to cry in front of Mark. Not when it sounded like he was about to ask her out. "Couple stuff?"

Mark took two steps closer to her. "Yes. If you'll have me."

She nodded.

He closed the distance and took her hands in his. "What about the divas?"

"Hang the divas. This time, we have to agree to ignore them. We can't give them the power over us like we did the last time." Leah had felt guilty lately over allowing them to influence her life so much. She was going to have a talk with the ladies and let them know how much damage they had done to people in town with their gossip. And how their gossiping wasn't something God liked.

The Bible was clear about gossiping women. God did not appreciate them. He loved them, but gossip was a sin. It was one more way the enemy got ahold of people. Those ladies really needed to find something worthwhile to jump into. It might take some time, but Leah would get her friends involved and they'd find a way for the four older women to stay busy.

"Loose lips certainly do sink ships." Mark chuckled. "I think we have to agree to talk to one another if we're feeling outside pressure."

Leah nodded. "Yeah. I remember when Logan and Lizzie got back together. They were hounded by the Diner Divas, too. But now that I think about it, they got the ladies involved in extra activities to keep them from gossiping so much."

Mark nodded. "I remember. It does help when they have activities to keep them busy. Maybe as part of the punishment for the three boys they can go over and help each lady. One day a week they go to one house and help out. I know for a fact that Mrs. Stanhope needs help with her garden."

Leah laughed. "Poor boys. That's worse than working on the ranch."

He chuckled. "But it would be good for them. As well as for the divas."

"True." Leah smiled. "The widows need extra help around the yard. Maybe they'll even focus on your young charges instead of us?"

Mark leaned down, and with his lips just centimeters from hers, he replied, "Bonus."

When their lips finally met, Leah felt it all the way to her toes. She wrapped her arms around his neck and pulled him in closer. Mark wrapped his arms around her waist and deepened the kiss.

Leah's right foot popped up like in those cute rom coms, and she finally understood why the girls always did that at the end of the movies.

Chapter 31

One week later and too many kisses to count, Leah and Mark were still seeing each other every day. He continued to spend his evenings in the store with her when she closed. But they were always chaperoned by Flynn when Leah closed.

"I swear, my brother just wants to torment us." Leah sighed and looked at next week's schedule. "Every night that I close, Flynn is listed as closing with me."

Mark came up behind her. "Darlin', he's doing it to make sure I'm here with you."

She turned around and wrapped her arms around his neck. "But you don't need an excuse to come by and visit with me anymore."

"I know that." He kissed her cheek. "You know that." Mark kissed her other cheek. "But it seems he doesn't yet." He kissed her sweetly on the lips.

Leah sighed into his kiss and all thoughts of schedules and brothers and anything else left her brain.

"Ugh, not again!" Flynn's complaint was loud enough to penetrate the haze of foggy bliss that surrounded both Leah and Mark.

They pulled away and looked at the young man.

"You know, if you wanted to get in good with the owner, interrupting her isn't the way to do it." Mark raised a brow.

Flynn chuckled. "Actually, Logan said I should keep an eye on you two."

"Of course he did." Leah was going to have to have a talk with her big brother.

The bell above the front door of the general store rang, and all eyes turned to see who was coming in right before they closed.

"Oh, good. You're both here." Sheriff Roscoe chuckled. "I should have known where one of you was, the other would be."

"What can we do for you, Sheriff?" Leah walked out from behind the counter and toward Roscoe.

"I have some good news." He took his hat off and ran a hand through his messy hair.

"Really? You caught Big Bart and he's going away for a very long time?" Mark turned hopeful eyes on the sheriff.

"No, not that good, but close." He grinned. "It seems that Big Bart's associates have convinced him that Rocko is a bad friend to have."

"Wait, Rocko's not getting out?" Leah's spirits soared at the good news. If Rocko wasn't getting out, that meant she'd be safe again.

The sheriff nodded. "It seems his high-priced attorney has dropped him as a client, and the judge in Missoula thinks Rocko is too dangerous to let out on bail. He was informed about what the criminal did to you both the last time he was out on bail."

"So, you think Bart's turned his back on him?" Mark asked.

"I do. And the Bozeman sheriff agrees with me. He had a talk with Bart earlier today, and the resident homeless wrangler has asked that you all come back out and help those living on the streets. He won't get in your way when you bring them food, clothes, and money." Roscoe raised an eye.

"Sounds like Bart wants us to bring gift cards again," Leah said.

"I'd have to agree." The sheriff put his hat back on.

"Then, that means we just bring food and essentials, like the last few times we went out there. No gift cards." Mark pursed his lips. "Do you really think Bart and his gang will leave us alone?"

"I do. I think that whatever they're up to, they need to get the local law off their backs. Which is why they turned their backs on Rocko. He couldn't stay out of trouble and brought a spotlight to whatever is going on." Roscoe grinned. "Now, be careful the next time you go to Bozeman, but keep an eye and an ear out for whatever is going on."

"Will do, Sheriff." Mark was already thinking about when they could go back. He wanted to check in on a few of the men he'd been trying to befriend for a while. As well as a few women who had almost decided to leave the streets, and Big Bart, in their dust.

Before the sheriff walked out the door, he turned back. "Just be careful. I don't trust Bart."

"Got it. And thanks." Leah grinned from ear to ear. This meant she was free. But it also meant that Mark no longer needed to spend his evenings with her when she closed. Her smile didn't last long.

After Roscoe left, Mark turned to Leah with a giant smile, but it fled his face when he caught sight of the worry crossing her features. "What's wrong?"

She looked at Flynn and shook her head. "Nothing."

"Come on, we agreed we were in this together and we'd talk about things that bothered us." Mark put his arms around her waist and pulled Leah close.

She sighed. "Not here." Leah pulled out of his warmth and took his hand. She led him to the back office. Once they were inside, she closed the door and turned to Mark. "Does this mean I won't be seeing you very often?" She bit her lip.

"Oh, darlin'." Mark pulled her in for a hug. "I may not spend all of my nights here at the store with you, but we will still be together. When Flynn closes with you, I'll do my best to be the one who picks him up." He kissed the top of her head, which fit perfectly under his chin.

Leah hugged him tighter. "I know you can't work with me, but I am going to miss spending so much time with you." She leaned into his warmth, and arms. She knew she shouldn't have gotten used to him being around all the time, but she couldn't help it. He was so much fun. The way they bantered, and then the way he held her, had given her hope over the past week.

Hope was something she was lacking lately. Leah didn't want to lose that warm feeling she had every day when she caught sight of the handsome cowboy, or when his scintillating scent wafted her way. His whole being infused her with warmth and happiness, something she'd never felt with anyone else before.

"Leah, darlin', don't you know how I feel about you yet?" Mark whispered in her hair.

She shook her head.

Leah knew how she felt about the cowboy, and she hoped he felt the same, but she also knew it was too soon for him to fall for her so hard. He couldn't return her feelings—not yet, anyway. But the hope that filled her heart told her it was possible in the future if they could just get through this current trial, and avoid being the top gossip.

He held her tighter. "You're my everything. You're the sunrise on a warm summer morning, and my sunset on a beautiful wintry evening." Mark pulled back and looked her in the eyes. "You are my North Star, the compass that gets me through the storm."

Leah felt the tears stream down her cheeks and she smiled from ear to ear. Her heart was overflowing with the love she'd felt for Mark since...who knew when. All she knew was that she'd been in love with the cowboy for ages. Maybe even since she was a teenager.

She cupped his cheek. "Mark, you're my knight in shining spurs..."

Before she could finish her thoughts, Mark pulled her tight against his chest and kissed her with everything he had. It was a good thing he held her so tight, as her knees wobbled partway through the kiss that changed her world.

When she couldn't even think anymore, Mark pulled back and whispered against her lips, "I love you, Leah. I've loved you for so long that I don't know what life is like without you in my heart."

She whimpered. Then pulled back and looked him the eyes. "I love you, Mark Manning. You are more than my hero, you're my best friend, my confidant, and I can't wait to see what God has in store for us, my faith-filled cowboy."

After he kissed her again, he grinned. "I knew God would bring you to me when the time was right."

She furrowed her brows. "What do you mean? We weren't apart that long. You prayed about us getting back together during that week?"

"I've prayed about you a bit longer, my love." Mark kissed the tip of her nose. "I started praying about the woman I'd fall in love with back in high school. I chose to believe in God when I was a kid, but I didn't have faith in my future love until one day when I was riding through the ranch."

Leah pulled back a little more and waited for him to continue his story.

"I was riding the fence lines alone, just checking that everything was alright. I started praying and asked God about some girl I was dating." He chuckled. "You know, I don't even remember who she was. But I do remember that as I prayed to God and asked him about that girl, it wasn't her face that flitted through my mind."

"Really? Whose was it?"

"Yours."

Leah's eyes widened. "What?"

Mark chuckled. "Of course, at the time I had no idea it would be you that I'd fall in love with one day. But back then I realized that if I was thinking about another girl while praying for a different one, then I was on the wrong path."

"You prayed for a relationship with someone else and thought of me instead?" Leah wasn't just shocked, she was overjoyed that Mark had always had her on his mind. Even when he was still teasing her.

"It wasn't like that. You're two years younger than me, so back then you seemed too young for me to like. But we were close. We always were. So I figured that God used your image to remind me that there were other girls out there, and the girl I wanted at the time wasn't the one for me." He smiled into her loving face. "In fact, whenever I prayed for a specific girl over the years, it was your face that kept running through my mind."

"So, God told you all the way back in high school that you and I would end up together?" Leah wished God had told her that as well. It would have saved her a lot of heartache. Although, she doubted Mark would have been ready before now. She wasn't even sure he was ready now. But she'd have the faith of a cowgirl and trust in God to ensure she got her cowboy in His timing, not hers.

Mark thought about it a moment and chuckled. "I guess so. Maybe my faith wasn't as strong as I thought all these years. If I had listened to God back then, we would have been together this entire time."

Leah wound her arms loosely around Mark's neck. "Listen here, cowboy. Don't go second-guessing your faith. I think all things happen in God's perfect timing, and neither of us were ready for anything this intense before now." She arched a brow, just waiting for him to deny it.

Mark's hands went up her back and he leaned down for another kiss.

After only a few brief pecks on her lips, Mark pulled back and Leah noted the serious expression on his face, and his chin dimple caught her eye. "Why so serious, cowboy?"

"If I had the faith of a cowboy, a true cowboy, I would have recognized *us* sooner." He tilted his head. "Can you forgive me for taking so long?"

"There's nothing to forgive, my faithful cowboy. Like I said, God's timing is perfect. All of our experiences have made us who we are today. If we had changed anything, we wouldn't be the people we are now." She kissed the dimple in his chin.

When she pulled back, his chin dimple was gone. But it was replaced with a soft smile and watery eyes.

"You really are beautiful, inside and out." He got down on one knee. "I don't have a ring yet, but Leah Hayes, I've loved you for years. I want to love you for the rest of our lives. Will you marry me?"

Someone cleared their throat from the open door and the couple turned their heads.

"Dad!" Leah jumped and put a hand to her mouth.

"Don't you think a cowboy should ask a father's permission before proposing to a man's only daughter?" Mr. Hayes walked into the office with his wife and Logan following him.

Mark stood up. "Sir, I'm sorry I didn't plan ahead. You're right, I should have asked you first." He looked between Leah and her dad. Then he took her hand in his and squeezed it. "Mr. Hayes, I love your daughter. I have for years, only I didn't realize it until recently." He cleared his throat.

Mr. Hayes pursed his lips and stared daggers at Mark.

Mark was grateful that the man didn't have a gun in his possession at that moment. He felt like the kid coming to take the girl to prom and her dad was sitting there at the table cleaning his rifle. Only in this scenario, Mark was certain that if he made one wrong step, Mr. Hayes wouldn't hesitate to use his weapon.

"May I have your permission to marry your daughter?" The words came out in a garbled, throaty whisper, but they did come out.

Mrs. Hayes exclaimed and put a hand to her heart. "Oh, honey." She put a hand on her husband's shoulder.

A huge smile covered Logan's face, and he walked around his parents and slapped Mark's back. "It's about time."

"I didn't give my permission." Mr. Hayes' loud voice stopped everyone in their tracks.

"Daddy." Leah pursed her lips and put her fists on her hips. About to give him the riot act if he said no.

"Pops, you know as well as I do that Mark is the best cowboy for Leah. Stop torturing them and give your approval." Logan chuckled. Apparently he was the only one in the room who didn't think Leah's dad was going to say no.

Slowly, ever so slowly, the tense expression on Mr. Hayes' face softened. And when the tension in the room was so thick it could be cut with a bowie knife, his lips turned up in a smile and he walked to Mark with his hand outstretched.

Mark took a tentative step forward and took the man's hand.

"Welcome to the family, son." Mr. Hayes grinned and pulled Mark in for a manly hug.

When he let Mark go, Mr. Hayes turned toward his only daughter. "Well, don't make the man wait all night. Give him your answer."

Leah laughed and cried all at the same time. "Yes, of course I'll marry you, Mark." She ran into his arms and he held her tight.

"So, when ya gonna get my daughter a proper ring?" Mr. Hayes laughed and slapped Mark on the back.

"I was thinking I'd drive into Bozeman tomorrow."

The rest of the room moaned. "No, not Bozeman."

Mark and Leah laughed.

He looked down into the eyes of the woman he was going to marry. "Would you like to join me on a trip to Missoula for a ring?"

Mrs. Hayes stepped forward. "Might I make a suggestion?"

Leah and Mark looked to her.

"Grandma's ring would be perfect." Teary eyes met her daughter's.

Leah began to tear up again, and she wiped away at the pesky leak in her eyes. "I don't think I've ever cried so much in one day before." She took her mom's hands. "And yes, I'd love to have Grandma's ring." She turned her gaze to Mark. "Do you mind?"

"If it's what you want, then I'm happy to put that ring on your finger."

"It is." She giggled. "Wait until you see it."

Mark wasn't sure what he had expected, but this wasn't it. He held the beautiful diamond and ruby ring in his hand and whistled. "Most ranchers' wives only wear a simple gold band." The diamond had to be at least one karat, if not more. Then it was surrounded by small, princess-cut rubies. Even he knew the ring was beautiful and expensive. He never would be able to afford something like this on his salary.

"That's because of all the hard work they do on the ranch. They don't want to ruin a diamond. Or lose it." Leah grinned. "The women in my family weren't ranchers, they were storeowners."

"But your mom wears a simple band and runs a small ranch," Mark countered.

"True, but she grew up on a ranch. In the beginning they lived in the apartment above the store. Then when they could, they bought this land and Mom ran the ranch, so to speak." Leah put her left hand out.

Mark took in a deep breath. The ring must have cost a fortune. Her grandparents had to have come from wealth. Or maybe it was a family heirloom? Either way, he hoped she'd not wear it when working on their ranch. He didn't even want to think about trying to replace it.

When Leah's hand came up, he slipped the ring on her finger and smiled. Then leaned down and kissed her hand. "I'll understand if you want a long engagement, but please don't torture me with waiting too long."

What happened to the man who feared marriage? Wasn't he the one who had said it would take a long time before he would settle down? Now he was the one who wanted to get married right away?

She grinned and kissed her fiancé. "Don't worry. I don't want a long engagement. Just one long enough for you to build us a house somewhere."

He jerked back. "But that could take up to a year." Mark had planned on building a house for them on the ranch, but he didn't want to wait that long to make her his wife.

Leah laughed. "Gotcha!"

"So, how long do you want to wait?" he asked.

"Just long enough for us to plan a wedding and clean out the upstairs apartment. I think we should live above the store until you have a house for us." She scrunched her nose. "I love your family, but I don't want to live in your parents' house. And I don't want to live with mine, either."

Mark kissed his future wife. "I completely agree. So, what? A week? Will that be enough time?"

Now it was her turn to jerk back. "What? I need more than a week to plan a wedding. It takes longer than that just to get a dress!"

"Gotcha!"

Epilogue

After their wedding, which only took a month to plan, Mark gave Leah a piece of paper.

"What's this?"

"Your wedding present." Mark beamed.

"Oh." She raised her brows. "I thought paper was for the one-year anniversary, not the wedding day."

He wrapped his arms around his new wife. "Leah, darlin', open the paper." He kissed her neck as she attempted to open it.

His kisses sent shivers down her spine and her hands trembled. "I don't think I can focus if you keep doing that."

His deep chuckle sent a thrill all the way to her bones. "Then I guess you won't see what your gift is." Mark nibbled on her ear.

"Oh, man." She pulled out of his grasp. If he didn't stop, she wasn't going to be able to stay at her own wedding reception. "Let me read this."

He grinned.

"OH!" She clamped a hand over the paper and tears ran down her cheeks. "You didn't."

"I did."

She scanned the paper and realized their honeymoon was going to take six weeks. Six weeks of them together twenty-four seven with no one to interrupt them. The big lug had booked them a four-week cruise on the Mediterranean, and then two weeks going through Greece and Turkey. "How'd you know?"

"Your brother told me you had once mentioned this trip was your dream." He pulled her back into his arms. "I want to give you everything your heart desires for the rest of our lives. You deserve it."

She leaned up on her toes and kissed him deeply. "Thank you so much. This means the world to me." Leah chuckled. "No pun intended."

"And we are going to see the entire world. Every anniversary we'll travel somewhere new. It might not always be to Europe or even another continent, but I promise, we will see somewhere new every year."

"I love you so much." She kissed him again.

"But," he warned, "this is going to set me back with building you our own ranch house. I hope you don't mind living in the apartment for a little while longer?"

"As long as I'm with you in our own space, it won't matter if it's a small apartment or our own ranch home."

She kissed his cheek. "Home is wherever you and I are together."

They were able to build their own ranch home on Triple J land and move in before their first child arrived.

And every year for their anniversary they did travel somewhere new and exotic, until they began having kids. Then, the trips were more local. One year they even took a family trip to Orlando and did all of the amusement parks there as a family.

As their family grew, their love grew, and Leah's desire to see the world waned. Her desire for her family and her hometown grew, until one day she told Mark that she didn't want to go anywhere for their anniversary. She wanted instead to do a staycation with her husband and children.

Life had thrown them some curveballs along the way, but as long as they worked together, they hit them out of the park. Family had quickly become their passion.

Author's Notes

S o, what did you think? For those of you who've read Her Montana Christmas Cowboy, did you pick up on the little tidbits of the other series? If you haven't, it's such a fun set of books! Don't miss it.

This book was written during November and finished in early December, 2020. It came back from the editor the middle of December, but by then I was really sick with a sinus infection so I did very little with the edits. Then once I started getting better, I spent a few hours one day working on it. The next day, I couldn't work because I had contracted a bad case of Covid.

I live in Southern California where we ended up having the 3rd worst amount of cases in the world per capita. The hospitals were overflowing with patients. My temperature got up to 102.4 and wouldn't break for 4 days. But, since there weren't any beds in any hospitals, I had to stay home and pray that God would heal me. He sent an angel my way with a very simple tea – ginger root and lemon. My whole house had Covid, so when we got this tea, my aunt immediately made it for all of us. She had mostly recovered by this time. I was the lucky one with the worst case out of all 3 of us.

But what was interesting was that my fever began to break the next day, only after drinking one cup of the tea. Of course, on day 2 I started drinking it twice a day. Then my fever dropped by a whole degree each day and within a few days I no longer had a fever. I'll share the tea in case you, or anyone you know, has Covid. But, please, check with your doctor before taking anything anyone suggests. Even homeopathic options. You never know when someone is going to have a reaction to something. I also used Vick's VapoRub on my chest every night and slept elevated. It really helped to keep my chest clearer and breathing easier.

I ended up being sick for a month, and then it took another 2 weeks for me to get my strength back. I'm sitting in Western Washington at my sister's house as I finish this up and publish book 4 in the Triple J Ranch series. I'm almost all better, a few lingering issues, but I no longer feel like I'm going to die.

God is good!

I missed Christmas on Dec 25, so I finally felt good enough to drive up to see my immediate family and celebrate Christmas. I got a Cricut! Woot Woot! Once I get home and get settled, I'm going to start crafting. And I'll share pictures of my crafts once they are good enough to show people. LOL I hope you all will share your crafting pictures with me as well! And any tips or tricks you have for using Cricut.

And I plan on releasing book 5 of the Triple J Ranch the first week of March, 2021, or sooner if possible. Keep an eye out for a pre-release option coming soon! Or, if it's after March 2021, then book 5 should be live now.

I pray for you all to have a blessed and healthy new year!

Keep reading for a recipe from Leah as well as the ginger root tea recipe and a sneaky peek at Her Montana Christmas Cowboy, book 1 in the Big Sky Christmas series.

Contact Me

For those of you who love social media, here are the various ways to follow or contact me:

Newsletter:https://jennahendricks.com/newsletter/
BookBub: https://www.bookbub.com/authors/jenna
-hendricks
TikTok: https://www.tiktok.com/@jennacleanauthor
Instagram: https://www.instagram.com/j.l.hendricks/
Twitter: https://twitter.com/TinkFan25
Facebook: https://www.facebook.com/JLHendricks
Author
Website: https://jennahendricks.com/

Ginger Root Tea

2 inches of fresh ginger root, peeled and chopped into chunks. (It's alright if some of the skin is left on. It can be difficult to get it all off)

½ fresh lemon, quartered

3 cups water

Bring to a boil, then lower temp and continue to boil for 7-8 minutes. A lot of the water will boil away, and it should leave you with at least one good cup of tea. Maybe 2. If you need more, then just add more of the ginger root and lemon along with water.

Be sure to keep the lemon rind on. There are nutrients that you need in the outer part of the lemon.

To sweeten it, use honey, or your favorite sugar. I used Stevia in The Raw.

Drink this 2 – 3 times a day while you are sick and keep doing it at least once a day after you no longer have Covid until you have your energy back.

**Remember to check with your doctor before taking the tea to ensure that you won't have any issues.

Leah's Chicken Enchilada Casserole

2 boneless, skinless chicken breasts (An easy short-cut - I prefer to pick up a rotisserie chicken from either Costco or Sam's Club as they are larger than the grocery store ones)

1 package of corn tortillas (at least 18 tortillas)

1 - 48 oz can of Old El Paso red enchilada sauce (I use mild)

1 - 10 oz can of Old El Paso red enchilada sauce (this is just in case you need a little extra sauce)

3 Cups shredded Mexican cheese (or your favorite cheese)

13x9 rectangle baking dish

Pre-heat oven to 350 degrees Fahrenheit.

If you use my shortcut, then pull the chicken breast apart, or cut into pieces. If you don't use my shortcut of a rotisseries chicken, then cook the chicken breasts at 350 for 30 – 45 minutes, depending on the size of your chicken breasts. When they are done, cut into bite sized pieces.

Empty the can of enchilada sauce into a large bowl.

Pour a small amount into a 13 x 9 rectangle baking dish. Just enough to cover the bottom.

Take 6 corn tortillas and dunk into the bowl of red sauce. Then put them on the bottom of the pan. They need to cover the bottom. They will overlap each other and that is fine.

Take 1/3 of the chicken and spread out on top of the tortillas.

Take 1 cup of cheese and spread on top of the chicken.

Then drizzle a little bit of the sauce on top. Don't pour it or drench it, just drizzle it across the layer.

Then do 2 more layers of tortillas, chicken, cheese, and sauce.

Sometimes, I need a little bit more sauce, so I always buy a second smaller can of the enchilada sauce to have on hand just in case. Sometimes I don't need it. But, I highly recommend having it on hand when you make this for your first time.

Bake at 350 for 30 – 35 minutes. You'll know it's ready when the cheese on top is bubbling. Remove from the oven and let sit for 5 minutes. Then cut into pieces. I usually get 8 pieces from this size of pan. It also makes for great leftovers.

You can pair this with a salad, and you'll have a nice meal.

Bon appetite!

Sneak Peek

H er Montana Christmas Cowboy

Chloe Manning's first Christmas in Frenchtown was heartbreaking. Will Santa give her her heart's desire during her second?

Brandon Beck left behind a woman for the benefit of his family ranch last Christmas. Now that he's back, why can't he get her out of his heart and mind?

When Santa and Mrs. Claus play matchmaker, will Chloe and Brandon fall under their Christmas Magic? Or will past hurts and fears keep them apart?

Don't miss out on the first Christmas story of the heart-warming Christmas Cowboy romance series, Big Sky Christmas. Where the romance is clean, and Christmas takes center stage!

Prologue

"Oh!" Chloe Manning yelled as her foot slipped where the driveway met wet grass. The water pooling on the concrete driveway wasn't something she'd planned on when scheduling her move. Since it had rained early that morning, she could not have foreseen the hazard and rescheduled. But, she also knew that her brothers and sister had scheduled their week to help on this one day. "Great, just what I ne—"

A strong, masculine hand reached down and offered to help her up.

"Thanks," she said without looking up.

"My pleasure." A husky voice that Chloe didn't recognize turned her face up just as she stood, and she yanked her hand out of his. "Ah!" Not looking where she was going, Chloe fell over the headboard she had dropped when she'd fallen the first time. This time she fell on the wooden headboard and smacked her knee good.

"I'm sorry, I shouldn't have let go until you were steady." The stranger furrowed his brow and bent down to help her get back up, again.

"No, no. It was all my fault." Chloe's face heated up, and she did her best to stand. She inhaled a quick breath when she put pressure on her right leg. While she knew enough medicine to know she hadn't broken anything, she was going to be sore.

In addition, she'd fallen flat on her face not once, but twice, in front of a very handsome cowboy. Her pride had also taken a huge hit. To make matters worse, Chloe hadn't dressed to impress; she was wearing an oversized, faded University of Montana sweatshirt and yoga pants. Her blonde hair was up in a messy ponytail, and she had zero makeup on. The only upside was that she doubted this handsome cowboy would recognize her again.

A bright, white smile greeted her when she stopped wobbling and took a step away from him. "Thank you. I don't know what's gotten into me today."

"Are you the one moving in?" The cowboy looked between her and the house.

Chloe nodded. "Yup."

"Well, welcome to Frenchtown. You must be the new medical billing manager everyone has been talking about." The cute cowboy put his hand out. "I'm Brandon Beck."

Well, there went that thought. He knew exactly who she was. No way was she going to be able to hide her embarrassment behind anonymity.

Standing taller, she straightened her sweatshirt and blew her bangs out of her eyes. When she took his hand, a jolt of electricity swept through her entire being. "Ah, I'm..." She cleared her throat. "I'm Chloe Manning." She shook his hand and noted the calluses, but also the strength in his warm touch.

"Nice to meet you, Miss Manning." When he ended the handshake, he touched the brim of his hat and nodded.

"This is my sister, Elizabeth, and our brothers." Chloe pointed to them all and introduced her five brothers to Brandon.

Elizabeth looked between Chloe and Brandon and gave her twin sister a sly smile. If Elizabeth didn't know better, she'd think Chloe already had an admirer. But really, who *wouldn't* be attracted to Chloe, even in moving clothes? The men of Beacon Creek had always admired her sister. The only reason Chloe wasn't already married was because she had made it known far and wide that she wanted to move away as soon as possible.

Brandon took a closer look at the newest resident to Frenchtown, and something in his gut told him to watch out for this little filly. She just might cause *him* to fall at *her* feet. He wondered if that would be so bad.

Once Brandon had moved on, the sisters went inside with the headboard and set it up in Chloe's new bedroom.

"Wow, sis. You did good. This is a rental?" Elizabeth Manning walked around the room checking out the wooden floor and blocked wainscoting on all the walls. "There's so much potential with this place."

Chloe Manning agreed. She couldn't wait until the day the owners let her buy it. This was exactly what she wanted. The deal she'd made was to rent for a year, and if everyone was happy then she would buy it. The owners wanted to make sure she stayed there with her job and didn't go home. Mr. and Mrs. Rice, who owned the quaint house, lived next door and felt it was important to like their neighbors. They worried if they sold her the house now, she would leave and sell to someone they may not like.

Chloe knew she was home and wouldn't be going anywhere. "Yes, I think I'm going to be very happy in this house, and in this town." She beamed at her sister as they unloaded their boxes into a spare room.

Chloe and Elizabeth were twins. While Chloe had always wanted to get out of Beacon Creek, Elizabeth was happy to live there for the rest of her life. When Chloe was offered the chance to move to Frenchtown and manage the local medical clinic's administrative side, she'd jumped at the chance to leave her small home-town. Not that Frenchtown was much bigger, but it did offer her a chance at new experiences and a promotion at work.

The plan was to work in the Frenchtown Clinic and manage it for the next five to seven years, and then she could start applying for jobs in the big cities, like

Bozeman or Helena. Then, she would be doing exactly what she had wanted her entire life—get out of Dodge, so to speak.

"What about the men? If they're all as handsome as that cowboy we just met, then I think I won't be the only one getting married next year," Elizabeth teased her sister.

Heat shot up Chloe's neck and face. She deserved the ribbing after everything she'd put Elizabeth through when her now fiancé came back to town last summer.

The man who had helped Chloe up from the ground was gorgeous. Too bad he'd met her when she was at her worst. No makeup, hair a mess, and then to fall flat on her backside? She knew he wouldn't be back.

Just thinking about slipping and falling in front of the handsome Brandon Beck caused her face to heat up again. She wasn't normally a klutz, but today seemed to be her day of making a fool out of herself.

Even after he'd helped her up, she'd still tripped over the headboard because she wasn't looking where she was going. Instead, she was focused on the very good-looking and tall cowboy with chocolate-brown eyes and medium-brown hair that looked as though it needed a cut. His hair curled around his ears and above the back of his collar, which only served to make Chloe even more attracted to the cowboy.

All she could think of was running her fingers through his soft hair. Where that thought came from, she couldn't say. But when she'd realized where her mind was, that was when she'd tripped over the headboard.

Does this sound like fun? If you enjoy reading about the faith and fun surrounding a small town at Christmas, then this book is for you! And it can be read year-round. So check it out today! You'll be glad you did.